AFTERNOON AT BERGDORF'S

RICHARD M. MILLS

Edited by Vince Font
Cover design by Cover design by Judith S. Design & Creativity
www.judithsdesign.com
Produced by Glass Spider Publishing
www.glassspiderpublishing.com

For my daughter, Laike.

Chambers Street

"Well, if it isn't Joe Tiller."

The voice summons me from behind. Subtly I peek, pretending I don't hear him, holding my stare at the *New York Times* sports section; it's the beginning of football season. Pushing my face deeper into the paper like an ostrich to sand, I hear him again.

"Joe!"

He's questioning himself now, wondering if he's mistaken me for someone else. I feel his eyes burning a hole through the back of my suit and now something is poking my right arm—repeatedly.

"Joe, it's me, it's Barney Williams!" he says enthusiastically, as if he's discovered something life-changing.

Not wanting to appear confused, even though I am, I grimace. "Oh, yes," I say, and pause.

"We met in December at the Randolphs' holiday party. Up on 92nd Street," he adds reluctantly.

"Oh, yes, I remember now." I stare down at his hand to see if I can make up something quickly. He's wearing a wedding band. "Oh, yes, with your wife."

"JC. Oh, she's doing great, Joe. We're expecting in a few months. I guess she drank a little too much that night, if you know what I mean." He nudges his elbow deep into the side of my arm like we're old college pals. "That was the night Milo was conceived. Anywho, I'm having a party on the Fourth of July," he says, writing down his address on the back of his business card, "and we would love it if you could make it. My cousin from Goshen is in town and looking for someone to show her a nice time. It's always great to have a connection with those Indiana roots." He seems somewhat relieved at the thought that he can somehow pawn his distant niece off on me to play entertainer.

Anticipating the next stop, Chambers Street, I can't get away quickly enough. "Sounds like a real good time. Unfortunately, I'll be out."

"You know, it's not a problem because she'll be in town for weeks," he says, assuming I'd carve out time from my busy schedule to 'show her a good ol' time.'

"I do wish I could help. I'm sure she's . . ." I pause. ". . . but I'm an extremely busy man these days with the New Year approaching. I recently took over the Goldstein account, which demands a great deal of my time and attention."

"Oh, okay, I guess I understand. I'll just have to let her know." A look of disappointment appears as his eyes stare down at his feet.

"Next stop Chambers Street," the automated voice came over the speaker.

"This is my stop," I say. "It was great seeing you."

"It's okay," Barney says sadly. He looks like a disappointed kid staring out the window waiting for his father to pick him up. "Really! Now that JC is expecting, I guess it's more important that Sandra help focus her attention on baby Milo."

I recognize the signs of an approaching guilt trip. "Well, sure . . . I mean, I guess. But only for the—"

"That's great, Joe! I'll let her know. You won't be disappointed. She's a real midwestern looker."

"Look, it's just dinner, nothing more. Like I said, I have a big account to look after and really need to keep focused." I notice a change in his demeanor.

"Perfect," Barney says, "We'll see you then!"

The train stops at Chambers Street and I immediately exit onto the crowded platform. Behind me, Barney stands like someone who's just been caught with his cock exposed, still holding his business card. Before I can turn back to pretend to try to take the card, the train car is gone—like that, I successfully dodged the bullet of Barney Williams.

*   *   *

I've always enjoyed New York in late spring. It's absolutely beautiful. Although the subways are packed this time of year, at least it's not overflowing to the rafters with French tourists stinking up the trains because they don't wear deodorant or bathe. I don't know how people do it. After an hour on the subway, I can feel the sweat on my balls begin to seep onto the yellow and orange seats. I'm always persistent when powdering the inside of my underwear. It could be worse; I could be riding the bus.

The cultural epicenter of the universe with lights, music, and a limitless number of restaurants, it has crossed my mind (once or twice) that maybe I should purchase a timeshare in Jersey City.

February is an ideal time to visit the city. By then the tourists have gone, yet those big-city travel buses continue to run. I can see how New York at this time of year wouldn't appear as exciting: It's cold and wet, and nobody likes that.

Street vendors sell *Cosmopolitan* and *LIFE* while storefronts are seemingly magical. In twenty minutes, you could find yourself in Times Square, or Rockefeller Center to observe the annual Black Friday tree-lighting ceremony. I often avoid those parts of the city. They're tourist traps—overcrowded and impossible to maneuver.

New York once seemed overwhelming. But now, it's my reality.

Peter and I often joke that on Sunday, trains should designate one of the cars for families so parents with strollers can listen to their screaming children. I've always wondered why someone would choose to raise their children here. The kids grow up with weird accents—not quite like those who live in Jersey, but a definite East Coast twang with a shot of sass.

I'd never raise children here. But then I don't plan on having any anyway.

Tourists are easily spotted. It's not hard, as nobody from here would ever be caught dead with a Nikon strung around their neck or, better yet, hugging their purse so tightly that it bleeds the leather raw. I've never actually witnessed anyone getting mugged in Manhattan, although I assume someone on some drunken night—the idiot who passes out on a Brooklyn-bound L train or the 6 Train and is rolled by some hoodlum on their way to the Bronx—is easy prey, but never in the city. Once I was that idiot who passed out on an uptown 2 Train and ended up in Wakefield. Still, I wasn't assaulted. Call it luck or just a glitch. I still don't understand why anyone would live in the Bronx.

New York can be a difficult city to manage. At first it felt unfamiliar, foreign. Sometimes, impossible. It seems like every day someone moves out and a queer moves in to seek out fame on Broadway, only to realize working three jobs to pay for a shoebox apartment with three other roommates isn't for them.

"It just takes time, faith, and a good effort," they say.

If you can make it through your first year, chances are you'll make it three. And if you can make it three, well, you can make it five. Finally, after ten years of hard work and dedication, you can finally call yourself a New Yorker.

When I first moved here, I thought, "Great! A new city. A new start. New beginnings." Little did I realize having an MBA from one of the top ten business schools in the Midwest doesn't even guarantee a job waiting tables. Every job ad required a minimum of one year of serving experience. I did some bartending in college (four years to be exact), but that didn't matter: "It's not New York experience!" they would say. Fuck them, I said back.

The majority of people in the service industry are aspiring actors without agents, and they're a lot like dogs. They beg for even the smallest parts and savor what scraps they can get. They think someday a big director will see them performing off-off-off-off-off-off Broadway and declare, "This kid is going to be a star!"

It's narcissistic. Sure, it could happen. *Anything* is possible, yet many find themselves without representation, which makes it almost impossible, as those who do are given priority during auditions—they could find themselves going to open calls, arriving early in the morning, and never getting seen. I've always wondered if I could be an actor. But nah. That life isn't for me.

I've decided instead to cherry-pick the finer things in life. Taking the easier path. And if I regret it? At least I have a stage in my living room where I'm always accompanied by my dog, Potter, and my goldfish, Maria Delgado.

*   *   *

"Gloria, I'm running late," I say over the phone. "Can you . . . *No, I can't!* Gloria . . . I need you to move my noon appointment with Festerson to—I know, let him know I need . . . no, I cannot. Just do it!"

Gloria may have graduated from college, but she clearly lacks emotional intelligence. I constantly entertain the idea of firing her but quickly realize how easily she's brought to tears, so I've decided—for entertainment purposes—to keep her around.

She used to come in wearing low-top blouses and super-short miniskirts, but soon I realized if I looked at her the wrong way it could be misconstrued as sexual harassment and I'd end up like Harvey Weinstein, the sacrificial lamb for the #MeToo movement.

After a week of being tortured by her big rack, I had her draft and send out a company-wide memo laying out the new dress code policy.

Attention All Tiller & Associates Employees:

Employees are now required to adhere to a professional dress attire policy. This includes but is not limited to garments where any type of skin is exposed. Also, please refrain from wearing excessive amounts of loud colors, as it has been reported a distraction to members of upper management. Denim jean skirts and dark-green turtlenecks are acceptable. In addition, long hair should be braided.

Truly Yours,
Joe Tiller, CEO/CFO/President

Adjusting her style to observe this company-wide policy, I noticed Gloria was feeling self-conscious, like one of those sister-wives in a polygamist cult sect in Utah.

*　　*　　*

Damn it! It's pouring. That's the thing about living here. You must be ready for the elements. I spend quality time with myself most mornings, but particularly this one—fixing my hair, ironing my shirt with organic starch, and making sure I'm presentable—as you never know when you'll end up in someone's family vacation album or social media newsfeed. I wouldn't want to be found looking reprehensible with my face splashed across the cover of the *New York Times*.

I've worked hard to preserve my image—contacted my attorney to ensure my right-side profile is patented and has the appropriate copyright. The legalities of using my image without permission could cost you a year's salary.

I've placed this protocol in action to avoid any unwanted attention or advancements from women who might claim I'm the father of their bi-racial child—a kid everyone knows was the result of a late night out with Tyrone, the Starbucks barista on Avenues of the Americas.

What she doesn't know is I've been shooting blanks since 1998, after *the accident* while playing football in high school. Thankfully, I was smart enough to have my guys cryofreezed to ensure the future of the Tiller estate lives on.

Women think they can easily trap a man this way, but I'm smart. I'm Joe Tiller.

I've seen it played out too many times. Knocking a woman up only to be forced into financing an abortion or dishing out the cash for the next eighteen years while little Jenny's mother uses the money to get her hair and nails *did*. It's really sick to think that women operate this way.

Nine times out of ten, I'm wearing a jockstrap at the gym to secure my boys in place. After an intense workout I like to hit the shower and experience the sensation of warm water running through my hair, down my body, and through the crack of my ass, which sometimes brings up the urge to rub one out.

Soap from the dispenser can sometimes leave a lingering burning sensation when I try to urinate, but I've realized you have to pick your battles. Sometimes I have to go dry; an empty dispenser is often a clear indicator I'm not the first to experience this type of release.

Once, I worked myself into exhaustion to the point my shirt stuck to my chest. My body odor was so overwhelming that I ended my workout early to shower. Moving toward the locker room, I watched another guy also end his workout.

I didn't think much of it at first. I grabbed my towel and toiletries and headed for the shower. From the corner of my eye, I saw him headed there too.

I felt an increase in my heart rate. The pent-up storage of testosterone was overwhelming, and something about that felt uncomfortable.

I often allow the water to run a few seconds to avoid cold pellets shooting at my body, but due to the unwanted company I decided to jump in quickly. I disrobed, threw my underwear and towel on the shower rod, and waited.

There was a tiny snag in the middle of the curtain. Curious, I looked through it and saw him naked, disrobing. As there were five private showers, I assumed he would've taken the one opposite of me, but he didn't.

His backside was exposed. An exhibitionist of sorts, he opened the curtain, turned on the faucet, and provided full-frontal exposure. He knew I was there; he'd seen me walk in. Now we found ourselves separated by a thin latex barrier and the noise of the water against the porcelain tiles.

I stood under the water, wondering if he was like me—a bit carnal, vulnerable, and exposed. Strangely, I wanted to hear him hitting the dispenser. I listened for periodic suction sounds that syncopated in an offbeat rhythmic motion. I felt aroused that I could experience potential exposure from a stranger while engaged in this animalistic yet normal ritual.

I waited for him to leave so I could be alone, but he took forever. I didn't know what to do, but I assumed he wanted to see me. *How sick*, I thought. I quickly turned off the water, grabbed my underwear and towel, and headed back to my locker.

I felt myself growing annoyed. I understood it was a public shower, yet I needed privacy. Why else did I always come in the later hours of the morning? I came up with the brilliant idea to go to the sauna. People didn't usually go in there that early in the morning, and I figured I'd be alone.

I walked in. It was perfect: dark, muffled, and relaxing. It didn't appear anyone was there, but it was difficult to see through the clouded steam. I went to the very back, where even if someone was there, it would be difficult for them to see me. The only thing separating my naked body from the seat of the bench was the towel provided by Guest Services.

It felt nice. The steam made contact with my body as I laid my head against the wall. The silence made me feel less self-conscious; I decided to expose myself. I touched my chest, pinching my nipples, sensually and without distraction. Down below, John Deer (the name I gave my member—reminds me of a tractor) began to come alive.

"Woooo, boy," I said to him.

After I was sure I was alone, I began squeezing him harder. I imagined him thanking me for the service I provided and hoped he would return the favor by shooting a load like one of those amateur porn stars on X-Tube, which the ladies seem to enjoy as well.

Just then, I heard a voice. "Joe! Is that Joe Tiller?"

I immediately covered my body, wondering if it was the guy who'd followed me into the shower.

Hampton Grove

"Oh, and Marshal, please arrange for car service to arrive no later than half-past seven," the voice spoke in what sounded like a British accent.

"Why, certainly, Katheryn."

Sitting at her vanity, Katheryn applied the same shade of lipstick she'd used since she was a young woman, which was similar to the way she did her hair. Not much had changed for her. Just that she was much older.

"And please inform Roderick that I will meet him at our usual place," she added.

Roman sighed. "Well, we'll have to hurry and begin to get ready, now, won't we," he said, more of an expression than a question.

Katheryn began mentally assembling her wardrobe. She wondered if she should wear Chanel or Saint Laurent. "Marshal, darling, please afford me a precious libation. My kickie-poo."

He went across the room to the bar cart and prepared the virgin vodka martini, dry and with a splash of water and a twist of lemon He handed her the glass.

She took it and sipped. "Divine! Absolutely divine."

He smiled and turned to search through the wardrobe to find something more suitable that would please her. "Vuitton or Chanel?"

"I'm thinking the Chanel would be appropriate for tonight's event."

Returning the original selection, he picked out a few dresses to choose from.

"Oh, Marshal, thinking about it again, would you mind fetching me that Vuitton you had? It looked absolutely splendid."

Appearing frustrated, he did as she asked. *This old woman has lost her mind, running me around like the help.* "Here you go, Katheryn. I hope you find this to be fitting."

She looked in the vanity and began to hum an old Billie Holiday standard that transitioned into Ella Fitzgerald.

"Here are these," Roman said, holding out a vintage metal tray with a few pills on it.

Passive-aggressively, she looked back at him and continued to hum. "Marshal, darling, could you please hand me my white gloves?"

"I need you to take these first." Seeing that she was annoyed, he quickly changed the direction of his approach. "You want to be ready for your performance, don't you? These will help your voice. You can't let your fans down."

She nodded and took the pills from the tray, continued to hum, and began to look at herself in the mirror the same way she'd done since she was a little girl. Her hair was gray and falling out, and she often wore a wig when leaving the house.

She couldn't let her fans down.

*   *   *

I know that I said I wanted the Vuitton, but I'm not sure it will match the aesthetic of my gloves. Chanel, maybe that is what I should consider this evening, but then again the Vuitton feels natural.

I hope they like me. I hope they applaud for an ovation. It always makes me nervous with the contract, having to be off stage by 10:30.

I feel natural, yet I know what they want: a big show, something that will make them come back when I return to their city. I feel insignificant at times and wonder if someone will pick me up at the end of the evening: my darling Roderick.

Marshal is absolutely divine. The best manager I've had in years. Everything I ask for is there. I don't have to ask; it's just there. He reminds me of a man I used to date, a handsome and renowned Negro, Marques. I've always wondered what happened to him after the war. He left me like many of the men I've known. They all leave in the end.

"Marshal, darling, will you bring me my broach . . . the silver one."

I hope he called to ensure the details are in order. I must be there no later than a quarter past eight. The soundcheck is most important, as if I don't have a good soundcheck I can tell how the entire evening will go. I'm a bit meticulous, but then again, I don't care. I've hired Marshal to ensure the show goes on without a mishap.

"Marshal, darling, will you find me that number . . . The one I've been working . . ."

"Yes, Katheryn. And the car has been called."

"Thank you, darling. And what time should they arrive?"

"Thirty 'til."

I don't question him, as he's never been one to disappoint. I've always thought about how he reminds me of Roderick—polite and always loving.

The phone is ringing. I should probably answer. I don't want to be taken by surprise.

"Yes, this is Katheryn. Yes, umm-hmm . . . I do . . . and it should be ready . . . No, I don't think so. Maybe I should . . . I do always worry about that . . . that makes perfect sense. Yes, I understand. Okay . . . so maybe later, then. Yes, I will inform him . . . Send Rebecca and the children my love."

"Who was that?" Roman inquires.

"That was Vernon, the manager of the venue. Apparently there has been some mix-up with the deposit. We got bought out by another act."

"That's a shame. Would you like me to cancel the car?"

"Yes, darling. It looks like it's just going to be us old birds tonight. Please pour me another libation. And please ring Roderick and let him know the situation. We cannot keep him waiting in this confusion."

I'm livid and beyond irritated. I specifically told Vernon we'd have the money two weeks ago. I just don't know what could have happened. I need to make a call to my finance manager. I'm sure he can clear this mess up. My fans will be disappointed, and all over a simple mix-up.

I wonder when Roderick will return home. Maybe he is getting me flowers, as he always does. White daffodils; my favorite. He's always been such a dear to me. After fifty years of marriage, it's amazing how we survived. Such a gentle soul, with such patience. I couldn't have asked for anything better in this life.

I wonder if he will still bring me flowers.

"I couldn't get a hold of him at his office," Marshal says, handing me a cocktail. "Left a message with his secretary, who told me he has a busy schedule. But I let her know tonight's performance was canceled and that he should return home after work."

I can't wait to see him and show him that old standard I revived.

*   *   *

I can see Katheryn is disappointed and confused. I feel bad for her. We go through this every day. Luckily, Ronny is a good sport about the whole thing. At first I would giggle because it all seemed so . . . well, it just seemed ridiculous. But it became sad knowing she might spend her entire life reliving this same moment. Ms. Katheryn seems oblivious at times, but I feel if I replay that moment over and over it might spark memories. The medication seems to be helping, but I remain uncertain how effective her treatment is.

Marshal is the name she's given me. I used to get frustrated, as my name tag clearly states my name: Roman White, RN. But after speaking to her therapist I learned it's just a part of the disease.

From what I've gathered, Marshal was the personal assistant who managed her affairs. Here at Hampton Grove we've been informed not to wear a nurse's uniform. This place is high-end, boutique. A twenty-four-hour supervised nursing home. Here, they hold the philosophy that patients shouldn't be triggered. So regardless of what she wants to call me, I've grown a tolerance. At the end of the day, my paycheck is written out to Roman White.

The phone rings. "Yes . . . why, certainly, yes. I will let her know."

Every day at eleven o'clock, someone calls and I say the same thing. She is oblivious and will forget by tomorrow.

"Who was that, darling?"

"It was Roderick. He wanted me to inform you that he's terribly sorry but doesn't expect he will make it home in time for dinner. He said you should go on without him."

Flowers are sent to her apartment every day before I leave. I am sure to take them with me and dispose of them in the dumpster outside. She hasn't caught on, but why would she? I can't imagine what it must be like to have this tiny glimmer in her memory that keeps her coming back to 1953 when she was at her prime. Maybe it provides her peace of mind.

"Katheryn, what shall we order tonight? What is your desire?"

I ask, knowing full well her response.

"Salmon and potatoes."

It's the same thing every night and has not changed. I've tried a million times to make other suggestions, but she doesn't latch onto any of them.

"Then salmon and potatoes it will be."

She looks delighted and amused for a moment. Then the disappointment returns. She doesn't realize her darling Roderick is never coming home. Maybe it's better this way, to have never fallen out of love, believing things in life are constant and your deceased husband is still alive.

"Oh, my, what have you done with yourself?" I say as her hair tangles in her brush. "Here, let Marshal help you." What a complete and utter mess—a rat's nest. I just hope I don't have to grab the shears.

"I was just trying to . . ."

"I know, and you did a great job. Now let me fix this so you can be presentable for . . . We mustn't allow a lady of leisure such as yourself to live under these conditions."

* * *

Roman was kind to her. He was a compassionate person, which is why he became a nurse. He looked at Katheryn and wondered about her life and how she'd entered this condition.

It must be difficult, he thought, but he understood this to be a progression of old age. He hoped he would never find himself living like her, disassociated and removed from reality.

Katheryn looked at herself in the mirror, appearing confused. It was as if the fog would soon be lifted, like something rising on the tip of her tongue, yet she was unable to put into words what she was thinking. She felt she was being held back by something invisible yet recognizable within her.

"Have you ordered the salmon?" she asked.

"I did. It will be delivered no later than five."

Ass and Balls, Upper Back

"**G**loria, can you get Bitterman on the phone?"
What an incompetent waste of talk space. I ask her to do one thing, just one, and she can't even do that. I should just fire her, but something within me says she's the type to file a harassment suit. I don't know what these secretarial programs are teaching women these days—they'll let anyone in. You spend your efforts, time, and money working with an executive search firm and they send you girls like Gloria.

"I'm waiting . . ."

"Mr. Tiller, Mr. Bitterman is in a meeting."

"Well, did you explain its urgent and imperative I speak with him?"

"Yes, sir. Mr. Till—"

"And," I interrupt. Silence follows. "AND . . ."

"And his assistant said he is in meetings all day."

"Gloria, I don't think you understand how many girls would kill for this job, but you, well. I don't know what they taught you back at Secretaries 'R' Us, but this is *real life*! I need you to do better."

"Yes, Mr. Tiller."

"So call his assistant back and tell her it's urgent. Lives are on the line here!"

"Yes, Mr. Tiller, I'll let her know."

You think she'd get the message. It's not difficult to follow. She just needs to answer the phone and be one step ahead of the game. It isn't hard, but she does smell nice. The last assistant lasted for about seventy-two hours, and now I've ended up with Gloria.

She'll be easy to train, they said. Yeah fucking right.

"Mr. Tiller, I have Bitterman on line one."

See? That wasn't difficult. Maybe her nails are too long. Time for someone to get a clipping.

"Gloria, please place Bitterman on hold and let him know I'll be with him momentarily."

"Yes, sir, Mr. Tiller. Mr. Bitterman, please hold. Mr. Tiller will be with you in just a moment."

"Oh, and please put out a company-wide memo that acrylic nails are no longer permitted at Tiller & Associates. If anyone is observed violating this policy, they will be sent home for the day without pay. The *L.A. Times* just released a report that people are suffering hearing loss due to loud clanking on the keyboard. And please make sure you sit silently on the call to transcribe our entire conversation and have the document sent to the Library of Congress to avoid theft of my intellectual property."

"Yes, Mr. Tiller."

"Bitterman, old chap," I say with an exaggerated level of excitement, "how are you? Umm-hmm . . . yes . . . oh, most certainly. Tell me, how are Bunny and the children? Is that so? Well, congratulations, old chap . . . yes . . . umm-hmm. I was thinking the same thing."

The old fat bastard keeps droning on about his litter of children and his slut wife who's been fucking one of our mutual colleagues—the poor bastard doesn't even know the little shit she is carrying is probably Baker's.

" . . . that does sound interesting. I'm wondering . . . umm-hmm . . . we really need to be a bit more progressive with your portfolio. I recently received some intel from a very reliable source . . . Yes, yes . . . they say the dividends are going to be massive. It's not at all risky . . . a smart financial move if you ask me. Bitterman . . . Bitterman, have I ever steered you wrong?"

I don't really understand people. Incompetent. They ask for your advice, and when given, they begin to doubt your abilities. I'm in the money business. If they don't get paid, neither do I. It's that simple.

"Bitterman, I hear what you're saying, but you just have to trust me on this one!"

He doesn't sound convinced.

"No, unfortunately I'm unable to tell you the source, but just know that it's very reliable . . . Alright, well, if you change your mind, let me know. Let's have Gloria set up a dinner in the next week to go over the numbers . . . Alright, old chap. Please send Bunny and the kids my regards."

What a fucking idiot! That guy needs a stiff cock up his ass.

"Gloria, get Mr. Barney Williams on the phone."

My tolerance is running low right now, but maybe it's my blood sugar.

"Mr. Tiller, there isn't a contact for a Mr. Barney Williams in our system."

"Gloria . . . GLORIA . . . there was this thing invented years ago, it's called Google. You enter a few keywords into the search bar, and thousands upon thousands of hyperlinks appear. Or maybe they didn't teach you about that back in school?"

"Yes, Mr. Tiller."

I tell ya, she's not that bright. I bet she wouldn't even recognize her face in the mirror if she saw it. The only thing she's got working for her is that oversized rack and voluptuous ass, which I'm sure many guys have explored.

"Gloria . . . Gloria . . . please call the day spa and schedule an appointment with Robert. I'm feeling a lot of tension in my upper body after that phone call."

"Yes, Mr. Tiller."

I wish more people understood and valued the likes of Joe

Tiller. I provide a certain level of personalized attention that you don't get with one of those bigger firms. I'm sure he's been brainwashed by that cunt wife of his. She's got him by the balls, and now I'm the one suffering.

"Gloria . . . GLORIA . . . did you make my appointment?"

"Yes, Mr. Tiller, Robert has you scheduled for noon."

At least she can do one thing right. I've been seeing Robert for years. He's a good-looking guy, but I look better. He's a queer, and I know how fags like to rub their hands on other men. I mean, who wouldn't? I'm sure he thinks about me at night when he is lying beside his queer lover. Rubbing one out and revisiting his thoughts of me. I feel it's only right to provide my fans with something to fantasize about later. I get aroused thinking about how others want a piece of me. Something I find myself thinking about when I'm alone at home.

*   *   *

"Mr. Tiller, how are you this afternoon?"

"I'm fine, thanks. A few minutes early, but I'm fine."

"Robert is just finishing up with his last appointment. He'll be with you momentarily. Please feel free to help yourself to a beverage while you wait."

If it weren't already enough that I pay a monthly membership fee, I'm expected to leave a tip, which, if I were in Europe, would not be common practice. You tip for *everything* in New York, from the doorman at your apartment to cab drivers. Everyone expects a handout.

They're like those welfare mothers with children from five different fathers, who expect everyone else to pick up the tab. All those Sharitas and their heathens should be thanking Joe Tiller for his contribution to the Unwed Mothers National Slush Fund. I hope Robert's sterilized his entire body before even thinking about touching me.

"Mr. Tiller, Robert is ready."

It's about time—ten minutes later and two diet cokes in.

"Thanks."

*   *   *

"Mr. Tiller, what can I do for you today?"

What can he do . . . didn't he ask the Maria working the front desk why I'm here?

"A massage and wax."

"Certainly. And what areas will we be working on today?"

"The usual, you know."

I'm not one who likes to repeat myself. I shouldn't have to. You think Robert would already come in prepared and ready to begin: ass and balls, upper back.

"Okay, Mr. Tiller. Please remove as much clothing as you feel comfortable." He motions to the white robe that's folded on a chair.

I take off everything and don't even bother with the robe, then slide into the blanket on the table. I lay my head down, close my eyes, and concentrate on the ambiance within the room, focusing my attention on the background music. If I could stay here all day, I would, but I realize it's not feasible. I've thought about calling Gloria and having her cancel all my afternoon appointments, but I've been known to just not show up, and I'm trying to turn a new leaf.

There are eight million people in this city. Honestly, who would even notice?

The door creeps open and I find myself distracted by Robert as he fumbles around in what sounds like a drawer. You think he would've set everything up before I got here, but that would assume he thought that far in advance. I wonder if he and Gloria are related.

"Mr. Tiller, we are going to begin," he says.

I should've requested one of the other workers, but I've got a bush the size of Africa growing on my ass and need someone who enjoys nothing more than to caress my body—that queer who last time probably stole my moist boxers and smelled where my ass crack was. You can't trust a faggot in that area.

Robert's hand touches my shoulder, and something about it sends a shiver down my spine. He touches my pecs, and then my abs. I'm sure this is why he went to school for massage therapy— to have contact with someone who will never want him. I'm sure this has made his day.

"There is a lot of tension in your chest," he says and continues to rub my extremities. "I'm going to use a different kind of oil. It will further help relax you."

He is right. I am starting to feel relaxed. I'm sure that's a classic fag pickup line: "tension in your chest."

I take a deep breath and exhale loudly to send a message that he's "doing a great job." I would get up, but I think it may leave him feeling offended. I wonder what he and his fag boyfriend do at night. How does that even work? Your asshole is where shit comes out. I wonder who's the man and who's the woman. I bet his lover dresses up in women's clothing while Robert fucks him from behind.

I feel the sheet being lifted, and my right leg is now exposed. I can feel the side of his polyester-cotton blend scrubs rubbing up against my arm.

"Just relax and allow your body to melt into the mattress," he says in a soft, low voice.

The hairs on my arm feel like they're starting to stand up. He's touching my calf muscle. I can only imagine what he's thinking: *I'm going to turn him.*

"I'm going to move to your left side. Just continue to relax."

Again, I feel his pants rubbing against my arm. I'm going to act like I just had a reaction to his touch and flinch. This will allow me to see if he's getting aroused.

I'm sure he wants to touch it, and if I were feeling generous today I might let him. I'd bet you a hundred bucks that after I leave he imagines what it looks like. He's probably one of those sick fucks who, when you walk into an empty bathroom lined with urinals, stands next to the only guy taking a piss. I'm sure he glances to his side to check out what the dude next to him is packing. I've seen plenty of guys like him before. This is why when the bathroom is empty I go into one of the stalls. Next time he goes for a long-winded lunge on my leg, I'm going to extend my arm to see if his tiny pecker is hard.

"I need to turn you over onto your stomach to begin the second half of your treatment. Then we'll move to the waxing portion of the session."

I think he was on to me. That's why he decided to turn me over. With my eyes closed, I hear him moving to the other side of the table and he begins rubbing my shoulders. I think about Gloria's big tits and how they would feel on my back, not Robert.

My head is lying in this little donut. I open my eyes to notice he's wearing yellow tube socks and white shoes, which match his pants. The cuffs of each pant leg are rolled up, but his ankles aren't exposed.

These fags love their capris. Gloria used to wear them often until I sent a company-wide memo addressing professional attire in the workplace. As Robert sits in the swivel chair, I'm in direct gaze of his crotch.

Fucking sick. I don't want to look at his junk. I wonder if he prefers briefs to boxers. If I were a queer, I would make sure to wear the tightest undergarments in case I got aroused, but then Robert probably has a tiny pecker and doesn't need tight underwear.

"So, tell me there, Robert. How's the lady?"

"He's great. Celebrating our two-year anniversary next month," he says and chuckles.

"Interesting."

It was, indeed, interesting, as I think he's making the entire thing up. These queers. It seems a little off to me, unnatural, and something I'm sure his mother was extremely disappointed about.

I'm still locked in on his crotch, and I think this whole conversation has gotten him aroused. He continues to rub my shoulders and begins moving down to the middle of my back. He stands up and I can feel his junk rubbing up against the crown of my head, but I still can't tell if he's hard.

"That feels real nice, Robert," I say to make him think I'm somehow interested, luring this queerbait into my trap. He's now standing on my left side, so I think I'm going to try one more time to act like I'm having a reflexive reaction so I can see if this twisted fuck is getting his jollies rocked from touching my body.

One . . . two . . . three. I hit my target and stay there for a moment. "Oh, excuse me, Robert. I think I had a knee-jerk reaction."

"That's okay, Mr. Tiller. It happens from time to time. If you find you're having these types of reactions, please let me know. It could be that you are becoming over-stimulated."

I'm sure he says that to everyone. I feel like he's related to one of those senators you hear about on the local news who gets caught having sex in some dirty bathroom at JFK. I'm not sure, but I think he liked it. I'm going to do it again, but this time I'm going to let him know it's intentional.

One . . . two . . . three. I dive in deep and leave my hand there. It gets completely silent. He walks to the other side of the room. The door opens and closes.

"Mr. Tiller." This time it's not Robert speaking.

The lights are now on full-blast, and my ability to relax feels impossible. I don't understand why they promise a "serene and peaceful environment" when what the advertisement on the subway doesn't match what happens in a place like this.

"Mr. Tiller." I lift my head. "Please get dressed, gather your things, and come with me."

I'm confused as to why the bossman feels the need to disrupt me. I'm sure that little faggot Robert complained to the management.

If anything is said, I assure you it will come down to his word against mine. The customer is always right.

Showtime

She continued to stare at herself in the vanity mirror, feeling a sense of peace. Still, something within her felt unsettled. She recognized the woman before her but was taken with another thought of Roderick.

Why does he have to work so late? Maybe he's screwing his secretary.

She found herself obsessing about him, wondering how he spent his day. She understood how married men sometimes strayed from their wives.

If she had never met Roderick, she thought, she might have married Marques—then reminded herself: *It was never in our cards.*

"Marshal, darling, did I ever tell you about my first love?"

"No, you never did." Roman played along as if he hadn't heard this story repeatedly for the past six months. "Please, do continue."

"Swear to me this, that you will never tell Rodrick, as it could break him," she said and took in a deep breath. "It was the summer of '53 and the world was beginning to change. Everything was changing. I was a regular at the Polly Parker Club in Harlem. Negroes weren't allowed in most white establishments back then. It was magical! Marques played that bass like the women he loved. The moment I saw him, I was immediately taken."

Katheryn took a moment to pause, then continued. "He wore a charcoal pinstriped suit and fedora. He was handsome, intriguing, and full of energy. I just watched him play and was taken on a mental journey, as he was accompanied by that jazz band. Occasionally we would perform on the same bill, but on my nights off . . . if I'd not seen him for a while, I would head on over and order a drink," she held up her martini glass, "and sit amazed by the ambiance of the club. I was just eighteen then and felt so free . . . There was something about that time that has continued to stick with me."

Roman looked at her with amusement. "It sure sounds like you had yourself some great times."

She appeared fragile and temperamental. "It sure was. Before my record deal . . . I was freer back then. It feels as if it were just yesterday."

Katheryn continued to yammer, and he just listened to her reminisce about her life back in 1953.

A part of him felt sad for her, as there were certain things she remembered more frequently than others. *I hope this never happens to me*, he thought, wondering what it would feel like to forget almost everything and have nothing solid to connect with.

This felt strange and unusual. Their lives couldn't have been more different, yet he felt a sudden surge of compassion. He saw her as someone who was narcissistic, as she never inquired about his life, and thought maybe she saw him as nothing more than the help. He found their generational difference to be strange yet refreshing.

"Yes, darling," she said with an expressive movement of the martini glass, "Marques was divine. I've never met a kinder soul. I believe we were kindred spirits."

She seemed to be a woman who didn't recognize herself anymore or the people she encountered in life.

"He sounds pleasant," Roman said to demonstrate he'd been listening.

She would usually stop at this point. It was common for her to become distracted and lost in her train of thought. But today she continued.

"I loved him, Marshal. And I often wonder what our lives

would have been like if we'd lived in a different time."

Roman knew very little about Marques with the exception of what Katheryn had told him. "Oh, really?" His ears perked.

She began to fan herself. "Yes, darling. Again, not a word of this is to reach Roderick's ears."

"Of course, your secret is safe with me."

Her eyes began to water as she looked down and grabbed a gold chain from the jewelry box. She brought it to her chest and closed her eyes, deep in thought.

"I've missed him for what seems an eternity," she said, clasping her hands together and bringing the chain to her lap. The whites of her eyes had reddened, and she noticed it when she looked in the mirror. "Oh, the hay fever! It's that time of year."

It was clear she didn't want to admit to her sadness—to herself or to Roman.

"Well, that sounds like a really nice story."

"It was. He had this way about him . . . to captivate an entire audience. When he walked on stage, the entire room stopped. He was a very handsome Negro."

Roman caught her passive use of the word Negro but understood she wasn't trying to be derogatory. She was just trying to be culturally relevant, as he himself was black.

"I remember that night as if it were yesterday. He'd just finished up his second set, and I, my drink. As a white woman, I got looks. White girls didn't come to this part of the city and spend an afternoon at a speakeasy with a room full of Negro men. But I didn't care. This was the only place Marques and I could fully be ourselves. My mother and father would never have approved of this arrangement. They'd never visited Harlem, let alone associate with a Negro. It was just the way it was."

Roman was intrigued; he wanted to know more. It never occurred to him that Katheryn had lived this life. Their worlds were extremely different, and if he were not employed here he would never have met her.

"Darling, will you fix me another drink?"

He moved to the bar cart and refilled her libation. "That sounds like quite the story. I must say, you're a woman full of surprises!"

She smiled and continued. "I knew all Negroes weren't bad. I knew this because I was raised by Effie, may her soul rest in peace. My mother wasn't the woman who raised me, no. It was Effie. She changed my pampers, cooked, and taught me how to French braid my hair. I remember those evenings when my parents would sit in the other room entertaining their friends. She would pick me up and place me on the counter and sing those old spirituals as she brushed my hair. She was a woman of faith who was always kind. When she died, they hired another woman, but I don't think anyone could have ever replaced her."

Roman felt an extent of emotional transference, revisiting those times his grandmother would sing to him as a child while taking a bath, then grew sad when he thought of how she'd died a year ago from cancer.

"Here you are, Katheryn. And here's something for your voice."

She was hesitant to take the medication but trusted him nonetheless.

*   *   *

If I have to hear this woman rattle on "Negro" one more time . . . Is she completely unaware I'm standing ten feet away and can hear everything she says? My mama never let me forget that her grandparents were released from the plantation years ago. I have a name.

"Darling . . . darling . . . can you be a dear and fetch me

another?"

Fetch her. If I wasn't being paid, I would've probably strangled this woman by now. "Yes, Katheryn."

I'm not assuming she would care to inquire about my life, which is probably the way she's treated most of the people in hers, not caring about anyone but herself. I never met Marques, but from the sound of it he got out at the perfect time. This woman has never worked a day in her life. She had a mama, a daddy, and a nanny. You think with everything she's had she would have learned a few valuable skills.

We've been informed that under no circumstances are we to interrupt a patient during moments of storytelling. Rather, we are to make a clinical notation, the date, and provide as much detail of what the patient disclosed. Later, the doctor will revisit this during individual therapy. It's believed that if we can trigger older memories, we can mentally walk the patient into the present, addressing loss or anything that remains unresolved.

While it's extremely sad to think one day everyone could forget who they are, I do wonder how much of this is a reality. It appears she observed much in her life, and yet it seems as if something about her feels undocumented.

From what I gather, she lived an interesting life. Regardless of whether this memory is an actual moment from her past or something she made up, it is hers.

Getting old seems difficult, but it is something I realize happens to each of us. I hope that when I'm leaning on death's door, I will have lived a purpose-driven life.

*   *   *

I'm feeling unresolved in this moment. As long as I've known Marshal, I've never let him see me in this condition. At any moment I feel as though I could go into a fit of hysteria, the flu, or even worse. Maybe I'm coming down with the consumption. I need to find rest. Maybe I should go to bed.

I'm still not certain why Vernon wasn't paid and why the show has been canceled. When Roderick arrives this evening, I'm going to have him make me a bath that we may discuss this. He must speak with Vernon to ensure something like this never happens again.

Even if there was a problem, I've got enough money in the bank to buy that theater. Vernon should be thanking me for even deciding to grace that dump of an establishment with my presence. I have many places I can perform, and for some reason I always return there.

Marshal doesn't seem to care that my career and the dedication of my fans are going down the toilet, or for that matter what the tabloids write. I need him to place a call to my accountant and check on my finances. I may have lost everything, but I haven't lost my mind.

"Marshal, darling, can you please contact my financial advisor and let him know that I've requested a meeting to discuss my portfolio?"

"Of course, Katheryn."

Financial problems! I think not. I receive a quarterly payment for all my royalties. I refuse to accept the notion that I'm bankrupt. They're going to get an earful from Roderick when I tell him about this.

I would like to think this was just some sort of mishap, that possibly there has been a huge misunderstanding. This is clearly a breach of my contract. I made this industry millions. The least they could do is allow me to perform.

The show is sold out. My name in lights and across the marquee. This all seems trivial and unfortunate. I've done nothing but give my sweat, blood, and tears for this industry, and this is how I'm repaid. I'm respected and a legend, only to find out I've been thrown away and placed in some rummage bin. I wish they understood who they were messing with—and they will, once I'm through with them.

"Grab my coat, darling. It's time to go pay someone a visit."

*　　*　　*

Roman looked confused and didn't understand what was happening but dared not to question her.

"Okay, Katheryn. And where are we headed on this fine afternoon?" he asked, to which she appeared contemplative and disoriented.

"Please call my driver and have him arrive no later than three. It's imperative that we leave within the next hour before the bank has closed." A smidge of agitation and discontent laid in her response, yet it was clear she could not fully form her thoughts as she attempted to remain concentrated.

"But what about dinner . . . what will you have?"

"I'll order something else. Please, just gather my coat and purse."

Roman knew this might lead to an unneeded embarrassment and realized he had to act quickly to prevent any further disruption.

This crazy white woman wants to go to a bank? he thought, then texted Ronnie: *SHE WANTS TO GO TO THE BANK. I NEED A DIVERSION. CALL HER ROOM! PRETEND YOU'RE SHAPIRO. IT'S SHOWTIME* ☺ ☺ ☺

The landline began to ring. "Why, yes," he said into his phone. "Umm-hmm. Certainly . . . you would . . . I'll see if she is available." Roman turned to Katheryn. "Vernon is on the line."

She stopped abruptly and looked at Roman. "Who?"

"Vernon," he said, then added: "Vernon Shapiro."

"Ah, yes, that old bastard. What does he want?"

"He didn't say. Just that it was urgent and he needs to speak with you."

She took the phone. "Kathryn York speaking."

"Katheryn, it's Vernon."

"Yes, I gathered that. What is it you want?"

"It appears there has been some mix-up. I was able to locate the money that was used to pay the deposit. A glitch in the system, I suppose."

"Glitch in the system," she said. "Well, that doesn't sound very reassuring, now, does it?" She put her hand over the receiver and mouthed to Roman, "They misplaced the deposit" and continued on. "Well, is that really my problem? I think it's time to get my lawyer involved. You can't dismiss a legally binding contract." She took a deep pause. "So what you're saying is if this were my error, I would be spanked like a dog, but when it's yours I'm just supposed to sit back and grin. Well, I'm just not comfortable with this. You will be hearing from Roderick and, better yet, my lawyer. Good day, Mr. Shapiro. Send my regards to your wife and children."

She slammed down the phone.

"It appears the entire thing was a huge mix-up in accounting," she said. "Mr. Shapiro apologized but told me the sound engineer was sent home and they have no one who has the capability to run the system, so the show is canceled."

Roman looked at her and began to smirk. "Is that so?"

"Yes, darling, it is. Please fix me another libation. I need to think on this for a moment!"

He looked relieved but wondered what she might have planned. She'd never gotten to this point. Usually by now she'd drift back into her normal state of confusion. It felt cruel to create this new addition to her story, but it was likely she wouldn't remember tomorrow anyway. Yes, she was privileged, and yes, she had never lifted a finger her entire life, but one day we would all find ourselves limited and losing our minds.

"Darling, how is my drink coming along? That last one you made really sang to me."

"I'm glad you enjoyed it. I guess I'm a mixologist of sorts!"

"Marques used to love bourbon on the rocks, but sometimes he would have it neat!"

Roman looked to see Katheryn glancing down at her hands, still clasping the gold chain in her palm.

"Sometimes it's difficult to think about what my life would have been like if I continued down that path."

It was clear she felt deep sorrow—something many people experience.

"That sounds like a fascinating story," Roman said.

He didn't know how to respond or in what way he should provide comfort. He could see the back of her head and the side of her profile in the mirror and watched as she took a handkerchief hidden under the cufflink of her blouse and wiped her eyes to keep the mascara from running. He realized this was not something she'd concocted. It was indeed a recollection from 1957.

"It doesn't matter now, darling. He's long since passed. I wish I would have stopped him that evening, but I found myself distracted by the thought that one day I would be famous. If only I'd been there . . . maybe, just maybe, he'd still be alive."

"If I Don't Get Paid, She Doesn't Get Paid"

Can you believe that bullshit?

I mean, honestly, the little faggot told his manager I tried to grab his junk. He truly doesn't think someone like Joe Tiller would grab someone's cock, does he?

A pussy, maybe, but never a cock.

That dipshit of a manager said, "It is highly inappropriate to molest our staff."

Fuck him and that rub-and-tug—I'm a good-paying customer. When I get back to the office, I'm going to ask Gloria to draft up a grievance letter to the corporate office.

I feel violated to be accused of something so grotesque. I'm not a queer; he is. They both are.

If you ask me I think he's just angry that I left him a shitty tip the last time I was there. My ass hair is growing like the Amazon rainforest, and I was looking forward to a nice, clean wax.

I'm going to have Gloria make some calls when I return to the office. I'm sure she's gotten her asshole waxed in the past. Maybe she can give me a referral.

She better have trimmed those acrylic claws. The last thing I need is to hear her clanking on that keyboard. I'm wondering if she was able to contact that waste of space, Barney Williams. At the end of the day, if I don't get paid, she doesn't get paid—so she better up her game.

*   *   *

"Gloria. *Gloria!* When I get back to the office, you better have set up an appointment with Barney Williams for this evening. It's imperative that he and I meet today."

"But Mr. Tiller," she said, appearing shaken, "it appears we don't have a contact number for Mr. Williams."

"Gloria, I pay you good money not to think. You've got to rise above the adversity. One day you are going to thank me and tell people I was a major influence in shaping your character and work ethic. I'm sure you can find him on one of those social media sites you sit on all day when you should be working."

"Yes, Mr. Tiller!"

"And, Gloria, one more thing. I need the number to a spa!"

"Yes, Mr. Tiller. Would you like me to reschedule with Robert?"

"Gloria, did I ask for the number of *that* spa? I said *a* spa! I specifically provided an indication that I was looking for *a spa*, not *the* spa!"

"Yes, sir."

"And, Gloria, if you aren't able to locate Mr. Williams, it may be in your best interest to go down to the basement, grab one of those paper boxes, and never return to Tiller & Associates. This is solid grounds for termination, you know, not fulfilling your duties. Also, please transcribe this conversation and send it off to the Library of Congress."

*   *   *

I know she wants me, but I also understand that most women do. She's a "butter face"—a banging body, ass, and rack. But her face! I always crack myself up telling that joke . . . a "butter face."

It's no wonder she's single. When a guy fucks her, I'm sure he pushes her head into a pillow to avoid throwing up. Her pussy probably tastes like tuna. I thought I smelled something the other day. It was probably her rank cunt stinking up the office. When I get back, I'm going to have her send out a company-wide memo to address this.

"Gloria, I need you to draft up a memo that specifically addresses the issue of hygiene in the workplace. I don't know what it is, but something smells like it died. Under no circumstances will this be tolerated. Employees found to be in violation of this policy will be sent home immediately. Also, what's the status on Williams?"

Let's hope she takes the hint. I can't have clients coming into the office with that smell hanging around. With all the money she spends on her nails and hair, you think she'd take better care of herself.

I'm sure she'll use this to push for a raise. I can hear her now: "Sir, I'm in need of a raise. I can't afford to manage my PH levels."

The only thing she's going to get is a pink slip, not a paycheck. This is the last time I use that agency. The least they could do is send one of those good-looking girls they showcase in the advertisements. I should just hire a model. Maybe then it would draw in more business. They don't have to be smart, just pretty. That's all I need.

*　　*　　*

Gloria sat at her desk, panicked.

He's going to fire me! she thought.

She conducted a Google search and nothing viable came up. The only thing she had to go on was the information Joe provided, which was very little.

It was unclear why she stayed working for him. Maybe it was

because this was her first job out of college, and being unemployed was not anything one should have to experience living in New York. The thought of moving back to her parents' house in Ohio and admitting to everyone she knew that she'd failed and to hear the words "we told you so"—the nagging voice of her mother—terrified her.

She'd graduated with high distinction from Ohio State and desired nothing more than to one day become a successful writer. She told herself that if she survived Joe Tiller for one year, maybe she could get a real job at one of those luxurious publishing companies. She'd recently read *The Devil Wears Prada*, only to find it was now her reality.

It all seemed bleak and without end. *Who the hell is Barney Williams? There has to be some reason he appears this desperate. But it's not really any of my concern.*

She rummaged through Facebook but came up with many people named Barney Williams. For a moment she began to disassociate, thinking about the date she'd scheduled after work, thinking, *I hope he's nice.*

She assumed Mr. Tiller was being his typical self and would become easily distracted with his next crisis. She decided she'd give him a piece of her mind and thought about secretly videotaping the entire conversation—at least that way she would have some evidence when applying for unemployment, which she would be rightfully entitled to.

She began to file her nails and disregarded the directive of the memo she was supposed to write. *He'll probably forget about that, too,* she thought and wondered what his hang-ups were and why he centered the focus of his attacks on her—targeting her for the simple fact he had unresolved issues with women.

She wondered if he felt threatened by her and that was why he was so crass. It didn't make sense, and she wondered if maybe he wasn't loved enough as a child—that he needed mothering, the thing he'd missed out on as a toddler.

She'd spent the afternoon applying to jobs and heard the best time to submit your resume was during the late afternoons on Tuesdays. She thought about what she would do if she failed. Moving back home was not an option.

Like other young women before her, she wanted two things: a career and a husband. She wanted to marry a successful man she could spend time with in the Hamptons on weekends.

She could tell her boss to screw himself and take a vacation. She refused to accept that her destiny would end at Tiller & Associates. In fact, she didn't see herself here for more than a year but realized the options were minimal. Everyone was looking for "New York experience."

She thought about waiting tables at a restaurant in the West Village, but they required two years, which she didn't have. She'd waited tables in college at a Steak 'n Shake near the bypass close to her house but wasn't abreast to the hip lingo for kale and chorizo, or what those meant.

Growing distracted, she took a peek into the company share drive. She saw a folder labeled MEMOS which was where the previous victim of Joe Tiller saved and documented the fax confirmations sent to the Library of Congress.

Gloria clicked on another folder labeled Joe Tiller (PRIVATE), which she assumed would be interesting, and found a spreadsheet labeled ACCOUNTS.

Opening the document, she saw there were ten names listed. She found Barney Williams at Williams Innovations and his direct number with a 212 area code and address.

She felt bad for snooping but also realized her boss was a sociopath. She hoped he would show a little gratitude, but she also understood he was limited in his capacity to show anyone kindness. It occurred to her that she'd need to make up a story about how she found the information. She had to be cautious.

He's impulsively unable to manage his emotions, she thought. *I'm sure he'll just rant and move on.*

She started to obsess over whether she'd overstepped. She really didn't care if he fired her—she could collect unemployment and treat herself to something nice like a deep-tissue massage. It was almost as if she wanted to be chastised, and she wondered if she'd done something horrible in a past life. Regardless, she had to come up with a story he'd find believable.

What a fat fuck. His penis is probably really small. Nothing more than a man with Napoleon syndrome. Maybe he'll slip, fall, and be placed on bed rest.

It was apparent that she needed to figure things out. Clear her head and take a deep breath. She anticipated he would come in— ragging about something irrelevant that mattered little. In his emphatic response he would scream, "GLORIA! GLORIA!" as he often did.

She was reminded this was temporary but understood that if she were going to make it in New York City, she had to play nice.

*　　*　　*

I forgot my wallet and need to go back. I probably need to cancel all my plastic, too. They're hard up for business these days; it doesn't look like they have much traffic now that I'm gone. That little faggot will go through my wallet looking for a cash tip.

When I withdraw bills from the ATM I mark them on the right corner with a ballpoint pen. I'm wondering how many lucky motherfuckers have had the honor of touching what I've touched. I'm sure I've started a trend, and I'll need to copyright this idea. I'm sure it's difficult to come up with something this brilliant. I need to call Gloria, have her type up a memo and document the fax confirmation that it's been submitted to the Library of Congress.

"Gloria . . . Gloria! Damn it, Gloria, why do you have to let the phone ring more than once? Remember when I trained you? I told you to never let it ring more than once! I need you to type up a memo regarding the phone policy. Also, how's it coming with Mr. Williams?"

"I was able to find his contact information."

Interesting! I wonder how a dumb broad like her was able to locate his fat ass. She's not that bright.

"Well, that sounds perfect. Please have his secretary set up a meeting for this afternoon. Let her know it's urgent. He'll be ecstatic to hear from me."

The fat bastard probably hasn't been laid in a couple of years.

Gloria needs to come through on this one. She needs to be focused, talk nice to her friend over at Williams Innovations, and work her magic.

It's her job.

* * *

"Williams, you old bastard, how are you?" he said in a British accent, raising an invisible glass of bourbon on ice. "How are JC and Million? . . . That's what I said, Milo! Well, let me tell you, the market is doing well. I have information from a reliable intel source . . . Yes, a potential lead. Have you thought about expanding your portfolio? . . . Interesting. Well, let's meet over dinner sometime this week . . . Oh, really? Well, I think I have some time in the late afternoon today. I forgot to grab your card this morning . . . Yeah, my assistant Gloria was able to track you down . . . Yes, of course. Oh, and if I'm still invited, I would very much like to meet that darling niece of yours . . . Perfect! I will see you then!"

*   *   *

What he doesn't realize is that this reliable tip was taken directly from *The Wolf of Wall Street*: Nothing more than penny stocks. I just need to massage this for a bit longer, make him eager and then invest his cash into my bank account. From what I hear, Williams has a big wad and is eager to take the risk.

I wonder how someone like him ties his shoestrings in the morning. I bet his wife has to doublecheck his work, like going over math with a child. And speaking of his poor wife, although I can't place her face at the moment, I have a feeling she wasn't blessed with looks if he is her consolation prize. I feel sorry for that child. Miles . . . Martin . . . I can't remember. But without even seeing the offspring I can assume it ain't a pretty sight.

"Gloria . . . *Gloria* . . ."

"Yes, Mr. Tiller."

"Gloria, thank you for moving at a snail's pace. I need you to contact Mr. Williams' assistant and have her set up our meeting for drinks at that bar on Lexington. When you call the bar, please inform them the table should be far away from the door. Please let them know the table is for Mr. Tiller. They'll know what to do!"

"Yes, Mr. Tiller."

They certainly will know what to do. People think when you take them out for drinks that you're going to pay for top shelf. Not on Joe Tiller's dime. Maria knows the routine—Gloria will set up the appointment, and an hour before I arrive, Maria will take an empty bottle of Belvedere and pour in some cheap well liquor.

When I'm in need of a refill, I'll signal the cocktail waitress, who has a martini made for me with only the finest. I always make sure to pick up the tab and have dimwits like Barney leave a large tip. Maria's happy, I'm happy, and Mr. Williams thinks he got treated like royalty—except when he's vomiting his brains out the next morning.

"Gloria . . . GLORIA . . . I'm leaving the office to find something for Williams' wife. A little something to express my gratitude. And remember, under no condition are you to leave your post. Remember, the phone should never ring more than once and that you, my dear, are expendable."

*   *   *

Gloria stared out the window and thought about how Mr. Tiller might choke on his lunch, or better yet laugh so hard and find himself gasping for air. She hated it when he called her "dear"; it felt demeaning. Maybe it was because she'd been harassed so much during high school that she didn't believe any of the men who thought she was attractive in college. She hated the thought of him, but still had hope one day a man, maybe the one she was going on a date with, would think she was someone special. Not just a receptionist from Ohio.

Her grandmother used to talk about her sister, Martha, how she used to entertain crowds ("Thousands upon thousands," she would often say). Gloria wondered why she was never blessed with fame like Martha. Her grandmother used to ask Gloria to sing those old jazz standards, which she did as she'd minored in jazz performance while an undergraduate. It was always on the Holidays with the entire family gathered that her grandmother would say, "Gloria, can you perform something you're practicing in school?"

Gloria was always kind to entertain those around her, closing her eyes and imagining what it would be like to sing those old standards as Martha had done when she was in her twenties. Unfortunately, Martha had made some bad deals which left her bankrupt and nearly homeless. Gloria never met Martha, who died a slow death in her forties.

"The bottle," her grandmother would say. "She loved the bottle."

God's Waiting Room

It was clear to Roman that Katheryn was visibly irritated and noticeably restless.

"Katheryn," he said, attempting to distract her.

Unresponsive, she continued to stare into the mirror, brushing her hair. He didn't want to interrupt her and felt a sudden sadness come over him. He was told that if she appeared dazed, under no circumstances should he intervene, as it could send her into a state of panic and further disassociation.

So he sat back, parked in contemplation, and observed her interactions with the hairbrush—thinking about what was important, what he should report to her psychiatrist, but more importantly when his shift would be over.

"Marshal, darling." She laid the brush on the vanity. "Let's go on a walk. I would like to visit one of my favorite places in the park. Feed the geese some seed and ponder upon the memorial statue that was designed for the woman who loved *Alice In Wonderland*."

He'd never taken her outside of the apartment. Most of the time she'd spend her afternoons listening to Billie Holiday or Ella Fitzgerald on the record player. He wondered what might happen if he took her to the park—would she become confused and emotional, or maybe not recognize him at all?

"Yes, darling," she said, "a stroll in Central Park would lift my spirits. I used to find myself there in the late afternoon on the corner of 96th and Broadway before heading over to the Polly Parker, as I had to cut through the park to the West Side. Often times I found myself distracted by that statue and wondered if my life would ever be that relevant, that maybe someone would remember the way he did."

She was only thinking out loud, but Roman understood how someone might feel cooped up in this lavish apartment. He found himself distracted by the thought of what it was like to live in the 1950s, how the subway systems ran, what dating was like before cellphones and dating apps. One day, he realized, all those things would be fictional tales, never again to be told, and possibly forgotten.

He wondered what his grandmother's life had been like living in Harlem at the same time; they were similar in age—yet unlike Katheryn, his grandmother had survived segregation.

It was difficult for him to translate her experience to his own, as he was only in high school when Obama was elected. He had a deep understanding of racism and discrimination, but nothing like what his mother or grandmother had experienced.

He never wanted to forget the black plight, yet he'd graduated at the top of his class with a nursing degree from Columbia University—a practicing nurse working in a high-profile facility on the Upper East Side.

"Are you ready to go to the park?"

"Why, yes, darling, let me just finish this libation . . . freshen up my face and we shall be on our way. Please gather my billfold and evening coat. I'm thinking it's time to see Julian at Bergdorf Goodman. Please have car service ready, as we may decide to forego the park and head directly to Bergdorf's. Then again, I think we shall have time to do both."

While she had many bags, she fancied one in particular—the vintage Vuitton she acquired in 1981 at an auction. The leather straps were faded with discoloration and scratch marks from her fingernails and other objects, but like an aged wine, it only improved with time. Roman assumed she might want to go out in something less casual and laid out a black pair of flats and a few other options.

"What is that, darling?" she asked, providing a look of trepidation.

"It's . . . umm," he said, examining the tag, "Sascha Jason. Some upcoming designer in New York. Her assistant was here a few days ago and wanted to leave you some samples of her work."

She examined its print. "I do absolutely love this one, but not so much that," feeling the texture of the material with her fingertips, ". . . Darling, we're going to Bergdorf's. I couldn't possibly show up in some no-name frock by . . . what's her name?"

"Sascha Jason, madam."

"Do they even sell this at Bergdorf's?"

"This dress retails for $765," he said, picking up his phone and searching Sascha Jason and Bergdorf Goodman. Unable to find the name, he searched for something similar. "I don't know if they carry her there, but I do see she has an entire line at Barneys."

"Hmmm, rather interesting. Maybe she is one of those up-and-coming designers." She paused. "Let's go ahead, then, and take a chance on this Sascha Jason. Julian will have to be the one to decide. And if he says it's trash, I'm going to have it sent back and provide that designer a cease and desist."

He handed her the dress and shoes; gathered her Burberry cane, scarf, and pair of Manolo Blahniks and Chanel sunglasses, then waited patiently by the door. Even for a woman who was almost one hundred, she was stunning—put together and finally with somewhere to go.

It was as if this day was meant to be, that they were to share in her memories and venture out to meet Julian at Bergdorf Goodman.

*   *   *

It's approaching the afternoon on a Friday, and I hope we can see Julian and Central Park. I'm just wondering what my fans will say when they find out. Probably, "There she goes again, what a no-show!" I should have Vernon send out a press release letting all of New York know I had a family emergency, but what type of emergency would this be? A distant cousin, or maybe my sister? I suppose. Honestly, it really doesn't matter at this point. I just hope this isn't splashed across the entertainment section of the *New York Times*, but then again most people don't read.

There is something about this dress that attaches perfectly to my body—the print is divine, a green pattern with specks of yellow—and provides a certain point of reference to my life . . . just like my life. The indentations from the fabric flows naturally are reminders of myself as a little girl when life was simple and I remained ignorant to most things.

I wonder how my sister is doing these days. It has been a while since I last saw her. I need to schedule a date for afternoon tea— yes, myself, Roderick, Lilian, and her husband. I should have Marshal schedule this sooner than later, yet I will let tomorrow worry about itself; today I have a date with Bergdorf Goodman.

"Marshal, darling, can you please phone Julian and let him know that we are coming, and to have all the newest fashions ready for my viewing? Also, please call Lilian and let her know I'm thinking of her, and to call me later this evening to discuss when we can schedule an engagement for a late lunch."

Maybe I should call her myself, but then again Marshal is such a darling. "And, darling, please have Julian schedule this in one of those private rooms. I can't handle the odd looks I might receive when they see a handsome Negro such as yourself escorting me into the dressing room. That's all we need is for the *Times* to begin making up a story. If it were up to them, I would've been history long ago."

"Yes, Katheryn. I will let him know."

Honestly, I don't know what I would do without him. I wish Roderick didn't work so much and spent more time at home. I make more than enough with my royalties from that first album that he doesn't need to work, but whenever I mention it, he insists that we "live above the normal life," which is the way he always phrases it.

I need to find some new additions to my wardrobe. "Darling, any word from my Lilian? Also, have you called the driver? Ensure he knows we will be ready to leave in just a few moments and should be waiting."

"I thought we were going to Central Park."

"Yes, dear, I stand corrected. Let him know that we may be phoning him should we need to be carried."

I do that sometimes—find myself fixated on a certain thing. It feels as though I'm losing my mind, but I do know this: I must find a few additions for my collection, something in sequins, but possibly something similar to what I'm currently wearing.

I would say let's head down to Seventh Avenue, yet for the life of me I don't understand why Marshal would see a woman like me in a men's ready-to-wear store. Maybe he was thinking I would want to go to Barneys to gather up some ideas for Roderick, but then again maybe he is losing his mind.

"Darling . . . yes, I'm almost ready. Let's find ourselves, or maybe lose ourselves, in this city."

*　*　*

When she walked through the door she looked pieced together, like a package that would be opened on Christmas Eve. I thought maybe she might get further distracted with thoughts of Lilian. Just last week she was sobbing that they hadn't before her death, but today she's wanting to plan a tea party. I feel it's better this way; to be flooded with only present reminders of the past.

"Well, well, well, look at what the cat dragged in. If it isn't Mrs. Katheryn York!" I say.

She appears amused and entertained. "I think I'm ready," she says, and I hand her the purse, glasses, hat, and additional accessories. She dismisses the cane but approves of the Chanel sunglasses and the vintage gloves that stretch up her forearm. She grabs the recently purchased Philip Treacy from the hatbox in her closet, only to find herself distracted as she stares into the oval mirror in the foyer.

"This does seem grand, darling. Such a nice, relaxing day for a stroll. I'm feeling a bit unsure about these shoes . . . I know what I'm missing." She pulls a scarf that further enhances her color palette and focuses again on the mirror as she wraps it around her neck. "There we are, darling. I think I'm all put together now."

I smile and open the door. She hands me the keys and begins to walk toward the elevator in the hallway—believing it to be her old apartment, the one she left twenty years ago. The apartment where she'd return from the theater to find her husband waiting at the door to remove her coat and kiss her on the cheek.

"We mustn't be too late for his return. I must be home to greet Roderick."

I don't question her. "Of course, Katheryn. We have plenty of time."

It seems cruel, in a way, to dismiss the reality that he's never returning, yet she seems happy and alert. I wonder how she might feel if she were able to fast-forward through the decades of her life and past the generational differences that stand between us.

It seems complicated yet easy to imagine. I wonder if tomorrow she'll remember me. It's difficult to think that someone's life can end up this way, to eventually return to a childlike state and find yourself lingering in God's waiting room, where death awaits us all . . . to be left with the thoughts of what could have been, yet understanding this is the hand we've been dealt. Hers was nothing less than moments of happiness dressed in wealth.

In certain ways I envy her and wonder what it would be like to have her experiences. But I am someone who has worked for everything in life. She never worked a day in hers.

*   *   *

They took the elevator to the lobby where she was greeted by the bellhop. "Good day, ma'am," he said and tipped his hat.

"Good day to you as well, Joseph."

"What do you have planned for the afternoon?"

"We're headed to Central Park and then to Bergdorf's," she said excitedly.

"That sounds delightful! Well, enjoy yourself and do not hesitate to let us know if you need anything," He opened the door and directed her outside.

She looked at Joseph and began to move forward, putting on the sunglasses that were in her hand. "It's unexpectedly loud for this time of the afternoon," she said, to which Roman directed her to the way of the park. She motioned for his left arm and he obliged.

"I'm sorry, darling," she said, staring down at the concrete.

Roman was confused. He held her arm as they walked.

"It was never supposed to end that way," she continued. "I tried, but I guess sometimes you can only rock the system so far before it breaks you. Never let it break you, darling, regardless of what happens."

57

Roman listened as they walked down Park Avenue. He wasn't sure where she was mentally but realized she was reminiscing of a certain time in her history—a time when the world was simple, yet complex, where racial epithets were commonly used in many parts of the South, even today.

"I once sang for Martin backstage at a show in Birmingham. Billie Holiday was supposed to perform that evening. She was the headlining act, but we were informed by the venue manager that 'Negroes must use the back door.' Well, that was problematic as she and I were to perform with Nina Simone. I was the only white person in the facility and managed to convince Mr. Paul Walters that slavery had ended years ago and the Negro was free to do as they chose. Martin walked in right before my set and I was humming. I found out later he'd been shot by some man who hated him and the movement. For the life of me, I still don't understand why someone would want to take another person's life, but then again there was so much happening at that time."

Roman processed the complexity of what she'd just said. Either she was a good storyteller or she had sung to Dr. King before his death.

"It looks like we're almost there," he said, motioning to her mentally to begin processing what it would take to successfully cross the street.

She continued to hold on to his arm as he towered over her; he could only see the top of her hat. He knew her ability to remain coherent could be difficult, so he tested her to see if her faculties were intact.

"Central Park is a vast wonderland. How will we spend our time?"

"There's this place I want to take you," she said, remaining focused.

He didn't question her, rather just allowed her to guide them wherever she intended they go. He wondered if she truly understood where she was, and if she would manage to remain present for the remainder of the afternoon. Maybe he would understand more about her and her condition, but then again life is a complex process that leads us on various journeys and adventures.

She feared he might become bored but felt it was imperative they be here today, in this secret, undisclosed location. "Marshal, darling, today is a special day. One that has brought me much pain, but also joy . . ."

Roman could hear the sadness in her voice but didn't know who or what she was referring to. He stood mentally beside himself, realizing he could provide her a space to be free, regardless of whether it was reality or fiction. He escorted her through an entrance encased in green ivy—one he'd never seen before. Or maybe just never noticed. It reminded him of a portal children step through when making their way into another dimension.

Her experiences were foreign to him yet were familiar to her— a story from the days when she was younger—a destination to somewhere more relevant and meaningful, something that did not make sense to him yet was a reminder of something bigger, decorated with memories that could be felt; something tangible and specific.

"We're almost there, my darling," she said and continued to guide him along the path near the road. From the top of the hill he could see a large pond surrounded by tourist maneuvering remote control water boats: yellow, blue, green, and red. The boats and those driving them appeared somehow disengaged yet fully attentive to this activity.

"This is one of my favorite places," she said, looking up at him. "I haven't been here for quite some time. But it feels like a fleeting memory . . . from a time when I was most happy in life."

He didn't know what to expect but determined to be present in the moment.

*   *   *

I do hope I can find this—it appears I've forgotten where I am. I wonder what Marshal will think. He may consider it to be irrelevant to his own life experience, only to realize we are all connected and everything has a purpose. I just want to see it, yet something seems out of place—this feels a bit queer. It's as if I've woken from an extended period of sleep. Parts of this life have changed, or maybe it's that I wasn't providing it my attention. Regardless, I will continue to search for what I came.

"I'm certain it's here, darling."

I know he thinks I'm mad, but I am not. This was our meeting place, the place we found ourselves in the cool of those late summer nights—left with all the unknowns and possibilities. I wish he were here to love and hold me, to provide me reassurance that everything will be okay, and that I can finally rest at night knowing everything will be fine.

*   *   *

She continued to walk along the water, taking an inventory of her surroundings, anticipating something that might trigger her memory and remind her what it was she came here for. The cool breeze from the Hudson River made its way into the park and hit her with excitement and pause.

"It's here, darling, I just know it!" she said, yet Roman remained unsure she would ever find it.

She refused to accept this defeat, that something this important and memorable could be misplaced within a sea of tourists. She smiled at him, to which the expression on her face appeared as if she were beginning to experience panic. Her ability to have a point of reference seemed important and something she wouldn't allow herself to be separated from—remaining focused for a moment longer should she miss her appointment at Bergdorf's. It seemed of greater importance. Something that she needed to achieve, something that would provide her comfort. They continued ahead.

Her attention was driven to a couple sitting on a bench. While there were many unoccupied, she became fixated upon them.

"There it is, darling! I knew I'd find it," she said and began to race forward.

The couple paid no attention, distracted by each other.

She attempted to grab their attention and began to wave. "Hello, there . . . hello there," she said from a slight distance.

They didn't hear her or anything else.

"Excuse me . . . hello there," she continued, dragging Roman by the arm. Not knowing what she wanted or why she was targeting them, he attempted to keep her from moving any closer.

"Katheryn, why don't we go this—"

"Marshal, darling, I need to be there. It's there."

"I don't think . . ."

"Shush, darling. Now, just follow me," she quickly interrupted him.

*   *   *

The only person she's going to make a fool of is herself. I'm sure when they see her in their peripheral view they'll entertain her. I doubt she even knows where she is or who she is—people like her tend to interrupt others.

If she were black, I don't think they would be amused. This woman is emotionally tiring, which provides me some insight into what my mama use to deal with raising seven children. I'm sure she went in her room most nights, shut the door, and drank. This woman, on the other hand, is certifiably crazy—running around, raising her hands up in the air and interrupting people.

I'm assuming this is how she ran her late husband into the grave, but I guess this is what happens when you get old. You start to lose your mind, and then before you know it you've ended up in some retirement community where they tell everyone who works there to play along. Who knows, maybe we're the ones who are crazy?

Honestly, it doesn't really matter. When I leave, she'll be left with what little memory she has. This is my fear of getting old. I hope I will never be left to linger in a past that doesn't exist, a reality that lacks something concrete and formal, left wondering what could have been. Then again, it must be joyous to live in a past that feels familiar and without flaws.

"Excuse me, I'm sorry to bother you," she said.

The expression on the faces of the people on the bench is absolutely priceless. I feel embarrassed for her that she's consumed with this new obsession, but maybe to her it all feels relevant.

*   *   *

They appeared amused, seeing a woman four times their age escorted by a caretaker. They sat there gazing at one another, drinking Starbucks coffee, fully immersed in the moment— looking up to the woman and smiling politely.

"Hello, gentlemen, I wanted to inquire," she said, "do you think it would be too much to ask that my companion and I be afforded the opportunity to occupy this space?"

They appeared confused. There were a dozen other benches that were empty.

"It's just that this bench," she continued, "if you'd be so kind to oblige a woman such as myself . . . I would be ever so appreciative."

The man on the left looked at the man on the right with a strange grin that was replaced with a look of annoyance. He shrugged his shoulders. "I suppose for a woman such as yourself, we would be honored."

Both stood at the same time, immediately embracing one another with a hug and peck on the cheek. "I think I should be going . . . It was really great to meet you. We should do this again sometime," to which the other appeared smitten and grinned.

"Certainly, what are you doing tomorrow?"

Katheryn began to tap the rubber part of her cane on the pavement impatiently, staring at them directly.

"Just a moment," one of them said.

"It's such a lovely day," she said, clearing her voice, "those children over there appear happy." She motioned at Roman to look.

Realizing she was passive-aggressively making random statements about children with their parents, one of the men said, "It's all yours."

"Thank you," she smiled and watched as they walked off, then immediately sat with a sigh that insinuated relief. Adjusting herself and clasping her hands together, she closed her eyes.

Roman said nothing but waited for her to respond. He didn't understand why it was so important they sat here, but honestly it didn't matter to him. He was consumed with the silence and his ability to remain present in the moment. He would not disturb her but allowed her to remain in contemplation, free of distraction.

ABC Carpet & Home

He didn't mention where Gloria should make the reservation or whom she should inform Joe Tiller would be gracing them with his presence—only that it was some bar on Lexington Avenue and that he wanted to have a drink.

He mentioned something about a gift, but it was unclear where someone like Joe would go to make a purchase for another man's wife. She thought it odd that he would go out of his way to do something nice for another human, but she understood his motive. It was difficult to understand or comprehend how someone like Joe became the person he was. She assumed it was unresolved mommy issues and a lack of affection from his father.

What she did understand was that he was narcissistic in nature and had limited emotional intelligence. He also lacked the luster needed to achieve a certain level of suave.

Like her, Joe was from the Midwest. He always talked about Indiana as if he'd walked out unscathed, but she figured if he were that bright and intelligent he would have gone to a school like Columbia or Stanford.

Joe Tiller was unbearable but survivable.

Gloria knew calling his phone was "a huge no-no," which was the way he always put it—she should never call, only wait for him to return to the office. The phone was never to ring more than once, and she should always "show a bit more excitement in her voice when answering."

This was often what he told her after yelling her name across the office, even though she was less than ten feet away.

The week before, he'd taped up the windows with wallpaper that mimicked the New York skyline.

"If you look at the window long enough, you might break the glass," he said laughingly. "We must take precautions to ensure the safety of all employees," he said, even though she was his only employee.

Gloria went into his office and saw he hadn't locked his computer. No password was needed. In some ways he was a private person, but she did know something else: He was eccentric and neurotic, paranoid and meticulous, and he recorded every appointment in his digital calendar. She began to think like him.

If I were Joe Tiller, where would someone like me go to take a potential client?

Nothing came to her. She felt she'd wandered into a dead end. Then she remembered the spreadsheet where she found Barney's contact information.

She sat down at the computer and opened the electronic folder, skimming the tabs at the bottom of the spreadsheet: Clients, Memos, Meeting History, LIB, and For Tiller's Eyes Only.

She opened Meeting History. There were about three hundred lines, which listed DATE, CLIENT NAMES (LAST/FIRST), ORGANIZATION, ESTABLISHMENT, ADDRESS, PHONE NUMBER, DURATION OF MEETING, AMOUNT SPENT, RECEIPT NUMBER, NOTES/COMMENTS.

There were about three years' worth of history sorted in chronological order.

He'd met with John Weaver—associate at Fisher & Bowing—on several occasions last year where he'd spent $150 at the Plaza Hotel, the same place he took many of his other clients. It was either that or Mr. Purple on the Lower East Side.

Scrolling down to the bottom, Gloria read the final entry:

DATE: 6/4/2017
Client Name: B. Williams
Organization: Williams Innovations
Establishment: Plaza Hotel (Champagne Bar)
Phone: 212-546-5309

In the notation, "Maria the airhead" was mentioned, the cocktail waitress he'd referred to earlier. The note also indicated the reservation itself should be under the name Barney Williams.

*   *   *

"Williams Innovations, this is Margaret speaking," a woman answered.

"Hi, this is Gloria, Joe Tiller's assistant. Mr. Tiller would like to confirm the appointment for this afternoon with Mr. Williams for 5 p.m. at the Champagne Bar."

"Let me confirm with Mr. Williams that he will be available this afternoon," Margaret said. "I see that he has a sonogram appointment with JC at 3 p.m. Please hold."

Gloria was nervous, as Joe never confirmed a time and she didn't want to be thought of as one of those pushy receptionists.

"Yes," Margaret said, "Mr. Williams should be available at that time. He and JC are finding out the sex of little Milo."

"Isn't it a . . ."

"They don't know the sex of the child. But Mr. Williams says he knows JC is carrying a boy because he read in some astrological book that if she's carrying high, it's a girl. If low, it's a boy. With their luck, the baby will probably be intersex. Anywho, yes, Mr. Williams confirmed 5 p.m. at the Champagne Bar. Please inform Mr. Tiller that Mr. Williams will only have until 6 p.m. as he and JC are having a gender reveal party at 6:30 where he and his friends will gather to celebrate the upcoming birth of little Milo."

Gloria said, "Please let Mr. Williams know the reservation has been placed under his name and Mr. Tiller will be waiting for him in the lobby at the bar."

Then she hung up and dialed the Plaza.

*　　*　　*

"Hello, this is Gloria from Tiller & Associates. I would like to confirm a reservation for two at 5 p.m. under the name Barney Williams. The reserving party has requested that he be placed in the lounge section of the bar, in the far back. It's important that they are provided with complete and total privacy. Also, he is requesting Maria be present to provide bottle service. Belvedere is preferred."

"Madame," the man on the other end of the line said in a British accent, "Maria is no longer an employee of our fine establishment, as she was found to have engaged in some questionable behavior."

"Questionable behavior?"

"Yes, madame, we here at the Plaza hold our employees to the highest standard. We wish her well in her future endeavors, yet she is no longer allowed on the premises."

"That's unfortunate . . ."

"Yes, madame, is most certainly is. Please let the reservation holder know Teresa will be providing accompaniment this evening, and that a bottle of Belvedere will be placed on ice with two rocks glasses that have been chilled. Please let the arriving party know they *must* be here at the time the reservation begins, as we will be closing the lounge area for a private party at 7:30 p.m."

Gloria hung up and began clicking on the tabs at the bottom of the spreadsheet. There were various transactions, some for massages, pedicures and manicures, catering that had been ordered. These went on for almost twelve hundred lines. The lengthy history made it clear Joe Tiller was bad with money.

There were multiple debits but not many deposits. She also saw multiple IOU notations in the last column. Joe hadn't received any payments since November of last year, which made sense as the only incoming calls were from debt collectors.

Examining the subtotal calculation at the bottom of the column, Gloria saw Joe was in the negative for almost thirty grand. This concerned her. She hadn't received her first paycheck, which he informed her would be paid out at the first of each month along with all bills. She would have to work a full month before being paid. Now even that was in doubt.

"It's easier to do it all at once," he'd constantly say, "getting one check a month should remind you of what it was like growing up. You know, being able to take a vacation at the nail salon."

Gloria didn't think much of it at first. She assumed this was New York and the way things were done around here.

When Joe returned, she would request a memo to address the salary she was offered upon her first day of employment at Tiller & Associates. If he began to dance around the subject, she would contact the employment agency and request to be moved. Part of her hoped that he was on the verge of bankruptcy.

*   *   *

They should just make it so people like JT can ride the trains for free—all the riff-raff congregates eating their lunches probably didn't bother to actually read the sign that clearly states it's not a cafeteria.

The woman next to me is stuffing her face with nachos. They smell like vomit, and I assume she asked for extra white sauce. She's rocking the little brat in the stroller while he sleeps. I'm sure she's collecting a monthly stipend from Uncle Sam, all while Joe Tiller is footing the bill. She probably bought her lunch with a food stamp card. They should have kept people paying with those paper coupons to experience the embarrassment of having to count out actual paper money. Maybe then she'd think twice before whipping out the fake ATM card. Then again, who wants the Mexicans holding up the line? I should call ICE on her ass! I heard her broken English. Obviously, she's an alien and crossed the border illegally. Thank you, Donald Trump!

The guff of some people. Fucking losers . . .

I have to find that bitch JC something that will impress her. Something her husband would never think of. Something that says, "I wish you were the one fucking me."

That fat bastard probably lays on his back holding his small pecker and thinking of all the ways his tranny wife will service him. I can picture it now, her mounting his fat ass—getting moist while he sticks his micro-penis in her snatch. I've heard it said the way to a man's wallet is through jealousy.

If this asshole in his failed attempt at life doesn't shut his mouth, I may just toss his portable speaker out the subway door at the next stop. It's too much. No one wants to hear the music or smell the lingering stench of the food you bought from a street vendor. I'm finally on a train where the air actually works but the eyesore hobos who smell like rotten cheese are sprawled out sleeping, taking up an entire bench of seats.

And then those annoying fucking train performers. You should see their faces when the NYPD hops on to randomly search a subway car. They scatter like cockroaches exposed to the light. That dirty beaner better watch herself and crawl back to her *casa*, stupid *puta*.

If I see that asshole Tony who normally works the 1 Train wearing that fake brace on his leg and crying about "I lost my home, can you spare a few dollars so my kids can eat tonight?" I may lose it and kick the fat bastard off the train platform.

I saw that asshole one time at the 59th Street stop about to hop on the train back downtown. He pulled out two wads of neatly folded bills held together by rubber bands. He was talking to his partner in crime. "The train will be here in the next five minutes. Use script number nine. I'll work the back and you work the front."

That's right, they had a script and a backpack full of medical supplies that had somehow fallen out at Columbus Circle. I give the waste of space credit for one thing—that fucker knew his craft and knew it well.

About a month later, I saw Tony and his bimbo girlfriend hop on the same train. I was running late for dinner and this asshole was screaming at the top of his lungs, "My name is Tony . . ."

He worked his audience hard that evening and managed to screw an old lady and a tourist out of a few bucks. When he got to me, I was at my end.

"Hey man, would you mind helping a brother out?"

"Is it the fire or the eviction?"

"What?"

"You know, yesterday. I thought it might have been the fire, but then again maybe it's the eviction."

I could see I'd gotten a rise out of him—that bastard knew I knew. He suddenly got quiet and turned to the door, waiting for the next stop.

"Which one is it . . . brother?"

He just continued to stare with his nose pressed up against the sliding door.

I looked up at the sign that read: *EMERGENCY BRAKE. Lift Cover. Alarm Will Sound. Pull Cord.*

I wanted to get up from my seat and do as instructed, bringing the train to a screeching halt.

We were approaching the next stop on the N at 34th Street, Herald Square, when a voice came over the intercom. "Please be advised that we are being held in the station because of a sick passenger."

Two minutes later, the conductor repeated the same announcement as if we'd missed it the first time.

Then the strangest thing happened. I looked up and there was Tony's girlfriend—motioning him in through the window of the next car.

"Please be advised backpacks and large objects are subject to random search by the police. If you see something, say something," the automated recording said over the PA.

You bet his ass I was going to say something. Maybe he'd think twice if he should encounter me in the future. I guess he didn't learn his lesson the first time.

He gave me a sarcastic look and said, "You better watch your ass."

"Next stop is 14th Street. Transfer is available to the 4, 5, 6, L, N, Q, or R trains. Stand clear of the closing doors," the conductor says, ridding me of Tony's memory.

I need to go somewhere classy. Find something that says, "JC Williams, you're a peach, you're special, I am your baby daddy."

I imagine when Barney leaves for work, JC surfs the internet to find decent headshots of celebrities like Brad Pitt or George Clooney, prints them out, opens up old photo albums of her and Barney on their wedding day, and pastes their heads on the wedding pictures—spending the afternoon rubbing her pussy and thinking what life would have been like if she never married him. I bet her curiosity will get the best of her and she'll find me online, cut out my picture, and add it to her spank bank.

The train doors open and I'm greeted by a homeless man who's managed to stink up the entire platform in a mixture of urine, vomit, and old cheese. I doubt he even realizes he stinks.

He's lying there, oblivious and disheveled. I could kick him from behind and push the old bastard onto the tracks and he wouldn't even know what hit him. Fucking drunk. He should be thanking me.

Shopping for a woman is difficult. The truth is, they're never truly happy until they've received the ultimate gift: nineteen years of uninterrupted child support to pay for their weaves and nails, and annual tax breaks from the federal government.

Women like JC probably throw men like Barney to the trash when something better comes along, something of greater financial gain. They've learned the following keys, from the cradle to the grave: manipulate, manipulate, and if at first you don't succeed, the third time is bound to be the charm.

ABC Carpet & Home has a plethora of knickknacks, but I don't know if she's a bohemian woman who would appreciate an international peace offering. Like most gold diggers, she probably prefers something uptown from the many department stores by the Plaza Hotel.

I'm feeling drenched. Perspiration lingers beneath my sportscoat and my brow is sweaty. To make it worse, a woman is trying to carry her stroller up the stairs. I could help her if we didn't live in such a sue-happy culture.

I can see the headline on *The Huffington Post* now: *JOE TILLER DROPS BABY AT UNION SQUARE.*

Instead I stop, tap my foot, say, "Excuse me" and race her to the top. When I get there maybe I'll cheer her on, as I'm sure she could use all the encouragement she can get.

I'll act like I'm holding open a door and point her to the top of the stairs—I'm sure she'd appreciate that.

*   *   *

He felt confused and bewildered—obsessed over finding the perfect gift. It was still unclear to him why he'd placed so much pressure on himself. He reached the top of the stairs and exited the train station only to find he was turned around. He walked toward 27th Street in the direction of Herald Square.

He always enjoyed the Flatiron District. The architecture served as a reminder of why he moved to New York. He wanted to be successful, a leader within the world of investments, and he believed one day he would. His mother had always told him, "You're special, Joe," but it wasn't long before he realized there were many special people who shared the same sidewalks.

He walked along Broadway, window shopping. (Speak of the Devil, there was Tony, his leg was wrapped up in an Ace bandage, crying crocodile tears and talking about how it would be amputated and he needed money to hire a babysitter.) Joe continued walking, paying him no attention. His goal was to impress JC Williams to the point she would become infatuated with Tiller & Associates and convince her husband to get in bed with him or else she would.

He walked past Club Monaco and some other department stores but saw they were having a sale at ABC Carpet. The A-frame sign outside read *70-80% off. EVERYTHING MUST GO* next to blue, yellow, and green balloons waving in the wind. He wanted to yank them from the sign and let them go because they attracted parents with strollers and toddler-aged children. Then he remembered that most of the children were white and being pushed by Jamaican women, and it wasn't as if they could afford anything in there anyway.

He took a picture of the sign so if there were any questions about what was or wasn't on sale he could whip it out at the register and accuse them of false advertising. He embodied the slogan "the customer is always right" and believed in it only as long the customers in question weren't his.

Joe had never been here but thought maybe he might find something of value for JC—an object of his affection that he could present to Barney, something that could loop him in, gain his trust, and move their business venture forward.

He was taken by the aesthetic of his surroundings but wondered about "the catch" and thought they must be really hard up for business—assuming one of two things: Their product didn't live up to its promise, or the lease was about to expire.

Not thinking much into this, he surveyed the department store. The only problem was that while he saw many trinkets he could pawn off as thoughtful, he knew not all women were the same.

"Hello, sir. Is there anything I might be able to help you with today?" asked the girl at the register, as she did with everyone who walked through the doors.

"Not sure," Joe said, looking at a basket filled with bundles of sage roughly nine dollars each.

"Looking for anything special?" she asked, seeing him as an opportunity to make a commission. "We have some wonderful selections. Maybe I can provide some suggestions . . ."

Joe avoided eye contact and picked up one of the silver bangles next to some wooden embroidered bracelets. "I think I'm okay."

"Those bracelets are handmade, from India. Everything from this line is handcrafted."

There was a Buddha statue that looked unique, but he didn't want to offend. He took out his phone.

"Gloria . . . GLORIA . . . could you please . . . yes, I know. Call Williams's secretary and ask about his theoretical orientation. I'm standing like a dumbass at ABC Carpet and need this pronto."

He wanted to make sure he got it right. All he needed was to screw it up, and his window of opportunity would close. He looked down at a tiny cardboard sign: *AUTHENTIC HANDCRAFTED BRACELETS & BANGLES. 1 for $20 or 3 for $50**

He was not amused. *What dumbass is going to pay that much for a piece of trash chachki made in India?* he thought.

He wandered the store until Gloria returned his call. "Jewish?" he said into the phone. "Did you say Jewish? Do me a favor and look up good gifts for Jewish women." He began to think creatively. "Fuck her, I'm going to focus on the unborn."

Walking around, he realized everything was marked up five times its actual value or worth and trying to find a gift for under ten bucks was going to be a challenge. Still, he couldn't show up empty-handed.

He remembered the sale, snatched up six bracelets, and went to the register. "I guess I'll take these."

"Perfect," the girl at the register said, "I'm sure the Mrs. will love them. They're one of our best sellers. Would you like them wrapped?"

"Sure," he said and began figuring in the discount and tax in his head. "That would be, umm, nice."

"That's going to be $31.80, plus a two-dollar surcharge for wrapping."

"I thought they were on sale. Surcharge?"

"Yes, they're on sale," she said. "You saved a little over seventy dollars."

"I don't need them gift wrapped," he said and reached for his wallet, mentally recalculating the total and wondering how this woman had reached that conclusion.

She removed the bangles from the gift box. "Okay, sir, that's going to be $31.80."

He looked unamused. He was determined to bring the total down twenty dollars and eighty cents. "Can I see them real quick," he said and began inspecting each one closely. "I'm just . . . you see that . . . they're damaged. Why do people have to be so careless?"

The girl looked confused. She was positive she'd handled them with care.

"You see that and that," Joe said, pointing to a nonexistent dent.

"I don't—"

"You don't . . . you don't . . . I specifically spent the last twenty minutes going through that basket to collect six perfect bracelets. I'm sorry, I meant bangles. Now please go over and find ones that are identical. The same color that the—how did you say it?—the Mrs. will not be triggered by and her condition agitated all because of your careless behavior."

The girl walked away from the register and headed to the handwoven basket in an attempt to find six bracelets that were identical.

"I'm waiting . . ."

She was terrified. This was her first job out of high school. "Give me just a moment," she said, rummaging through the basket. She didn't know what she should be looking for, as they all looked naturally worn and were supposed to have a rustic quality that looked vintage.

"Could you please hurry up?" Joe tapped his foot impatiently. "Some people have things to do in this life."

Growing increasingly irate, he began slamming his hands on the counter, making a scene. It caused the girl to become even more nervous and unable to concentrate. "Can you just do your fucking job?" he said, his volume increasing.

A woman who looked as if she'd just finished aerobics class was eying a hand-carved ivory statue. She quickly pushed her stroller with one hand, clenching her half-drunk coffee in the other, to protect her child from the commotion.

The cashier found six green bracelets at the bottom and returned to the register hoping he would be satisfied.

"Are you colorblind?" Joe said in a sarcastic tone.

"But I thought . . ."

"Well, you thought wrong. I'd like to speak to a manager."

She grabbed the wire clipped to her shirt and requested someone come up "to provide assistance."

A few moments later, a woman walked up and smiled at Joe. "How can I help you today, sir?"

"I honestly don't know where you get these people from," he said. "She looks like she's not a day past sixteen. Aren't there laws about children working during the day? Ah, I see, this is one of those welfare to work programs. You see, I wanted the blue ones and she returned with a bunch of green."

Joe proceeded to explain how the "bimbo banged them up and I can't possibly give these damaged items to my wife."

The manager surveyed the bracelets and then Joe. It was clear there was no difference in the variation in color and they were undamaged. "Gina, please assist Mr. . . ."

"It's Tiller. With two Ls."

"Yes, please help Mr. Tiller."

Gina looked down at the register on the verge of tears, then back to Joe and then to the register again. She assumed an additional discount would appease him but more importantly get him out of ABC Carpet & Home. "That will be $12.06."

He tossed her his credit card with an eye roll. "Much better!"

"I'm sorry, sir," Gina said, "but there is a $15 minimum for all transactions paid with a card. Unless it's a debit card."

Now enraged, Joe was becoming explosive. "What is this, some kind of Ponzi scheme? Just wait until the Better Business Bureau gets a whiff of this!"

He threw the bracelets past Gina's head, grabbed his credit card, turned around, and walked out the door. "You haven't seen the last of Joe Tiller," he shouted.

He'd drawn so much attention to himself that in-house security was standing close by. "Sir," one of them said, "we have been asked to have you removed from the premises."

"What is it you make?" Joe said, flashing his wallet in fount of their faces. "You only wish you had what I do."

Then he grabbed his crotch. Putting his wallet into his back pocket, he raised his hand and flipped Gina off. Then the security guards. Then Gina again.

"Dumb cunt!" he snarled and walked out the door.

Layers of Paint

"It's strange to think we would meet here every Saturday afternoon, regardless if Marques or I had a performance that evening," Katheryn said and smiled.

Roman wasn't sure if Marques had been real or a figment of her imagination. Maybe he was a mixture of her late husband.

She was hesitant to go into detail but began to make small talk to engage him. "You know, darling, I do love Central Park this time of year. There is just something absolutely magical about this space."

He nodded and stared forward, continuing to people watch. A woman was pushing a child in a stroller. An elderly man had his arm around a woman Roman assumed was his wife. A group of people were on the quad doing tai chi in synchronization. The remote control boats reflected the light of the sun. It all seemed trivial, the concept of hustling through life, and he wondered what it would be like to say, "I'm on holiday" in a European accent.

It felt strange to him that people moved through this life with such different experiences, yet everyone regardless of how much they'd obtained would eventually die, return to dust, their souls released into the atmosphere.

"Are you ready, Katheryn?" he asked, but upon examining closely he noticed her face was wet. The emotion she exhibited appeared genuine, and he wanted to allow her a moment to grieve. He imagined what she must be thinking, and for the first time he felt she didn't just see him as someone who was her caretaker. He felt her humanity and sorrow. The silence stated everything, and he thought about the person he once loved who lived on 190th and Wadsworth in Washington Heights. It didn't matter if Katheryn's reality was built on something fictitious. It only mattered that she was happy in the moment.

"This is the exact location where we would meet. Where he told me he loved me." Looking down, she touched the wood of the bench that had been painted over multiple times. She removed one of her gloves and then the other, opening her purse and removing a nail file.

"Katheryn, I believe we just filed your nails and put on a fresh coat."

"Hush, darling," she said and removed the nail file from its cover. "I need to concentrate now. I mustn't screw this up." She examined the seat closely. "Ah, here it is. They always try to cover it up, but I always seem to find it. It's as if their efforts are to erase such a defining time in our history."

She used the tip of the nail file to etch away the green layers of paint.

He didn't know if her use of the word "our" referred to him as himself, him as Marshal, or him as her late husband. He dared not interrupt her but sat in observance to make sure she didn't hurt herself or someone else.

"I could've sworn it was here. I've done this not once, not twice, but many times." She continued to dig, providing a verbal guide to break down her understanding of how she located the bench.

"The sun is always facing slightly to the west," she said and pointed to the sun. "You know a child drowned once in there," she added, pointing to the other end of the pond. "This woman, who I assume was his mother, was in an argument with some man I assumed was the father. I saw him walk to the edge but never assumed anything would happen. You should never assume, darling. He couldn't have been more than three years old. It was so quick . . . just a few moments before all life exited his body."

She continued to dig and appeared to be making traction—not hard or fast but rather slow and soft. "Gentle to the touch, darling."

He felt amused and began to judge her, but then he realized she had limited control over herself or how things changed from one moment to the next. He felt this to be what all people with money experienced—that while they controlled most aspects of their life, they were ultimately left like the poor, helpless and lacking control. He hoped when he was Kathryn's age all his senses would remain intact like his grandmother's had. She'd witnessed events that led to the evolution of humanity, experiencing life before email and the internet.

"Just one moment, my darling," she said as if a connection had somehow been made to something profound, all the while chipping away at layers of old paint that covered the flesh of the bench. Roman just stared out into the distance, hoping the NYPD or someone from the New York Parks Department didn't think he was trying to rob her.

"Katheryn, what in the world," he remarked with concern and looked away, trying not to bring attention or come off critical. He looked across the pond to see a man walking alongside his son.

She nudged him. "See, I told you I'd find it."

Roman didn't really see anything, just the accumulation of chipped paint, but decided to entertain her for a moment longer.

"I suppose that is something," he said and looked back up. The man and son he'd seen were no longer visible but were now replaced by what he assumed was a nanny pushing a child.

He never could wrap his mind around why anyone would go through having children and not raise them. When he was a child, he rode his bike down Amsterdam Avenue but always knew he should return home before dark, before the streetlamps turned on. He would often be greeted by his grandmother, who sat at the table cutting vegetables and preparing dinner for when his mother came home from work.

"It really does amaze me," he said, then quickly stopped himself.

'What's that, darling?"

"How someone would have children and then pass them off to a wet-nurse or another woman."

"Oh, the nannies. Yes, darling, it was just the times. When Brando was a toddler, when he was just two or three, we hired Hilda. He really developed a fondness, but as with everything, all good things eventually come to an end. He was sent off to a boarding school upstate, and we just no longer needed her."

Roman avoided engaging her; he felt her narrative to be non-relatable. He thought about how difficult it must have been for her son realizing that his mother had to pay for someone to love him.

She sensed his judgment and felt a sudden compulsion to explain. "I know what you're thinking. I'm such a horrible mother to bring some woman into my home to raise Brando. Well, it wasn't easy. I'd just released the new record and was set to tour in the fall. I couldn't imagine interrupting his life, nor mine. I know it sounds selfish, but it's just the way things were. I couldn't have done it without her."

Roman still didn't understand why she would do such a thing. Children need to be loved, he thought, they need a parent, but he felt Katheryn would never receive or understand his message, so instead he said politely, "I understand."

She continued to scrape off the paint and began to hum an old standard. She continued scraping, but it seemed she couldn't find what it was she was looking for.

*   *   *

I haven't received a letter in some time. I fear for his life, that maybe something might've happened during this war. Before he left, he promised at least one letter every other week, but sometimes they arrived weeks later. I warned him not to go, not to be brave, but he was determined to join the service the day after his eighteenth birthday.

I tried sending a care package, but when I phoned to ask for his forwarding address I was informed it could not be provided and under no circumstances would they. I even tried saying "Do you know who I am?" thinking they might oblige me, but it didn't work.

The gentleman informed me "this is for our safety and yours."

I've tried numerous times, thinking I might reach another human, only to be informed they would try their hardest to receive whatever I sent, and provided with the same address where all mail and other large packages were to be sent.

What kind of human would deny a mother access to their child?

I called Hilda the other day to see if she'd heard from him—they remained close even after she no longer worked for the family—but every time I try a man answers the phone and informs me there's no one there by that name. I can barely understand him, as every time I call it's inaudible from all the background noise.

I don't understand why every time I come here I'm forced to remove layers upon layers of paint. You think they would see their efforts are in vain—this bench has probably been painted over a dozen times or more, and every time I'm forced to find whatever object I can use and cause destruction to public property.

"Marshal, darling, I'm feeling parched. Do you think you could be a dear and hand me the canteen?"

I've always enjoyed him, the times we've shared and those close calls. I'm still confused as to why my show was canceled. I may need to hire an additional hand to keep an eye on my finances. I've suggested that I manage the books, but I assume the likes of Vernon Shapiro would understand I'm good for the money.

When I walk past a lit-up marquee where a show has been sold out . . . oh, the embarrassment, to think that me, a household name, is either broke or someone took off with all the profits. It's frustrating to know every bank in Manhattan will be closed for the weekend. I will call first thing Monday morning and have Marshal ensure a meeting is scheduled to speak with the bank president myself. He's gonna get an earful.

"Marshal, please call my bank first thing next week. I need to ensure all things are in order and that something like this never happens again."

This has to be the bench, as the sun always shines this direction in the early afternoon. I'm not sure how he will react knowing this story, who I truly am . . . but more so who I was. There is so much going on in this world, and one day I hope things will change. Tomorrow we could find a bomb has dropped and we'll all be wiped off this planet, having never truly lived.

I'm not scared, as I am impressed. I know our boys will bring home a big win for America. But I'm fearful that something has happened to my dear Brando, as I've not heard from him in some time. I must assume everything is fine, but I find myself becoming worrisome when I see the names in the obituary section of the *New York Times* of those who've lost their lives serving our country. I just worry one day I will be greeted by two men in uniform who will inform me that my son perished while fighting a war that in years to come will be seen as a lost effort to Vietnam.

I think about the new selections Julian will have available for me today. He knows me well enough that when I'm able to show up, one of his assistants brings a bottle of their finest Sauvignon

Blanc, a tray of grapes, cheese and crackers—the wardrobe rack is presented and filled with Chanel and Saint Laurent. I'm not picky, just particular, which he understands and seems to have grown a tolerance for.

I often wonder if I were an average woman who didn't have a rolling line of credit at Bergdorf's, would he still love me the same? I don't know, but then again I'm not an average person or housewife. I'm the incredible, unstoppable, and talented Katheryn James York, who's never cared what others think, but have always marched to the beat of my own drum—realizing that fashion, music, and art are not mutually exclusive.

"Well, I'm starting to run tired of this game, my darling. I think it's time to head to Bergdorf's, where we shall spend the afternoon looking at all the new lines. And, darling, maybe I might be generous and treat you to a shave."

*   *   *

She needs to spend less time focusing on me and more time focusing on herself. I assume this is something common for her in life—buying others' affections in anticipation they will love her back. Maybe after she kicks the bucket, I'll be left in her will—but then again, black folk aren't included in these types of arrangements. I wonder, if I were in her condition, what time would I remember? Hopefully something memorable.

"This way to the gate, my darling," she says.

It's as if nothing has changed and she's become invested in something bigger, something she can hold onto—a mirage of feelings that are distant and displaced. Maybe she's attempting to work through some unresolved trauma from her past, having little to no understanding that the world she lives in is nothing more than a past that's been bundled up into this present moment. If this were my life, I might be resentful, angry with God that I'd been left here alone, vulnerable, and without recollection of my yesterdays.

I believe there is something that can be gained from this situation, a lesson in life, to always treat the generations after you with respect, as they will be the ones who determine your fate and place you in a home like Hampton Grove. I assume this is why people have many children—they're like a life insurance policy that can be used to better the outcome. Even if you find yourself with dementia.

"Darling, this way. Or at least I believe it is."

She puts her hand on the back of my arm, leading the way through Central Park, headed toward Columbus Circle. I wonder if she has enough steam to make it past 59th Street.

"Come now, darling."

I just follow her lead. She's lived a lot longer than I, knows a bit more, and is a seasoned New Yorker.

A group of pigeons wobbles along, hunting for a morsel of bread or whatever leftovers they can scavenge, often resorting to the trash. It seems trivial that birds can be cannibalistic, pecking along in life without consequence or responsibility.

I remember those times when my grandmother would wake me up on Saturday mornings and take me to the bodega at our street corner, "What you got for me this morning?" addressing Freddy, who sold day-old loaves of bread for a quarter.

Saturday's fair was half-price and I rode for free, so she and I would take the train to Central Park where she'd remove a few pieces of bread from the bag and rip them into pieces.

"Space it out" she would remind me so no birds went to bed hungry. Not much has changed since then but the people, and she's no longer around. I always thought she'd live forever. But, like Katheryn said, "All good things eventually come to an end."

I sometimes find myself returning here to the park. Much like we are today, to encounter glimpses of those we've lost or the pigeons we will eventually meet again at Rainbow Bridge.

"Well, if it isn't something," she looked up and pointed to the bottom of the road. "I remember . . ." She stopped and returned to focus on her steps, one by one, feeling the sensation of the cobblestone on the soles of her shoes where horse carriages and rickshaw drivers charge by the minute—carting tourists who use words like "ain't" and aren't accustomed to walking such long distances in a city like New York.

I look at people like Katheryn and wonder why they would choose to spend thousands a month on an overpriced room with a window opening to city traffic—only to find you don't really own anything and are occupying space that will eventually be filled by another after you've died. I suppose it's her home. I've lived here my whole life and I've never felt like this was home.

"Let's take a seat, darling, I'm feeling a little worn." We haven't walked a quarter of a mile and she's already tired. "This looks like a good place to rest."

"Sorry to bother you," a man says, "but could you spare a dollar, quarter, dime, penny, nickel?"

She digs into her purse. "Marshal," she says and hands it to me, "please find my billfold to help this poor soul."

I grab the bag and rummage around. She has a tube of lipstick, some makeup, and a billfold. "How much?"

"Just a quarter. You should be able to get yourself a nice hot meal and have a little left for a shine," she says to the man.

At first I think she's being sarcastic but then I realize this was a significant amount of money in her time. I don't understand what she means by "a shine."

"Thank you, ma'am," the man says and pulls out a wad of crumpled bills. A syringe falls out of his pocket, to which he apologizes. He quickly picks it up and moves on to the couple sitting on the bench across the way.

"A shine?" I ask her.

"Yes, darling, a shine," she says, looking appalled that I didn't know what she meant, ". . . a shoeshine."

"It's important to watch out for people like that," I say. "They try to take advantage."

"Hosh-posh, I'm sure he needed it more than you or I. We sure are blessed, my dear, living this New York life."

I wonder if maybe she's forgotten about Bergdorf's and think not to mention it. I can call an Uber and we could head back to the apartment. She just stares off into the distance as if she's entertaining herself. I wonder if someone like her has a true concept of time, or does she have a different way in which she perceives it?

"I'm not one to complain, darling, but I really am finding these rays to be rather intrusive."

It's true; the sun is beginning to encroach through the tree branches.

"But I will survive. I just want to enjoy the afternoon to its fullest. I feel there is something we were supposed to be doing, but I can't place my finger on it."

My hypothesis is correct—distract her concentration, and she'll shift focus and attention.

"Ah, yes, Bergdorf's," she says.

I wonder if we'll eventually make it there. I hate going into stores like that. It angers me to think someone could ever throw away thousands of dollars on a dress, all for the name of fashion.

"Maybe we should just head back home. They say a storm is on the way." It's a partial truth.

"Over my dead—"

She stops, interrupted by a bird flying above and shitting all over her hat.

"Let's go, my darling. Please have Phillip ready should we need car service."

She walks off at a fast pace like one of those people you see spending their afternoons walking around a mall. I feel her urgency as we move past the homeless people congregating around a table playing chess. She's so far removed from reality that she fails to see a man urinating on a tree—or maybe she's just preoccupied with the concern over bad weather.

*   *   *

They walked along the bushes until they reached Sheep Meadow. People lay on blankets, drinking wine, having lunch, enjoying the scenery of the skyscrapers that surrounded them. It all seemed trivial that life would unfold this way, even for Kathryn and Roman who were spending the afternoon together; a world that was separated between them and everyone else. The only thing they had in common was the situational condition that was present and filled with various levels of connection.

"Marshal, darling, I think we should avoid this for today," she said, which he interpreted as they were turning around. "I don't think I have the correct shoes to be walking through the grass."

She pointed toward 5th and 54th. She put her hand on his elbow and nudged him to walk forward and guide her through the park.

He stood a foot taller than she so that if you cut him in half, he would still overshadow her.

"Honestly, darling, I just don't know what these young ladies were thinking when they walked out the door this morning. You never leave your home without a pair of long gloves and a decorative hat." She smirked, which was normal as she often muttered to herself.

She was fearful of the storm, yet the sky was clear. Roman felt bad about telling her it might rain but realized when she woke up tomorrow, her recollection would be limited—reminding him of the repeat cycle on the washer, experiencing each moment as if it were new. Only this time she'd managed to leave her apartment, go to the lobby, and out of Hampton Grove.

Roman was considering leaving Williamsburg and moving out of Brooklyn altogether. His neighborhood had slowly become gentrified, which meant developers were focused on buying out real estate, tearing down historic brownstones, and forcing people out of their apartments and onto the street.

I should've stayed in Harlem, he thought. He had recently found out his building went co-op and was no longer rent-stabilized. Last week, he received a letter in the mail from Grand City Management informing him that his building had been sold. When he called the old management office, it was true.

His lease was up for renewal in two months. When he asked how much rent would increase, he was told they were not renewing any of the leases in the building and he would need to be out by the first of August.

He called the New York Housing Authority, which sent him a report history on the apartment. Upon review, he found that because his unit had been vacant from 2012 to 2015, it was taken out of stabilization and Grand City could legally do as they pleased. He had a few thousand dollars saved up for a situation like this—"a nest egg for emergencies," as his mother would often say.

He walked beside Katheryn silently and sulked. Thinking about his own frustrations, he grew angry, believing she would never understand.

"We sure are blessed, my dear, living this New York life," he heard her say again, this time in his mind like a stuck record.

If he ever stopped working for Hampton Grove and she never saw him again, she wouldn't even remember. Then again, what did it matter? She never remembered anything anyway.

Mother's Day

"That stupid cunt! That will be the last time I . . ." Joe muttered under his breath, moving quickly past his frustration to focus his attention on the Colombian woman yelling, "One papaya three dolla!"

He approached her. "I'll take one."

She pulled out a small bottle of Tajin powder and shook it over the papaya.

"Here you go," he said and began to walk away with the half-sized Ziploc bag of chopped seasoned fruit.

"Sir, two more dolla," she waved.

Joe, who was already irritated, turned around. "Dumb spic," he muttered.

"Two more dolla, sir! Two mooo." She held up her hand to show the number two.

Her voice was drowned out by the sounds of car horns and emergency service vehicles.

"More dolla, more dolla, you want more dolla," he echoed sarcastically.

"Yes, sir, two more dolla," she said, still holding up her hand.

"I bet you don't have a permit to be selling this rancid trash. You probably got this shit out of the garbage at Whole Foods."

She looked confused and turned to the man next to her, who was also unable to translate English.

"Well, if you want to file a complaint," Joe said, grabbing a piece of paper and clicking a pen, "here's the number for ICE."

"Two dolla, sir," she kept on repeating.

He opened the plastic bag and took a bite, spit it out, dumped out what was remaining, and squashed the fruit on the concrete with his foot. The Colombian woman was terrified, as she'd seen lots of things in her life but never to this effect.

Realizing he was explosive and volatile, she stopped and began to swat at him. "GO AWAY . . . GO AWAY!"

"Dumb spic," he said again and threw the bag on the ground, walking in the direction of Union Square.

Why would anyone live in Queens? he asked himself as he walked down the stairs and through the turnstile to notice a group of elderly black men performing an old Motown standard, which Joe loved and believed, as he did of all good songs, had been written by white people. A larger than usual crowd was gathered in a semicircle, cheering them on, applauding when they finished "My Girl."

"Thank you, ladies and gentlemen," one of the men said and removed his hat, tipping it toward the audience.

Joe was not amused. This crowd felt like a barrier between him and the stairway that led to the train. He stood there, finding himself more irritated than he was with the Colombian woman he'd just insulted.

"Excuse me," his volume level increased, "EXCUSE ME!"— he was irritated, as at any moment the train would come and he would be left waiting for the next—"don't you people have jobs?" He used his arms to part the sea of people.

The crowd began to disperse, which meant that regardless of his strong-willed efforts he would be forced to move through a slew of people walking in the same direction. Each step felt increasingly difficult. Now there was an elderly woman in front of him headed in the same direction, and another woman walking up the stairs backwards with a stroller.

"That's fucking classic," he said underneath his breath. He

began tapping his foot and huffing loudly but became distracted by what he referred to as "Eurotrash," the nickname he used for women he found slightly attractive.

He looked at the woman and grinned to see if he could grab her attention, but she was distracted by her phone. He could smell her perfume, which reminded him of something his mother used to wear—providing a reminder of their life together and how on Sundays she would sit at her vanity, turn on the record player, and take out her curler rollers.

He was always amazed by how beautiful his mother was, and by the kindness and dignity she'd managed to retain after his father ran off with the secretary. He felt he should call her but realized she might not even pick up the phone or return his calls. He thought it best that he just remember those moments but not dwell on them—remembering her as he did when he was ten, avoiding at all cost the negative emotions he now associated her with.

Once they were close, but after his father left just after his thirteenth birthday, she never celebrated another. He and his father looked exactly alike, and he thought it was because of this that she secretly blamed Joe for the affair.

*　　*　　*

He went to the perfume display in the women's section of J.C. Penney and removed a crinkled wad of fives and ones and a bag of loose coins from his pocket and asked the woman at the counter, "What can I get with this?"

The woman had seen many cases like him during her career—trying to purchase something nice for their mothers on a shoestring budget.

"Who's the special lady?" she smiled, even though she knew full well what was happening.

"My mom. I'm trying to find something for Mother's Day."

"Well, let's see what you got," she said and motioned for him to pass over the loose bills and change. "One . . . six . . . seven . . . eight . . . eighteen . . . twenty-three . . . twenty-seven," she said with a false sense of excitement, realizing the commission would be nothing. "Twenty-seven dollars and eighty-six cents, to be exact."

He was amazed he'd managed to scrape all that together. One day he would learn to invest his money, as well as others', and be entrusted to make decisions that would impact the lives of many.

"Sounds about right," he said, then pulled out a dime he'd missed in the depths of his pants pocket and handed it to the woman.

"Twenty-seven dollars and ninety-six cents," she corrected herself.

He saw a dish partially filled with butterscotch candies and random change. He took four pennies from the dish, handed them to her, and said, "Makes twenty-eight."

"You're correct," she smirked, "so what will it be this year? What were you thinking?"

He looked down at the glass case and began eyeing all its contents. She could see he was becoming frazzled and redirected him to what he could afford. She pulled out a bottle of perfume that was labeled *TESTER* and squirted some on sample paper.

"Let's try this one," she said and waved the strip in the air. If this didn't work there were two other options in his price range.

His reaction was strange. The scent was different from what he expected it would be.

"That's okay, let's try another," she said and presented one of the other bottles.

"None of these remind me of her."

"But how could it remind you of her if she's never worn it?"

she said sarcastically and realized this was going to be much more difficult than she'd anticipated.

"What about that one?" he said and pointed to another more respected brand—a bottle of Burberry, which even the smallest bottle was forty dollars more than what he had. He wouldn't be able to afford it, not now or by Mother's Day.

"Are you sure you don't have any more money?" the woman asked, thinking that if he were eighteen she could offer to sign him up for a Penney's charge card. There was nothing she could do. "Maybe you can find her something else."

She returned the unwrapped perfume to the display case with the pink elastic keychain on her arm and handed him back his money. "That's twenty-seven," she said, handing him the loose change but not the four pennies. "We need these for . . . paying customers."

He turned and walked away. Talking himself through the possibilities, he began to mentally prepare how he would procure the perfume bottle—focused on its distinguished aroma and imagined it was already given to his mother on Mother's Day. He didn't know how this would happen but knew that it would.

Thanks for nothing, he thought and exited the revolving door which led to the street. As he looked back on what seemed an opportunity filled with possibility, he was blinded by the reflection of the sun against the glass.

He looked out into the street to the cars that passed and imagined how things might have been different if he had a job and could afford the perfume. He turned back and thought of defacing the revolving door as he passed through it and proceeded to the counter where the woman was wiping the glass with a cotton cloth.

"Excuse me, miss. Could you tell me the next day you're working?"

"Well," she said, "I was supposed to work this weekend, but

Randy is taking me to Indianapolis. He rented a room in one of those fancy hotels. He's gonna take me on a carriage ride. It's our one-year anniversary. I think he's going to pop the question."

He looked at her name tag and said, "Thanks, Jessica," and left.

That Saturday, he came back. There was another woman working at the counter.

"Yeah," he said, "My dad called earlier this week. He ordered a bottle of Burberry over the phone. He had it placed on hold."

The woman opened a drawer full of various decorative gift bags with receipts stapled to them. "It looks like a lot of men are thinking about their wives this year," she said. "What's the name?"

"Last name Tiller."

She searched for the package. "I'm sorry, hon, but we don't have a package on hold with that last name. What's the last name again?"

"It's Tiller. T-I-L-L-E-R. First name Paul."

The woman continued to search but appeared confused. "I'm sorry, but I'm not seeing that name. Are you sure the order was placed here?"

Joe looked annoyed and began asserting himself. "Miss," he said, staring down at her name tag, "my father, Paul Tiller, told me that he placed the order for my mother on Tuesday. The woman who took the order said it would be under his name, which is why I'm here!"

"Do you by chance have her name?" she pushed further.

"Let me think. I think her name was—I mean, she told me her name was Jessica. Like Jessica from *Roger Rabbit*."

"Oh, Jessica," she said and scratched her head. "Hmmm . . . I can't really call her as she is out of town this weekend. You might need to wait until she returns next week."

"Look, lady, my father is going to be pissed. Excuse my language," he said, adjusting his tone, "my father is going to be really upset if I return to his office empty-handed."

"Maybe I can call him and get a verification of the credit card number?"

"Verification . . . what do you mean by verification? He's out of town on business and won't be back until late this evening. There's no way to reach him, and if you call my mother it's going to send her into a panic. She might think you're some homewrecker who's trying to destroy our family."

The woman appeared confused and alarmed.

"And lady, that's all you need is for my father to return and find Mother's Day has been ruined. I don't think you want that message running around town. Being the woman who ruins people's lives."

She thought about calling the hotel where Jessica was staying in Indianapolis to confirm his story but worried she might be fired if it came back he was telling the truth, so she decided to trust the universe and let karma do her job.

"Here's what we're going to do," she said, grabbing for the phone and dialing. "Yes, Mr. Beater, sir, it appears there's been a mistake. A gentleman by the name of Paul Tiller made a purchase over the phone earlier this week and it seems Jessica didn't wrap the bottle that was purchased by Mr. Tiller. Yes, a boy by the name of . . . Mr. Tiller's son is here. I've looked and can't locate the package."

She looked down at Joe and then back into the distance. "Yes, certainly. No, it's a gift for his wife. We can't call to confirm . . . But sir, tomorrow is Mother's Day. Yes. I think that will work. Sounds great, yes. I'm sure it was just some mix-up. You're welcome."

She hung up the phone and looked at Joe.

"Well, I'm really sorry about all the confusion. I've explained everything to the store manager and he told me that under the circumstance, we'll provide a replacement—I'll just need your father's name, address, and telephone number."

Joe gave her the information, then told her what the gift was. "The Burberry."

"Excellent." She pulled out the box and wrapped it in tissue paper and placed it in a decorative bag. "Unfortunately, because your father purchased this with a credit card, he'll need to bring in the original card and a receipt. I'm sure Jessica just made a mistake. It's probably all the thoughts of engagement on her mind." She smiled and handed him the bag.

"Yeah, I know, she already told me," Joe said and left.

* * *

That fucking bitch better have her card, Joe thought as he continued down the stairs, providing silent judgment. The platform was crowded by a group of tourists headed uptown. He thought about turning around and taking the 4-5-6 Train. Then he heard an announcement:

"Please be advised that due to a police investigation at Grand Central, there is a delay on all northbound 4, 5, and 6 trains."

He looked down at his watch. It was quarter past two and his reservation was for five. He put his cell phone to his ear.

"Tiller & Associates," Gloria answered, even though she knew full well it was Joe calling.

"Gloria . . . GLORIA . . . what did I say about letting the phone ring more than once?"

"Sorry, Mr. Tiller."

"Gloria, I need to move the appointment with Williams to 5:30. I'm in a bit of a time crunch and think I might be late."

"Mr. Tiller, when I called his assistant, she said Mr. Will—"

"Gloria, if I paid you to think, I would be bankrupt. Just get on the phone and do your job!"

"Yes, Mr. Tiller!"

He hung up and Gloria began to panic. *What the fuck does he expect me to do, move a mountain?* She picked up the phone and dialed.

"Having a great day at Williams Innovations, this is Margo. How may I help you?"

"Margo, this is Gloria, Joe Tiller's assistant."

Feeling Gloria's pain, Margo listened.

"Mr. Tiller is running a bit behind," Gloria explained, "and has requested the meeting be moved to 5:30."

"No Bueno. Mr. Williams has a 6:30 gender reveal party for Milo. I was invited, but it conflicts with my hair appointment. Let me see what I can do." She put Gloria on hold and came back a minute later. "Sorry, it's still a no-go. If Mr. Tiller would like to reschedule for after the weekend, I'm sure Mr. Williams could squeeze him in. If anything changes, I'll be sure to let you know."

"Thank you. Let's keep the scheduled meeting and I'll let Mr. Tiller know."

"Sounds like a plan," Margo said and hung up as quickly as she'd answered.

Gloria panicked at the thought of telling her boss, the person who didn't take being told "no" well, that she had failed.

"Mr. Tiller," she said, "I tried to push the time, but it looks like Mr. Williams has a prior engagement that he's unable to move. Would you like me to cancel?"

"Gloria, if you learned anything at Secretaries 'R' Us, it's that you never cancel an appointment. It looks like I'll have to take this situation into my own hands," he snapped and hung up the phone.

Joe's level of irritation had grown. Between the delayed train, the crowded platform, and the smell of urine emanating from a homeless man parked on a bench with his shopping cart, Joe felt like screaming. He looked around for someone who appeared most vulnerable and wouldn't fight back.

He went to the digital kiosk and inquired about the arrival times of all trains, thinking, *This is really a shit-show!* It was true; the trains were delayed. It quickly reminded him why he hated the New York Transit Authority.

"Sir," a voice said, "I'm raising money to help support my high school football team and asking for any donations you could provide. This will go to help to bu—"

"Let me stop you right there, son." Joe pointed to the sleeping homeless man. "Keep on begging and you'll end up like him!"

The kid didn't know how to respond. Usually, people would just say no or that they didn't have any spare change, but Joe took it as an opportunity to provide the lad with an educational moment.

The kid attended a public school in the East Bronx that Andrew Cuomo and other state representatives refused to fund. Extracurricular activities, especially sports, were suffering. The boy's father worked two full-time jobs while his mother stayed home to raise their youngest, a boy who was delayed and on the spectrum. They weren't on public assistance because the father worked. So the boy had decided to peddle the platforms in Union Square where someone might hear his cry and hand him a few bucks.

What a dick, he thought, assuming Joe Tiller was the type who hadn't worked a day in his life.

"The next upbound Q Train will arrive in two minutes," the overhead announcement blared.

Joe rolled his eyes and let out a big sigh. The woman next to him was paying no attention. She had a pair of earphones buried deep in her ears and the volume was turned so high that if listened to closely enough, Joe could recognize the song.

"Hello!" came another announcement over the PA. "Soliciting on the New York City subway is illegal. Please donate to a local charity. Thank you for riding MTA."

Joe laughed. In a city filled with over eight million people, who had time to enforce such a policy? "That's rich."

He leaned out, looking for the distant reflection of the train headlights mirroring off the tracks, which was what everyone did as they waited. It seemed to happen only on those days when you really needed to be somewhere. Most of the people around him didn't live here and were most likely from some midwestern town where subway systems and mass transportation was not a way of life. He thought people with baby strollers should be forced to ride the last train car like the African Americans had before the end of segregation.

"Stand clear of the platform," the voice announced. "The next upbound Q Train is now arriving."

He felt relief when he stepped into the mostly empty car.

"Next stop is Herald Square, 34th Street, please stand clear of the closing doors,"

There were only two stops between him and 57th Street, his but tranquility was disrupted by the return of the overhead voice. "Attention, passengers, the train is being held by a stalled train at the next station."

"Stalled train my ass!" he said loudly and wondered in times like this why he lived here. "It's only when you need to be somewhere," he said to a woman seated nearby. He was the only one still standing by the doors but there were only a few people here: the woman, an elderly couple, a woman with a stroller, and a homeless man sprawled across an entire row of seats. Bags of trash and empty Wendy's cups laid on the floor.

"Attention, we still have traffic ahead and will be moving shortly," the announcer said.

"Is it stalled, or is it traffic?" Joe said to the woman. She clearly wasn't paying him any attention, preoccupied with a game of

Candy Crush and the music coming from her earbuds.

Joe felt ready to blow a gasket and went to sit down. He walked past the woman with the stroller, a Latina. She had her stroller out, blocking his way.

"Excuse me," Joe said, glaring at her, "could you please move this contraption?"

She shrugged and lifted her free hand. *"No Ingles."*

Joe felt his blood pressure rise and realized he was about to lose his composure. "PARDON YOU!" he growled. He assumed that meant "excuse me" in broken English. The woman moved the stroller, ignoring Joe and smiling at her baby.

"Why don't they neuter you bitches?" Joe barked.

The woman didn't respond, which only increased his irritation. He looked at the kiosk in front of him and put in his headphones. He needed to self-soothe with Rhye and refocus his attention on JC. He was overwhelmed by the idea of buying something for a woman he'd most likely never meet but possessed by the idea doing so could have influence over her husband to think fondly of him. Like the milkman his mother used to sleep with when his father was away on business.

"My name is Tony," came a voice. "I am homeless. I have two kids, Sheryl and John. We're living in a shelter. We lost our home in a fire."

Joe turned to see the familiar face holding up a crinkled photo that was barely discernible.

"Fuck me."

"If you would care to spare anything, my children, wife, and I would greatly appreciate it!"

Joe looked down at his shoes and saw a scuff, which he assumed someone had made by stepping on when he was trying to push through the crowd at Union Square. He filled his mouth with saliva and spit on the shoe. Then he brought his leg up and rubbed away the tiny mark with the bottom of his thumb. "There we go, all better."

What felt like an eternity was only a couple of minutes, yet it felt like so much more. Intolerable of this, he moved his attention to an attractive blonde who reminded him of his mother.

T.S. Eliot

"**D**arling, do you think we have enough time to stop and take a gander at the fountain?"

Roman assumed she was talking about either the one that could be seen at the south entrance of the park or slightly west where Tori Amos had once performed on Good Morning America—the same location featured in the opening credits of *Angels in America*.

"I suppose, darling," he said, echoing her.

Something about when she called him "darling" felt pleasant, but it was a nomenclature she used for everyone. It didn't matter if you were her doorman, a child, or a dog, she always started out her sentences with "darling."

She put her right arm around his and used the other to support the purse she held tightly. "Such a beautiful day for a walk."

He nodded and placed his hand on hers. "It sure is."

She continued to guide him, humming, and soon the hum turned into a whistle that mimicked the birds searching for pieces of bread or seed.

"That one right there," she said and pointed. "Come here, my darling."

She started making noises to a squirrel checking an empty acorn.

"You see that one?" she said, pointing. "Well, I think she's got a litter. Brando used to have one very similar that lived in our back yard. It would come up to the kitchen window and take seed from the bird feeder. After a long day at the park, we would return home and Brando would sit with me while I soaked in the bath while I puffed on a Virginia Slim. Eventually, he grew too old for his mother and we stopped going to the park. I was replaced by his first girlfriend." She sounded disturbed by the thought. "Yes, darling, that is every mother's worst nightmare—that eventually their innocent boys grow up to be men, join the military, and forget the women who raised them."

Roman could see this still felt fresh. He grabbed her hand and pulled her closer. "Well, I'm sure he grew up to be a wonderful young man."

She nodded. "Yes, I suppose he did. He went off to college and met a very nice young woman. That was after the war, of course. I tried to sway him away from joining the military and tried to get him to go directly to college. That way he could have avoided Vietnam, being the first born, but he absolutely insisted. He was never the same after he returned. But we were proud of him. I wonder what he and the kids are doing this weekend. Darling, can you do me a favor and remind me to have Hilda call and arrange a dinner party with Lilian, Brando, Veronica, Roderick, and myself? A dinner party sounds absolutely divine."

"Absolutely. So are we going to the fountain at Columbus Circle or the one in the middle of the park?" Looking down to make sure she didn't fall, he checked his watch.

Katheryn stopped and looked up at him. "You know, I think for today we will just visit the entrance of the park. When I was a little girl, we used to walk down there and find ourselves bathing in the fountain. My mother, rest her soul, would have had a heart attack if she knew we were diving into ponds and being soaked in bird and squirrel guano."

She stopped, looking troubled. "But Marshal, darling, we never did find the memento Marques left for me on that bench." Pulling a white handkerchief from her handbag, she attempted to offset the tears from her eyes. Roman could see she felt a moment in her history had been washed away.

"I was supposed to meet him that evening, but I wasn't . . . had I, maybe my life would be different today. We would have continued playing music together, but I don't think I would have been the star I am today. But then again, if I could go back I might have given all this up for just one more day. Just another moment to hear him say he loved me." She moved toward a bench near the south exit, wiped her eyes, and took in a deep breath. "It just wasn't accepted or legal for a colored man and a white woman . . . but then again," she said, beginning to smile, "I wouldn't have had Brando. I might have never made that album. I wouldn't have . . ."

Roman felt overwhelmed by her sorrow. "Katheryn, why don't we go over to that food cart?"

"No, thank you, my darling. Please just give me a moment." She looked the other way.

Realizing she deserved to have her dignity, Roman walked over to the hot dog vendor, bought a corn dog, and asked for extra mustard. When he turned around, he saw her from across the street with her hands covering her face, sobbing quietly. It was true that whatever she'd lost was something meaningful, something significant, something that couldn't be replaced with money. It didn't matter if what she was experiencing was real or perceptional. The only thing that mattered at that moment was that she was able to access her emotions.

*   *   *

He must think I'm a blubbering idiot, queer and unusual, as women should never ruin their faces in front of a man. I don't know why I continue to feel this way, as if something larger and more complex is upon me—yet I can't recall specifics or something to connect it with.

If Roderick knew, he would kill me, and all the years of marriage and what we've shared would have been for nothing, a waste. Something to consider in a larger light. If only I'd known what I do now, maybe my world would be different.

Marshal is always a support, someone I know I can depend and rely on. One strange thing about him is why he's never kept a woman longer than a season, but I realize finding something meaningful is difficult and at times impossible.

I do hope my fans are not disappointed and don't hate me. The last time I canceled a show was when Eliot was born—Luna was probably two months to full term. I was wrestling a cold and unable to focus. Her water broke and there was a puddle of embryo fluid that covered the entire back seat. Jersey City was just a few miles away, but it was clear we weren't making it that evening. Marques pulled off the highway and searched for a payphone but didn't have any change. He decided to call collect to the club owner—left the key in the ignition and left the car running.

"Luna's in labor!" he said ecstatically. "Isn't that something?"

Suddenly the car door flew open and a man who wasn't Marques jumped in the driver's seat. "Where we headed, ladies?"

I could see the fear in Luna's face, and she could see mine. I couldn't do anything but squeeze her hand and pray to God that we would be rescued.

The man smelled like urine; his hair was disheveled, in addition to his face. I told him to get out and began to fight, but realized that while there were two of us, Luna was not fully functional.

"Sir," I shouted, "this woman is in labor! We need to get to the hospital!" He didn't seem to care.

He placed the car in reverse, put his right arm along the front of the passenger seat, and faced the rear window to make sure he wasn't going to hit another car. The wheels began to squeal and spin.

"Fuck!" he screamed, "why don't you ladies put on a little weight back there . . ."

I looked to the phone booth for Marques but he was gone. Maybe he ran to get help—but knowing him, he probably ran off. Looking out the driver's side mirror, I saw him crouching. I wanted to scream. He crept closer to the driver's door and I distracted the driver.

"Sir!" I said, "I think there is someone waving."

Sometimes it's difficult to recall what exactly happened that night, but what I do know is the man didn't walk away alive. Marques pulled out a pistol from underneath his jacket, aimed it at the man's head, and screamed, "Freeze, motherfucker! Don't even think about moving! Put your hands in the air!"

The man seemed not to care. "Why should I listen to you?"

"Because if you don't, I'm going to be forced to splatter your brains all over the concrete."

The man seemed unfazed, as I'm assuming this wasn't the first time he'd tried to highjack a running car with two women in the back seat. My heart felt like it stopped, as that night could've been my last. The man was much bigger than Marques and overpowered him. He pushed him to the ground.

I couldn't see what was happening. I could only hear. Yelling, then a gunshot. I jumped into the front seat, rolled up the windows, and locked the door—trying to remember which was the clutch, the gas, and the brake. I'd never driven a car, let alone a stick.

"It's gonna be okay, darling," I said to Luna unconvincingly. "We're going to make it out of this."

Marques and the man were behind the car, rolling around in a complete struggle. "I'm going to shoot you, fucker," I heard Marques yell, and then another gunshot.

"Just stay calm, Luna," I said. "Just stay calm!"

She grabbed my shoulder, bellied up to the back of the front seat. "Katheryn . . . the baby is . . . comminnng!" she wailed. She started breathing rapidly, in and out with each contraction.

"Just sit tight, my darling," I told her and attempted to remember what Marques once taught me. I couldn't remember if it was the brake and the clutch, clutch and gas, or just the clutch. He always told me no matter what to keep my hands at ten and two. I put my foot on the clutch and brake and slowly let on the gas while putting the car into neutral. Then I put it into first. The car started to stall.

"Son of a bitch!" I yelled, adjusting the rearview mirror and attempting to operate the vehicle.

"It's coming!" Luna screamed. "I can feel it!"

"Just hold on for a moment more," I said and encouraged her to think about something pleasant. Then I heard another gunshot and saw flashes of light—my adrenaline was pumping and I felt myself beginning to disassociate. Then BANG BANG! I screamed.

"UNLOCK THE DOOR!"

With the combination of rain pounding on the hood of the car and condensation covering the windows, I couldn't see anything but the bare visibility of the headlights. "OPEN UP THE FUCKING DOOR!!!"

I used the sleeve of my cardigan to wipe the window. "Marques!" I froze, suddenly speechless. I couldn't move. I just focused on the steering wheel.

"Unlock the door, Kathy!"

I wrapped my fingers around the knob, pulled up, opened the door, and slid across to the other side. Marques jumped in and sparked the ignition multiple times. I prayed that it would turn over.

"Fuck this piece of shit!" he screamed, but the engine started and we spun off.

"What happened back there?" I asked.

"Don't worry about it, let's just keep driving!"

I hopped into the back seat to hold Luna and used my free arm to wipe away the remaining condensation so I could see out the back window. As we pulled away I saw the man lying on the ground, lifeless. "Did you kill him? Please say you didn't."

"Like I said, Kathy, let's just keep driving."

Minus the noise of Luna's verbal distress, Marques and I said nothing for the remainder of the ride. In fact, we never spoke again about what happened that evening. We found the nearest emergency room in Jersey City, where Eliot was born at 8:21 p.m.

Luna told me she named him after T. S. Eliot, one of her favorite poets.

We stayed in Jersey that evening and did not leave the hospital. Being white and a performer had its privileges, and I was free to go into the colored wing of the hospital. Yes, I received some stares, but it was mostly from Negro folk who questioned why someone like me was sitting in the colored section of the hospital.

"Just here visiting a friend," I'd tell them.

The next morning, the nurse asked Luna to fill out the birth certificate and told her that in twenty-four hours she and the baby would be free to return to New York. There was nothing worse than being colored, but it was even worse to be colored with a child that was a bastard.

"Who should I name as the father?" the nurse inquired.

"Me," Marques spoke up and smiled at Luna.

We knew he was not the father, but Marques decided to go along so that the world would have one less reason to hate the child.

*   *   *

Roman handed Katheryn a corn dog covered in mustard. "Here you go," he said. "My grandmother used to buy me one of these whenever I was having a tough time."

He was reminded of the time he skinned his knee and his grandmother placed him on the bench. "Just hush, now, my boy. Grandma is going to make it all better." It was something he would often hear from her when he felt scared, unsure of himself, or if she noticed something was off.

Grandma had walked over to the man standing at the concession booth and asked for two corn dogs. "It's for my grandson," she'd said, giving a few dollars and some change from her billfold, waving for the man to keep the change.

She had walked back to Roman and handed him the corn dog the same way Roman did with Katheryn. "Let me see your knee, son," she said and raised his pants leg. The pain intensified. "Now, now, now. Just hold still."

Roman closed his eyes tightly as his grandmother sang the hymn "Oh Happy Day." He wanted to look but knew seeing the gash might make the pain worse. "Well, it looks like you're all fixed up."

Slowly, he opened one eye and then the other. A small stain of blood had soaked through his pants, but his knee no longer stung. It seemed his grandmother had this power to distract him—and focus on the good.

* * *

Katheryn examined the corn dog.

Roman understood this was something she was accustomed to, and he tried not to experience her reaction as being rude or dismissive. Rather, he decided to sit next to her and focus his attention on how she was nothing like his grandmother, a kind soul that gave what she didn't have and never complained.

He sobered at the realization Katheryn was without excuse for her lack of lived experiences, which was how he saw her: a woman with many excuses, someone who lacked reason.

Through the corner of his eye he watched her. She did not want to indulge, remaining reserved. "You don't have to eat it," he said, offering her the option to politely refuse.

"It's not that, darling. I'm just confused as to what I'm expected to do here," she said, looking uncertain.

"It's a corn dog," he said and felt a sudden resurgence of confusion. "You've had one before, haven't you?"

"I can't say that I have, darling. Please explain this exotic gourmet street vendor concoction you refer to as a . . ."

"A corn dog," he finished for her.

"Yes, a . . . umm . . . corn dog!"

He wanted to offer her a moment of context but felt unsure of his ability to give an explanation and history of the corn dog. He pulled out his phone and Googled "history of the corn dog" and pulled open the first link that popped up. He handed her his phone.

"What is this, darling?"

"A cell phone, darling," he said sarcastically.

She looked confused and fragmented. "A what?"

Roman was taken aback that she didn't understand. Or maybe she didn't want to. "It's this magical box that is used for all forms of communication," he said and took the phone back, opened the link, and handed it back to her.

She looked confused and unsure of what to do. "I can't keep up with these changes," she said and sat there focusing on the brightly illuminated box.

"All you have to do is scroll." He reached over and put his

pointer finger on the screen. "That's all you have to do. Just scroll with your finger."

Katheryn scrolled down and read. "It does sound like this . . . corn dog . . . has such an extensive history." She handed back the phone. "I suppose I will try this, but I must warn you. If I'm repulsed, I will spit it out."

"Go on," he said encouragingly. "It's getting cold."

She took a nibble of the cornmeal and attempted to orient her senses. Thinking about what she'd just experienced, she said, "It does have a strange yet inviting texture."

"You haven't even gotten to the good part. Really allow yourself to experience it!"

She glanced up at him once more and took a larger bite, closing her eyes, then another, and swallowed. "This is an interesting mixture. I bet you the person who invented this is a millionaire." She put more in her mouth. "I must say I am surprised."

They sat together on the bench and ate in silence. Roman thought she was just being difficult but understood she needed someone to bring her into these experiences—that on her own she was limited, but with him the world was filled with possibility.

It felt queer for her to be present in that moment, as her entire life cycled between the stage and obligations to her husband's beliefs that "women aren't supposed to behave that way."

Because of these things she found herself more guarded and lacking the ability to really put her finger on who she believed herself to be.

"I wonder if he'll be home in time for dinner," Katheryn said, suddenly preoccupied with thoughts of dinner. "Marshal, darling, let's find a payphone to call the driver. I just don't think we'll make it there at the rate we are going."

*   *   *

At first I thought she was being fictitious, but it's clear she's confused and doesn't know we're just a few blocks away.

"We're going to have to go to the street. I'm sure we'll find one there."

If we did, I'm wondering if it would even work—I'm going to have to think about how to arrange this. Her driver is nothing more than an Uber, which I'm assuming I'll have to pay for.

"Alright, then, let's just focus on getting to the street."

"That sounds nice," she says. "I'm sure Harold will be more than happy to hear about how we spent this afternoon and how we intend to keep ourselves occupied. Also, please have him phone Bergdorf's and let Julian know I want to start out on the seventh floor and make my way down. And please let him know that the room should be ready and Gilroy should have my afternoon usual ready for consumption."

I assume Julian is long dead since showcasing the 1972 collection for Ms. Coco herself. One thing I do know for certain is that somewhere within this five-block radius she will become distracted, confused, and disassociated.

"I'll let him know," I say.

Something about me despises her, but I assume this is difficult for her, living at Hampton Grove.

We've basically spent the afternoon trying to track down some dead man's art project that he left on some bench, which she confuses with her now-dead husband and two dead children. She never found it and I don't think she ever will.

There are two things the Parks Department doesn't like: squatters and those who mutilate benches. I'm not going to be the one to break it to her. I'm assuming she probably thinks all the dead people from her past are going to show up at her luxury apartment on Park Avenue. I wonder if it would kill her to know

Joseph the doorman is really an orderly who wears a nice coat jacket and hat—an outfit that would be replaced with white scrubs if she were living in the Bronx, but she's never even been above 86th and Lexington.

"I'll try to find a phone when we get to the street," I tell her.

The next Uber is about five minutes away—call him Bob, Joe, Harold—I honestly don't really care at this point. What I do care about is ending this afternoon unscathed and not embarrassed for her. I'm going to make a fake phone call and come up with some story as to why Harold has been replaced with another driver. I'm not expecting her to connect the dots, but I hope she realizes she's living in a time where cell phones are commonplace.

"I really love afternoons at Bergdorf's," she goes on. "When I call, he always knows what I like. I need to find something for Lilian and Brando, as their birthdays are soon to approach. I think I'll get her some china."

Last time Katheryn wanted to go out for an afternoon of shopping we didn't make it out of the apartment, as I had to inject her with a PRN dose of Ativan. "I'm sure she will love whatever you get for her."

It doesn't really feel right lying to an old woman. Luckily, I took a vow to serve and protect the general public, which is similar to what the police take—as difficult it is to find a decent one. Usually you can catch them smoking out young black men like myself, having never gone to college and lacking insight into the bigger and more pressing issues impacting society. I wonder if they post a sign in the subway systems during stop-and-frisk attracting other racists to join their team so they can ticket poor black people for smoking pot or loitering in areas like the Upper East Side.

This is something Katheryn and her family never had to experience. More than likely they were the ones calling the cops and feeding their children stories about how to avoid places like

Harlem because Harlem consists of nothing more than crackheads and street pharmacologists.

"Life's a Bitch . . . Bitch!"

Tony looked at Joe and jingled his cup, which was partially filled with change. He said, "Please, sir. Anything you can give will help my family," to which Joe snarled—he wasn't feeling the holiday spirit in the month of June.

Joe looked Tony up and down, focusing on the saliva in his mouth, thinking *What if I . . .*

Just then two teenagers entered through the front subway car door. They were covering the bottom portions of their faces with the collars of their shirts.

"Yo, that fucking stinks!" one of them said, which was followed by laughter.

They weren't paying attention to anything that was happening but sat directly in front of Joe.

"Yo, that was a hot piece of ass," the other one said, referring to a woman he'd banged at their mother's house while she was out of town. "Her skins were fine, yo. I banged that shit for a couple hours and she wanted more."

"I wonder if she has a friend, dawg," his friend said and began to laugh.

Joe assumed they were headed to the Bronx and would transfer to the 6 Train at Lexington/59th Street, then head north to Woodlawn, Eastchester-Dyre Avenue, or Pelham Bay Park. Regardless of where they were going, he categorized them as hoodlums who were nothing more than Bronx trash. That was where he imagined blacktinos lived. Either there or Washington Heights.

"Next stop, Times Square 42nd Street," the intercom crackled. ". . . if you see something, say something."

Joe felt anxious. He felt as if he were being held hostage by illegal immigrants and boys in their late teens talking about how they'd gotten laid. "It's about time," he said to himself and refocused his attention to JC Williams. He thought of how Barney had fattened her up during the course of their relationship and wondered how someone with a little pecker like his could impregnate anyone.

I'm sure it's the size of a pencil. That's it, Pencil Dick. That's what I'll call him. Hey, there, Pencil Dick!

He began to laugh uncontrollably.

Pencil Dick! How classic!

The woman with the stroller and the blacktino kids avoided making eye contact when they heard him laughing.

"Yo, that dude is wack," one of them said.

The woman with the stroller readjusted her purse and slurped the rest of her Dr. Pepper. She tossed it into a McDonald's bag and redirected her attention to the baby in the stroller.

Joe regained his composure and flipped through the appointment listings on his phone. *I need to call Gloria and have her move that . . . and maybe this one, too.*

He felt a surge of impulsivity and thought maybe he should jump off the train to reconfirm his appointment for tonight, but he realized there was no reception between 34th and 42nd.

"You'd think with the increase in fares each year the MTA could provide wi-fi," he said to the woman and found himself distracted by an advertisement for overpriced luggage that could be purchased at a discount on 10 Bond Street. It read *EVERYONE WANTS TO GET AWAY* followed by *FOR YOUR CO-FOUNDER, FOR YOUR CO-CONSPIRATOR, FOR YOUR DESKMATE, FOR YOUR SOULMATE.*

How classy, Joe thought. *I'm sure some asshole wasted four years of his life in college to come up with that bullshit slogan.*

His thoughts were interrupted by the overhead voice informing everyone that the next stop was 57th and 7th. The subway doors flung open followed by a surge of people that packed the train, causing everyone to press against each other.

Too many people!

Joe moved to the far right of the bench. A mousy woman carrying a large bag from IKEA started yelling, "Hey guys! Hey guys! Can you move into the center? There's room!"

Annoyed, Joe shot back with "It's full!" before turning back to his phone.

"It's not! Some people have to work!"

"Looks like you went shopping instead," Joe pushed back.

The woman began pushing in even harder.

"Next stop 57th and 7th. Stand clear of the closing doors," the PA system called out.

The train stopped. The doors opened and then finally closed. The woman with the IKEA bag scowled toward the ceiling, holding onto the handlebar above her head so she wouldn't have to touch any metal surfaces.

"That's the problem with this new generation," Joe said, loud enough for the woman to hear, "they're too entitled. I wonder how they manage to get out of bed in the morning. Reminds me of my assistant, Gloria, who's probably back at the office sniffing whiteout."

He could see his comments were getting to the woman, who kept her focus on the ceiling and rolled her eyes.

"Next stop, 57th and 7th Avenue," the announcement over the PA repeated.

Joe looked at his phone and then back at the woman. "I'm assuming some people's parents never taught them how it's impolite to stare," he said to the man next to him concentrating on a book of crossword puzzles he'd picked up from a kiosk in Times Square.

"Hm?" He looked up at Joe and then back to his book.

"Yeah, these millennials," Joe said and nudged the man with his elbow, who in turn removed his bifocals and gave Joe a why-are-you-bothering-me look, which Joe ignored. "It's just a shame, you know. Self-entitled women think they're owed something in this life."

The man didn't engage him but put his glasses back on and returned to his book thinking *What an idiot.* Then he looked directly at Joe and chuckled.

"This is 57th and 7th Avenue," the intercom announced, which Joe took as an opportunity to provide a final performance for the woman and the entire train car. He stood up but didn't move, appearing frozen in place. The woman began to make her way toward the seat he'd just vacated but was still blocking.

"Excuse you," she said condescendingly and attempted to squeeze into the seat.

Joe didn't move but instead waited until the last possible moment before the doors closed, thinking about what he might say to her as he exited the train car.

"Thank you for riding MTA," the intercom remarked.

Joe and the IKEA woman were at a standoff. She expected him to give up and move, but instead he turned to the yuppie standing to his left and said, "Would you like this seat?"

Having been distracted by the music in his earbuds and unaware of the confrontation that had just taken place, the yuppie said, "Sure, thanks, man."

The woman went for the seat but didn't get there in time.

"Not so fast, Swift," Joe said, assuming she knew all the lyrics to Taylor Swift's "Red," and sat back down in the seat to block her with his body.

With the IKEA bag, she nudged herself between Joe and a random stranger sitting next to him.

Joe motioned the man over—"Sorry about that"—and began scooting her off the seat with his body.

Another man standing nearby caught her before she hit the ground.

Reorienting himself, the yuppie looked up from his phone and saw Joe motioning, urging him, "Quick, kid!"

The IKEA woman came up for round two, determined to wedge her body into the seat.

"Stand clear of the closing doors," the overhead voice ordered.

Joe motioned profusely, to which the yuppie sat and returned to his phone. Joe moved back to the door, putting his briefcase between the closing doors, waiting for them to reopen.

"Sometimes life's a bitch . . . Bitch!" Turning around, he extended his middle finger at the IKEA woman and added, "Take that!"

"Fucker!" she yelled and beat on the window. "Fucker!!!"

Joe felt a steady tap on his shoulder. "What seems to be the problem, sir?"

He turned to find two of New York's finest directly behind him—a man and woman. Joe shrugged and lowered his finger.

"The man over there says you pushed a woman on the train," the male officer said, to which the door flew open and the woman pushed her way through with her IKEA bag.

"That dick pushed me on the ground!"

The officers exchanged glances and the female officer said, "Is this true? Did you push her?"

"He sure fucking did! Blocked and pushed me to the ground!"

Joe held his composure and offered an explanation. "Clearly, this woman is delusional. I was simply holding the seat for a gentleman who had a visible disability. She just happened to be in the way. I never laid a hand on that woman. In fact, I don't even know what she is talking about."

"He's a motherfucking liar!" the woman screamed.

"Ma'am, we're going to need you to calm down."

"Are you just going to stand there?" she shouted at the female officer.

The officers looked at one another confusedly. The woman was the only one yelling. "We're going to have to gather each of your statements."

"I didn't do shit, officers! He pushed me!"

"Ma'am, we just need to take both of your statements. We'll figure out where to go from there. You say he pushed you?"

"Yes, he badgered me the entire ride."

"I did not," Joe protested, "that's a total distortion of what actually happened."

"Sir, we will speak with you in just one moment. Go on, ma'am."

"He was badgering me the whole ride," the woman said. "The train was coming to a stop. I was moving toward the seat he just got up off, and I took it as an opportunity—"

"An opportunity," the taller officer responded apprehensively.

"Yes, opportunity. You know, these seats can be hard to score during rush hour." She told the officers everything that had happened but couldn't resist adding, "Had you all been doing your job better, monitoring the subways . . ."

"Is that all, ma'am?" the male officer said and rolled his eyes. He looked at Joe. "And you, sir?"

Joe had been planning what he would say, configuring any loopholes he could create in her story. "Well, she has it partially correct. Honestly, as I said, I was just trying to give the seat to someone with a disability. I think Swift is a little confused, as the noise in her headphones was too loud. I'm thinking the volume tipped her balance. If you ask me, I think she had one too many before getting on."

"Is this true, ma'am, have you been drinking?"

"I had a couple of glasses of wine at brunch."

"Ma'am, I need you to come over here with us," the female officer said and ushered her to a discrete area to provide her privacy and avoid any further embarrassment.

"Please take a deep breath," Joe heard one of the police officers say.

I hope this will teach her a lesson, he thought and watched them administer the breathalyzer.

"Ma'am, please place your hands around your back, you are being charged with public intoxication," said the male officer.

"But I didn't do anything!" the woman cried, resisting. "I just . . . It wasn't me! Fuck you, pigs! I'm the victim here . . . he's the one who pushed me!"

They read aloud her Miranda rights and tried to turn her around. When she resisted, kicking at the air, they slammed her to the ground.

Joe watched as they hauled the woman up the stairs through the emergency exit at the turnstile. He stood in amazement, forgetting where he was, trying to orient himself. He headed east.

*　　*　　*

Life's a bitch . . . Bitch. I think I'm going to use that again in the near future. It really seems to get women going. I really need to find something special, something that says, "Joe Tiller cares." But I don't, really.

"Gloria . . . GLORIA . . . I need you to look up something reasonable, something that says Joe Tiller thinks ahead. That I'm someone you can depend on . . . No, Gloria, I don't really care about that baby. Ah, yes, I remember him saying something about that. Maybe I should get something for their ba . . ."

That's it! Honestly, who gives a shit about JC? But the baby! This is something I can capitalize on, something I can use as leverage to close this deal. Something that says I understand him, even though I don't, nor do I want to. I just need to keep things afloat, but I'm wondering what the alternative is if I can't make this happen? Indiana is always an option, and actually I'm a little tired and worn out from living in New York.

Here, you're not special. In fact, there are thousands of investors looking for that next opportunity that will land them big, but none of them are like me: handsome, endowed, with monthly credit card statements that go back as far as March 2012.

Unlike a lot of those kikes, Mr. and Mrs. Joseph Tiller II never prepared or thought about what their child's life should be or look like. No college fund set aside, let alone a trust. All while the Jews run this city and make it impossible for anyone to get ahead.

They own everything. Times Square, financial banking systems, colleges, universities, small businesses. I honestly don't need their support, nor do I want it. I've proven myself, and anything I do will have a long-lasting impact.

They'll be begging to lick my nuts: *Move over, sister. You can't have my balls. Not yet . . .*

If they're lucky and behave, I might teabag them and shoot my load all over their faces, in their eyes, and say, "Eat Daddy's cum, bitch! You know you want all of Daddy!" which drives them wild and leaves them asking for more. But it generally takes me a bit to go a second time, so I'll get a towel and help them wipe it up and throw it in the hamper, then reach for the small gold-plated padlock on the top shelf in the hall closet. Turn the combination—5-4-3—close the closet door, and return to her or them (depending on if there's more than one) and guide them to the restroom, where I watch them scrub their faces. If they think to complain, I let them know if they want round two they better wash with Noxzema. I then take another cloth and have them rinse out their pussy. It's probably been all the way up to Dyckman and down to Canal Street.

After they've washed out their snatch, I grab them by the hand, lead them back to my room, return to the closet, and throw the snatch cloth in a secured location. Back in the living room, I throw their purse and whatever articles they left in my room, letting them know I have an early morning. The classic but polite way of saying, "Thanks for stopping by, now get the fuck out of my house."

Generally, they're left scrambling to gather everything and double-checking to make sure there aren't any loose articles strung across the living room, through the hallway, or in my bedroom.

Once, I had this bitch who thought she was going to pull one over on me—slipping the used condom into her purse.

"Not so quick, bitch," was my immediate response.

I snatched that purse quicker than ICE at a beaner immigration bust and dumped it out on the floor. Caught red-handed with a stupid expression on her face.

"What do you think you're doing?" I asked.

She didn't have anything to say to explain why she'd stuffed a used condom into her purse. "I was going to throw it away on my way out."

I picked the condom off the floor, waved my future in front of her face, and sent her out packing. From the looks of it, she was probably one of those lesbians who poses as straight on Match.com, waiting for some stupid bastard to shoot his load into a rubber so she can collect it and take it to her lover Cyndi who'll carry the child for the next nine months—and later try to establish paternity in New York County Family Court.

I'm generally good about surveying the situation and putting it in the dispenser designated for used rubbers. I record each encounter in Excel. First and last initial, date and time of the encounter, what occurred (i.e., oral, anal, water sports, vaginal fisting, etc.), the type of condom style, lube used, how many times she said "give me more," and direct contact number.

That way, I'm well prepared if she decides to accuse me of being the father of her child, or forcible rape. Little do they know I have hidden cameras around my apartment that record every encounter. Let the bitch come back and say she didn't want it. The entire rendezvous has been tracked and cataloged.

*   *   *

He continued down 57th Street, thinking about a recent business meeting he had at The Roof across from Angelo's Coal Oven Pizzeria. He'd worked hard to land the new account, only to be told "you're too new" by one and "not enough experience" by the other.

Thinking about it infuriated Joe. He knew they were partially correct, but what he lacked in novelty and experience he made up for in good looks and the power of persuasion. That was when he decided to go out alone, hire an assistant, and build his reputation.

Upset by their reactions, he took one last swig of his drink, threw his resume on the table, and spit the remaining libations on the floor. "You're going to regret passing over Joe Tiller."

He thought New York was a place where people were given opportunities. Where someone would recognize he attended the Kelly School of Business where many East Coast Jews send their children. But apparently Indiana University is no Columbia or NYU.

He resented New York. They hadn't accepted him with open arms. What he didn't realize was that the city didn't really accept anyone. Not unless they'd lived there their whole lives. Only people with connections cultivated over decades were afforded the American Dream in the city that never sleeps.

Lennon Talent Agency

They found themselves on the west south tip of Central Park headed toward 5th Avenue.

"You really can experience the vitality of the city," Katheryn remarked and clutched onto his arm. "I think a nice afternoon cup of tea would be fitting on this windy afternoon."

She motioned for them to cross the street at 59th and 7th. She felt a sense of warmth and comfort as they walked in silence—only to be interrupted by the sirens of two firetrucks that whipped past, heading west.

"I sure do hope it's nothing serious, darling. But these buildings are old and sometimes cannot withstand the test of time."

Roman just listened as they walked together along the sidewalk closest to the edge of the park. He focused his attention on the lights as they changed in sequential motion—green to yellow to red—that moved along 7th, 6th, 5th, Madison, and Park.

"I've always thought it fascinating how the lights did that," he said, attempting to make small talk. He didn't know how he should engage her.

Katheryn looked up at him and back to her shoes, focusing on her steps and obsessing over the frock she wore. "Who is it you say that I'm wearing? I don't want to make a fool of myself when speaking to Julian."

"Sascha Jason."

"Sascha . . . what kind of name is Sascha?"

"Sascha Jason. She's an upcoming designer who's gaining popularity in places like DUMBO, Williamsburg, and is repped by one of the premier showrooms in SoHo."

He knew someone who worked there and represented other major upscale designers throughout the world—even places like Indianapolis—three hours south of Chicago, and other small boutiques in Miami. Her work was displayed next to designers like Patricia Costa of Stash.

"It just doesn't make sense how someone is randomly placed within the Bergdorf family of designs. If by chance, darling, this is some cruel idea of a joke, I will be forced to take it off immediately. When we arrive, Julian will place me in something more well-known amongst the general public," she said adamantly but also jokingly.

They continued to walk and eventually made it to 7th Avenue. "Shall we cross, darling?" she asked, to which he nodded. "Isn't it something . . . these lights. They just change together. It's as if the individual who designed this really understood movement and rhythm."

"Let's just focus on getting you that cup of tea," Roman said, annoyed that she hadn't listened to anything he'd just said or was just being dismissive. Then he sighed, realizing it didn't really matter what she thought.

She insisted they cross to the east side of the street. "I would love to see who is performing at Carnegie this evening." She focused her attention on a past memory triggered by the present. She held onto Roman's arm and began to walk past 58th and then 57th. Her eyes enlarged when examining the marquee that read *Presented by Mid-America Productions: New England Symphonic Ensemble.*

"Maybe we could get some box seats for this evening," she said, but her face filled with disappointment when she thought of the time she'd performed there. "I remember performing here back in 1972. I was accompanied by the New York Philharmonic, but now I can barely keep a venue to honor the contract that was set."

He could see she was becoming upset and wanted to avoid any further distress. "Well, look there!" he said to distract her. "Café Metro. I'm sure we can get a cup of English tea. There's also Park Café on 55th."

She looked at him. "The next time I see Vernon Shapiro, I'm gonna—"

"You will do no such thing," he interjected in an attempt to refocus her train of thought. "Shall we go to Café Metro or Park Café?"

She was angry and upset he wouldn't entertain her. "Why can't you just listen to what I have to say? That is the problem with you men!"

Roman tried not to take her insults personally. "Well, I suppose if that's the way you feel," he said and continued down the street, anticipating she'd pick one of the cafés he had recommended.

"Marshal, I'm going through a crisis. I'm uncertain as to why I decided to show my face in public today. All I need is for one of my fans to approach me, and then what? What am I supposed to say? All I need is for the *New York Times* to get wind of this. I'll be ruined. A laughingstock to the entire New York arts and culture community. I am Katheryn York. I've had platinum records."

She sounded like a broken record, and Roman was having difficulty expressing empathy. Then he remembered she was once someone's daughter. Someone's wife. "I think it would be best to refocus our attention. I'm sure Julian will be ecstatic to see you. Shall we make our way to Bergdorf's?"

Katheryn nodded, and they turned around a began to walk back to 59th. "When did it become this congested?" she said. "I remember those times we would walk midday, and all you would see was maybe a taxi or trolley car. Now the streets are congested with cars and traffic."

Roman grabbed her hand tightly, drawing her in close to ease her discomfort from the cars, double-decker tour buses, taxis, and people who were paying more attention to their phones than traffic.

"My darling," she said, "it feels like this entire area has become unfamiliar. It's as if they've made drastic changes overnight."

He didn't know what to say or how to explain that what she was witnessing was real. "I can see how it might seem that way," he said and attempted to redirect her: "I'm a bit turned around. Which way do we turn once we've reached 59th?"

"A right, my darling," she said with certainty. "Yes, and then it should be either on our left or right once we arrive at 7th. I remember that afternoon at the beginning of our courtship when Roderick took me on 7th. He said, 'Katheryn, the world will soon be your oyster.' But after that first album, it transitioned from 'will' to 'is.' He took me for an afternoon of shopping, and we visited the tiniest department stores. He told me I could purchase anything I wanted. That with the combined profits from the tour and royalties alone, it would cover anything I bought. That I shouldn't worry, as what was most important was my appearance. That I should never look back, and the Polly Parker Club would soon become a faded, distant memory. He told me I needed to prepare myself for an actual stage. Lights and a future. He told me I would no longer be playing in dangerous venues like the Polly Parker."

*　　*　　*

The day I signed with Lennon Talent Agency, a part of me felt I'd sold my soul. While it provided me with opportunities beyond my wildest dreams, allowing me to become accomplished, part of me wished I never signed that contract.

Roderick Weinberg was assigned as my manager. He told me,

"We are going to make all your dreams come true." I was presented a packet which must have been fifty or more pages of small fine print. "Don't worry about all that language," he said, "it's lawyer-speak. Just initial each page."

He told me, "You'll never have to worry about playing there ever again," which was strange, as I loved how it made me feel when I walked out on the stage. "No, my dear, you won't have to worry about a lot of things. You just follow my direction and you will be fine."

I worried about the ladies, if they would be able to join me—Luna had just given birth to little Eliot and was suffering with the emptiness. She came in a few months after and told me and Stella, one of the other backup singers, that she'd decided to give him up for adoption to a very nice colored couple in Harlem.

She told me the adoptive mother was a "friend of a friend" but assured me that he went to a nice family and that it was an open adoption. I could see this caused her pain, as if she'd lost a part of herself, but I knew she'd done the right thing. Bruno told her he'd offer the world and that she would eventually have a career as a solo performer, playing stages much bigger than the Polly Parker. It was the same thing Roderick told me.

"What about the ladies?" I asked. He knew exactly to whom I was referring: Luna, Berta, Candace, and Sandy. He didn't look at me but encouraged me to continue initialing. "You just let me take care of everything," he said and continued to motion the notary, who appeared impatient and restless.

I told him that only under one condition would I sign: He would need to provide assurance that Marshal would remain in the fold. "He's always taken care of me. I wouldn't be where I am today if he'd never given me that first spot."

Roderick went on to explain that Lennon Talent had a specific way in which they wanted to manage my brand. I stopped initialing and put down the pen. "It's Marshal and the girls, or I walk."

I was calling his bluff, and I knew at that moment I might lose everything. He insisted it would all work out but that for now I should just "sign" and that it could "always be adjusted later."

I wanted to trust him, but something didn't feel right. We went back and forth, and to this day I don't know why he became so adamantly invested in my career, trying to control the tiniest aspects.

"Well," I said, "before I do anything, darling, I need to speak with Marques." I knew Marques understood the industry, and I couldn't bear the thought of life without him. Roderick tried to stop me, but I told him I needed a day to think things over.

It was getting late and I was supposed to meet Marques, but I realized I was running an hour late. I assumed he had gone ahead to the Polly Parker to warm up. I hopped a cab to the park and waited for thirty minutes.

Marques would always say, "Kathy, you're going to be late to your own funeral," which was true—I always seemed to be running late. I hurried to meet him. I was excited to tell him about Lennon Talent and wanted him to read over the contract.

When I arrived, I asked Berta if she'd seen him.

"He hasn't shown up yet," she said and went back to talking to Jeremiah—something about a key change for a song where she had a partial solo. "This is where I come in. On the fourth measure. Do you think that's possible?" she asked, pointing at the sheet of music.

I headed to the bar to speak with the bartender about a libation.

"What's ya poison tonight, Cookie?" he asked. It always felt strange but endearing when he called me that, as he had special nicknames for each of the girls. He had a deep-rooted Bronx accent and always mixed drinks generously. Even then, I rarely found myself nursing a hangover the next morning.

"Good evening, Ralph, I'll have my regular." I removed my gloves and placed them in my purse.

"Coming right up," he said and began to prepare an extra dirty martini.

"Have you seen Marques, darling?"

Concentrating on making the perfect martini, he removed the chilled glass from ice. "I haven't, but I'm sure he'll be walking in at any moment." He presented the glass with two olives at the bottom.

"I just had something important to discuss with him," I said. "I'm going to find Candy, but if you should see him, please let him know it's important."

I finished the martini and went backstage where Sandy and Candace were applying their makeup, eyelashes, and wigs.

"What's new with you, ladies?"

"Nothing new," Sandy said. "I just know we're going to have a big turnout this evening."

I inquired if they'd seen Marques as I put my coat and scarf on the chair in front of the vanity and began to paint on my face.

Sandy let out a burst of laughter, which Candace followed. "He told me he would show me the world, but the only thing he had was a beat-up Cadillac and some busted teeth."

"Oh, my," Sandy said, "Well if my mama taught me anything, it was this: When a man tells you he's going to show you the world, you tell him about the acre of swampland you own in southern Mississippi."

"Ladies," I said and repeated myself, "have either of you heard from Marques?"

Sandy rolled her eyes and picked up a foldable fan with a hand-painted Oriental flower. "Don't you mean your loverboy?" She turned to Candace and laughed.

I stared at the mirror as I applied my lipstick. "Well, when you see him, let him know that Ms. Katheryn York is about to be signed with Lennon Talent Agency."

Candice leaned against Sandy, clutching her pearls. "A talent agency?"

"Yes, ladies, I'm being considered, and a man by the name of Roderick Weinberg will be managing me."

Sandy whipped out her boa, came over to my chair, and put it around my neck. "When pigs fly!"

"Well, looks like you better inquire with your mama about that swampland because we are soon to hit the big life."

I told them about the whole ordeal and stressed that if they weren't included, I wasn't signing.

"That's why I need to speak to Marques. To have him read over this contract." I pulled it out and placed it on the table.

Sandy picked it up and skimmed through the pages. "Well, it says here that you aren't allowed to play in Negro venues." She looked at me and then to Candace.

"That is why I need Marques," I said. "I know he's seen lots of these things, and I just want to see if there is anything I can do . . ."

"Now isn't the time to be pushing the envelope, Kathy," Sandy said and handed the contract back to me. "If that man is going to offer you something great, you better go ahead and take it. Us gals will be fine."

"Like hell she will," Candace interjected. "Honey, don't do anything until Marques gets here." She took the contract and looked it over. "It also says that you can only play venues booked by the agency, and specifically says that the talent is not permitted to ever return to the Polly Parker Club."

I felt conflicted, as a part of me wanted to go back and tell Mr. Weinberg and his agency that I would never sacrifice my morals or sell out my friends, that there would be others. But the question was: would there be? I wasn't too sure.

By signing, I was agreeing to become the property of Lennon Talent for the next seven years. I realized that while this was the dream of every aspiring artist in New York, Polly Parker was a big part of my story.

"Here it says," Candace said, pointing at the contract, "that you will only recoup ten percent of the profits that are retained after all expenses are paid back. Kathy, something doesn't smell right here."

I took the contract from her hands and put it back in my bag. "I know, I know. This is why I need Marques. Just forget I even brought it up."

We continued to get ready and put on our wigs—they each wore platinum blonde and I wore one similar to my natural color.

Berta walked in. "Well, ladies, I think I worked it out. Jeremiah was able to rearrange the number. I spoke to the person working the lights. When it's my solo, he's gonna put the spot directly on me. I heard a rumor from my cousin Nessy that a talent scout will be in the audience."

"Let's just finish up, ladies," I said, adjusting my wig and evaluating my contour in the reflection of the mirror. "It's gonna be a long night."

"Well," Berta said, "what's got into you, James? I ain't putting up with another one of your big ideas about how everyone needs to 'finish up' because I haven't even got started getting ready, and tonight is my big night."

Berta was always animated when she spoke, and I found it amusing that she used my middle name, James, as if I weren't present. If I was lucky, she would call me by my full Christian name: Katheryn James York. I never understood why my parents chose that for a middle name, but people do a lot of strange things when a baby is born, like giving the child the father's first name.

When I was younger, it was always embarrassing. Like the first day of my Freshman year in high school when Ms. Feinberg called me by my full name and ended with, "Well, that is rather peculiar." Everyone laughed, but by the time we reached the end of the alphabet, a girl named Dorkas (who went by Dorothy) from a good Catholic family took on the remaining brunt of the laughter. They called her Dork for the remainder of that year. It got so bad her mother moved her to another district. Years later, I tried to find her in the directory but there was no record of a Dorkas Zabble, only a Dorothy who lived in Bay Ridge. She had married the first man who proposed a week out of high school, had three children, and died of breast cancer in her mid-forties.

"Honey, you may laugh now, but Ms. Katheryn James has landed herself a contract with Lennon Talent," Candace said to Berta, who began to laugh.

"Well, well, well, if Ms. High and Mighty didn't kick us to the curb the first moment fame came knocking on her door."

I told her to calm down. "I haven't done anything yet," I said and continued to paint my face. "I met with a man by the name of Roderick Weinberg. I told him I wasn't doing anything if you ladies and Marshal weren't included."

She looked at me and then to Candace and Sandy. "You fool, you know Negroes don't get opportunities like that. You better—"

"Shush! I'll do no such thing. That's why I need to speak with Marques. I need him to read through this contract before I go back tomorrow. I want to make sure everything reads right."

"Well, regardless, I'm sure it's going to work out, and I'm sure he will be excited."

I kept thinking maybe he'd gotten preoccupied with something, as it wasn't unusual for Lenny to stand in at a moment's notice. His energy was good, but nothing like Marques. We played five standards that evening—many that were popular.

I wondered what it would be like to perform my own songs, to have families gather around the radio to listen while young girls brushed their hair, staring in the mirror and thinking, *I wonder what it's like to be her?*

I don't think I ever really understood what it would be like to never return to Polly Parker—to that stage, the one that represented a part of me before I became famous. The Polly Parker defined me, not only as a performer but also as a woman.

Lue and the boys would always stop in on the nights one of the ladies or I was performing. He'd always greet me with one of two phrases: "Kathy, you really know how to make a man's heart melt" or "There ya go, ya did it again," referring to the imaginary tear I'd brought to his eye. I didn't know if he was telling the truth or joshing—he probably believed he could chip away at me and find his way underneath my dress, which was never going to happen.

"Have you seen Marques?" I asked Lue.

Ralph interrupted. "Cookie, you hav'n anotha?"

"No, Ralph," I said, then corrected myself: "I mean yes, darling, please pour me another."

Lue began to joke with me and I told him tonight wasn't the night for joking. I asked again if any of them had seen Marques.

"I haven't," Lue said and turned to the men in his party. "Have any of you guys seen that old bastard?" He raised his beer stein and made a toasting gesture. "Long live Marques, may his soul rest in peace."

"That's really not called for," I said. I laid a buck on the bar counter and grabbed my martini, which I purposefully spilled on the sleeve of Lue's shirt. "Keep the change!"

Lue grabbed the side of my arm. "Calm down, toots. I spoke with him earlier. He told me he had something to do and that he was going to meet ya at Central Park."

"Did he say where?"

"Nah. Hey, if things don't work out between you twos, you can always give your old boy Lue a chance?"

"Are you being serious?" I felt my heart begin to panic, as this was not like Marques. "I don't really think I'm following. He said he was going to Central Park?"

"I don't know, toots, he just said youse would know where to meet him."

I didn't know what to do or say, so I went backstage where Berta was removing her earrings. "A talent scout my ass," she said. "More like a used car salesman."

"Like my mama used to tell me when I was younger . . ." Sandy chimed in.

"Yes, yes, we all know. An acre of swampland in southern Mississippi," I finished for her.

"Well, if something hasn't gotten into you, James," Berta said, but I cut her off.

"Seriously, I think there is something wrong. Marques isn't here. I was supposed to meet him this evening in Central Park, but I was late. He never showed up, which isn't like him."

"Kathy, we've told you a million times, men like Marques don't like to be chased around. I bet ya he got distracted with that hussy Minnie who comes in here all dolled up from time to time."

"Berta," I said, "would you do me a favor and give me a ride to Central Park? I just want to make sure everything's fine."

"Have you lost your damn mind, woman? You know it ain't safe for colored folk like me to be strolling through Central Park this late in the evening." She removed her wig and fake eyelashes. "No, you can ask that man who has been cat-calling ya all evening. I'm sure he will give you a ride anywhere you want."

"Fine," I said, "let's just hope I don't get murdered." I put my wig on the faceless mannequin head, stood up, put on my petticoat, opened my purse, took out my gloves, and checked in the mirror to see if there was any lipstick on my teeth.

"Damnit, Kathy!" Berta yelled. "I'll take you, but I ain't goin' in."

Guilt was always my greatest feature, but part of her knew that if she made it to the park, she'd escort me where no woman—let alone, a colored woman—should be after dinner hours. She appeared tough and mean, but deep down I knew she was just a scared woman who lived in a world that hated her just because she was Negro.

* * *

As they reached the corner of 59th and 7th, Roman began to guide her to make a right.

"If I've not said it," Katheryn said, "thank you, Marshal, for being with me on this day." She became tearful. "If I could do it all over, I think I would have made different choices. Sometimes I think what my life would have been like if I'd never been bitten with fame. What might have become of my life? Maybe I would have lived a life very much like Dorkas."

Roman realized she was referring to someone she may have known. Katheryn continued to walk, humming a tune that was unfamiliar to him. He assumed walking past Carnegie Hall had triggered something. He didn't really know if anything she told him was true or if she was just a woman who'd come from money and created a story about her life, her past, and her believed present.

"I sure do love the smell of June," she said. "The pollen from the flowers that string across 59th."

Her words triggered a memory in his mind. One of a time when he'd been in love and walking this very area. Window shopping and telling each other about how they would one day be able to afford the finer things in life and purchase anything they wanted from stores like Gucci, Louis Vuitton, or Barneys. "You know,"

Roman said, "I once was in love. But we were just . . . different."

"I know, darling. I always thought you should have worked harder to show Sandy your love," she told him and paused. "I'm sorry, my darling, I didn't mean to overstep . . . my mouth sometimes gets the best of me. Just spitting out whatever comes to me first."

"Oh, yes, Sandy," he said, indulging her. "I should have worked harder to show her my love." His irritation turned into a smile, and he bit his lip to avoid bursting into laughter. "I wonder how she keeps herself these days," he added, trying to sound as if he were Marshal: dignified, respected, and collected in thought.

"Oh, darling, you didn't hear. She passed away a few years ago in a tragic train accident after moving to Buffalo."

"That's right, I do remember something about that. I hadn't talked to her for some time."

"An absolute tragedy if you ask me. She had the voice of an angel. I'm guessing it was her time to go. I tried to warn her about leaving the city, but last I heard, before her death she was engaged to a very nice man who went to work in the factory. She'd always tell me that you should never trust a man who tells you they own an acre of swampland in the south of Mississippi because they're nothing more than used car salesmen. The irony is that he owned a used car lot, where he sold used cars." Katheryn chuckled.

They reached the corner of 59th and took an immediate right. "When we arrive, please have the door attendant ring Julian to let him know we are here. It's imperative we begin on the seventh floor to pick something out for Lilian and Veronica. I can't fathom the idea they'd arrive to dinner and be greeted empty-handed. My mother always told me what people present to you in adornment provides an accurate depiction of who you are . . . who Roderick is . . . the family crest."

Roman wanted to roll his eyes. *It must be nice to have a family crest,* he thought and grimaced. They continued down 5th and saw the entrance to the infamous Bergdorf Goodman.

"Isn't it absolutely divine! There is something about this place that brings me joy." Katheryn paused, thinking. "I need to make sure I'm not seen here, darling. We must avoid leaking this to the press and immediately squash any rumors that I was faking an illness . . . that I've made myself available to flounder my afternoon at Bergdorf's. When we arrive, please contact Gerard to provide him a detailed account of what occurred today, and how we should prepare if the paparazzi arrive to take some quick snaps and sell them to the *Times*, or even worse—use them to blackmail me."

"Gerard?" he asked. He'd never heard that name or detail.

"Gerard, darling. Gerard."

Roman didn't know what to say. "I'm drawing a blank."

She looked at him and took in a deep breath. "My publicist, darling. Gerard Feinberg. You seem to have become forgetful today. First Sandy and now Gerard. This could be early signs of dementia setting in," she said and laughed.

Roman just looked at her and smiled, as she was the one who was suffering, not him. "Ah, yes. I thought you said Gerald."

They crossed the street and Roman opened the door for Katheryn. They were greeted by a man in his twenties who wore a black suit and had a wire hanging off his left ear. "Thank you for shopping at Bergdorf Goodman," he said to a couple that was leaving, "have a wonderful day."

Katheryn waited for the couple to pass before she proceeded through the double door. "Wonderful day, darling," she said to the man. "I'm wondering if it would be at all possible—"

A man waltzed past her on his way to the elevator, leaving her with an impolite, "Excuse you."

Katheryn looked startled but rolled her eyes. "Here, take this, darling," she said and handed Roman her purse, then proceeded to remove her gloves and sunglasses. "Some people have no manners." She motioned for him to return the purse, where she opened the clasp and stuffed everything into the bag, attempting to compose herself. "Some people need to learn to show respect to the likes of Katheryn York. If that were Brando . . ."

"Welcome to Bergdorf Goodman"

I don't have time to deal with slow people—I'm assuming no one works or has no idea what the word even means.

I'm sure that was how Gloria was raised. She's lazy and would most likely be sitting on her fat ass collecting food stamps and living in the projects if it weren't for me.

I feel it's time to pay her a call and check in; find out if she was able to use her dewy-sweet voice to get the old bastard to push the appointment.

"Gloria . . . GLORIA! Gloria, what did I say about the phone? That's right, one ring, not two, not three, and next time be sure to emphasize the T in Tiller and A in Associate. Were you able to talk Williams' assistant into moving it? Well, that is unfortunate. I really need this to happen. Not yesterday, not tomorrow, rather today."

I'm surprised she even knows how to dress herself in the morning.

"Gloria . . . GLORIA . . . please send out a memo reminding everyone casual Fridays doesn't include wearing jeans. The only jeans material acceptable is long skirts. Oh, and please remind all the women that they should utilize a hairnet, which I've made available at the front desk. In fact, I believe we should begin this policy effective immediately. Oh, and Gloria, please remember to stress the T and A."

Her only job is to make a few phone calls and manage my daily itinerary, yet she's incompetent and finds the simplest task difficult.

I don't want to waste my time rummaging around some department store looking at women's panties and looking like a pervert. I need to find something to offer Williams to take to the baby shower—looks like JT is going to have to take matters into his own hands.

"Gloria, give me the number to Mr. Williams' office. I see I'll have to do what you can't."

* * *

Gloria gave him the number. *Good luck with that,* she thought and hung up. Her tolerance was running low, but she assumed he wouldn't be back until morning. She would put in her resignation.

You couldn't pay me enough to continue working for that asshole, she thought and began to draft the letter. She'd send it and copy herself to ensure she had a record of her two-week notice.

She could go back to the temp agency and find another position to get her through until she found something more permanent.

To: Joe Tiller & Associates, LLC
From: Gloria Fairbanks

re: Gloria Fairbanks (Letter of Resignation)

Mr. Joe Tiller,

I would like to start off by saying thank you for this opportunity. After much consideration, I've decided effective immediately I will not be returning to Tiller & Associates. While I'm grateful for this opportunity, I do not feel at this time I can continue working under these conditions.

She read over her words and decided not to give him the satisfaction of knowing he'd pushed her out, or that she wasn't strong enough to handle him. She came up with a brilliant idea. She had enough material to write a novel, which she imagined would be much like the movie *9 to 5*. But just thinking about it all long enough to get the words out on paper was intolerable.

She took a break and went to Joe's computer, brainstorming possible passwords to access the protected files. Maybe the name of his dog, Potter, or goldfish, Maria Delgado. She tried different spellings and variations of each unsuccessfully.

She put her hands down on his desk, leaned back, and took a deep breath. "He's not that smart," she said to herself. "Think, Gloria. Think!"

And then it came to her: GLORIA, in all caps. He loved yelling her name. She typed it in and the lock screen disappeared. She was in.

* * *

"Having a great day at Williams Innovations, this is Margaret speaking. How may I help you?"

"Yeah, this is Joe Tiller from Tiller & Associates."

Margaret wasn't amused. She took in a deep breath and let him continue.

"I have an appointment with Mr. Williams this evening at the Champagne Bar at the Plaza Hotel. I was wondering if the appointment could be moved?"

"Please hold," Margaret said and lay the receiver on the desk as she finished putting on a second coat of nail polish. "I'm sorry, sir, but Mr. Williams is on a tight schedule today and is unable to move any of his appointments. Would you like me to reschedule for another time?"

"No, that won't be necessary, I'm just in the middle of something and need to see if it's at all possible to move it back a half hour or so."

"Mr. Tiller and his wife JC are holding the gender reveal of Milo, who Mr. Williams said they will call Stacy if it's not a boy. Mrs. Williams' gynecologist will be present to announce the gender, and Mr. Williams has instructed me that under no circumstances is he to be late. So, Mr. Tiller, if you're unable to arrange your schedule to meet Mr. Williams, then you will have to reschedule to meet at a later date. Would you like me to reschedule?"

*   *   *

No, bitch, I want you to do your job. Call Pencil Dick and tell him my time is valuable and that I'm trying to find something for his fat-ass wife or unborn fetus.

"No, that won't be necessary. Just stress that it is important Mr. Williams be punctual. When he arrives, please let him know the reservation is under Barney Williams, not Joe Tiller."

Fuck! Why is it every time a woman gets a little power she thinks it's okay to talk down to a man?

I'm sure she and Gloria have met up after work on Wednesdays for happy hour where they go on about things that never actually happened, figments of their imagination.

If it were up to me, I would have every woman's IQ tested. If they didn't score above 110, they would be forced to wear a red cape, spread their legs, and their only job would be to conceive. Oh, that's right, we already have those. They're called welfare mamas. I wonder how Gloria and Williams' assistant managed to dodge that bullet.

*   *   *

Joe looked at the kiosk and skimmed the sign with his hand—starting at the bottom and moving his finger toward the top: Cosmetics, Designer Shoes, Advanced Designer Collections, Denim, Accessories, Lingerie, Decorative Home, the John Barrett Salon. All highlighted various access points of interest from the first to the ninth floor. He turned to a woman in her late twenties working behind the counter.

"Welcome to Bergdorf Goodman," she said. "Is there anything I can assist you with this afternoon?"

Joe scanned the makeup display, giving the woman little attention. "Not quite sure," he muttered and moved away.

Another woman working the counter farther down had a bottle of Windex in one hand and a cotton cloth in the other. "Welcome to Bergdorf Goodman," she said, "are you looking for anything in particular?"

Again, he didn't look up but was quickly reminded of the time he swindled that bottle of Burberry at J.C. Penney.

"My wife," he began, and the woman behind the counter looked down at his left hand and back to him with a smile. "I was here the other day and pre-ordered a bottle of perfume for my wife's birthday," he said, scanning the display case. "It was twenty ounces of your finest Burberry." It sounded to him as if he were ordering a bottle of expensive wine. "Yes, I was here the other day, and they were out of stock. I paid and I'm here to pick up my order."

"What name is your order under?"

"Tiller. T-I-double L-E-R. Joe Tiller."

"Give me just one moment," she said and searched for his name in the computer system. "I do apologize, sir, but we have no record of an order placed for a Mr. Joe Tiller. Could it be under another name?"

He took in a deep breath, exhaled, and stared at her. "I was here the other day. I placed an order with another one of your associates. Now, if you could please locate my order, I'm running late for a meeting." He looked down and began tapping on his wristwatch.

"Let me see," the woman said, "well, there is another way we can search. Can you provide me with the credit card number it was purchased with?"

Joe patted his blazer, pulled out his wallet, and rummaged through it. "Here," he said, throwing a credit card onto the counter, "use this one."

The woman put the card into the reader. "It looks like the last thing purchased on this card was sometime last year. I'm not seeing a recent order. Could you by chance have used another form of payment?"

"Let me see," he said and handed her a slightly used card.

With each card he provided, she came back with the same response: "Maybe it was purchased on another card?"

"I don't really understand what the problem is here," Joe said, his volume increasing. He tapped his finger in a cyclical rotation.

The woman pushed a button that activated her earpiece. "Mr. Tiller, a member of our management team will be here momentarily to speak with you."

A few moments later, a man wearing a Valentino suit arrived. "Nadia, what seems to be the problem?" he said, looking to Joe first and then to her.

"This is Mr. Tiller," Nadia said. She introduced her manager as Julian. "It seems there's been a mix-up within our system. Mr. Tiller informed me he was in the other day and pre-ordered a bottle of Burberry, but it doesn't appear to have been recorded in our system."

She went on to explain how she had tried to find his order through various credit cards but was unable to.

"Well, it seems we are in a bit of a predicament," Julian said, looking at Nadia. "Mr. Tiller, could you please come this way?" He directed him to the end of the counter. "I do apologize. This is highly abnormal, and we take all things seriously here at Bergdorf Goodman. I'll do some research to help rectify this issue."

He went on to explain how a few days prior there had been a systems crash.

"Give me a few minutes to find a resolution to this," Julian said. He walked over to Nadia and began speaking in a low voice. He turned back to Joe. "Mr. Tiller, please follow Nadia to the parlor area where she will provide you with a refreshment while you wait. I will be back momentarily."

Joe followed her, feeling important. "Nadia," he said, "any relationship to Naughty?"

Nadia looked back at him over her shoulder and continued to walk. Joe smirked like he'd gotten away with something, thinking she hadn't heard him, believing she secretly wanted him.

They walked into a secluded and refined lounge with a chaise, an abstract painting, two chairs, and a small table covered with a doily cloth and lamp.

"Could I interest you in a glass of Perrier?" she said.

"That will be fine," Joe said and continued to scan her body.

She left him sitting alone as she spoke into her headset. "Right away, yes, I'm on my way," she said and returned to the perfume counter.

*　　*　　*

151

Where in the fuck did she go? You'd think a broad like her with those big knockers would want to spend time with someone like me. I can tell she wants me. I saw her checking out my crotch the entire time. I'm sure she's one of those women who latch onto married men, trying to resolve some daddy issues. She probably picks them up all the time, lures them to her home, rips off her shirt, and lubes up her breasts to get those titties fucked.

*   *   *

A man in a suit entered the lounge with a bottle of Perrier. "Here you go, sir." He put down a napkin and glass on the table and began to pour.

"Where did Naughty . . . I mean, where did Nadia go?"

"She has become busy. Please know Julian is working to resolve your issue," the man said, holding the serving tray close to his chest and moving toward the door. "Please enjoy this from all of us at Bergdorf's."

Ten minutes later, Julian returned followed by his assistant. "Mr. Tiller, thank you for your patience. This is Julia," he said, offering no further information on who she was or what her position was. "Please tell us, from the beginning, about your previous visit."

"Well," Joe said, "I was here last weekend, and a woman . . . I can't remember her name . . . she was working the counter . . ."

"Was that on Saturday or Sunday?" Julia asked.

"It was on Saturday. No, no. Sunday. It was Sunday because the Mrs. was meeting her sister for Sunday brunch. Yes, I remember her saying 'Sunday' after brunch."

"Umm-hmm. Please proceed."

"I wanted to do something special for our fifth wedding anniversary," Joe said. "I know this is one of her favorite places to shop."

"That's interesting," Julian said. "I believe you told Nadia it was for your wife's birthday." He looked at Joe's ring finger, searching for a wedding band.

"It is. We got married on her birthday."

"I see," Julian said, piecing together the details of Joe's story.

Joe began to feel as though he were being interrogated. He straightened himself and scowled. "Honestly, I don't see how this is at all relevant. I was in your store, purchased a bottle of perfume. Your computer has crashed. And now I'm sitting here looking like an idiot."

Julian could see he was becoming irritated and attempted to calm him so as not to make a scene. "Mr. Tiller, we will need you to gain your composure. We are doing our best to resolve this and do not want to disturb any of our guests."

Wrapped in a Bow

"There's just something about being at Bergdorf's, darling. If you're really nice, I may treat you to something special. Now please go to the concierge and let them know we've arrived. They will know exactly what to do."

Kathryn walked ahead toward a woman working the counter.

"Welcome to Bergdorf Goodman, is there anything specific I can assist you with today?" the woman said, pointing at a line of recently released cosmetics.

"Not right now, dear," Katheryn said. "I'm just browsing while I wait for my companion to return."

"Well, if you should need anything, don't hesitate to ask!"

Katheryn turned around and walked to another counter where another woman was working. She gave Katheryn the same welcome, but Katheryn didn't respond. Instead, she stood evaluating the different shades that were somewhere between dark- and medium-red.

"Might I interest you in this wonderful new line of lipsticks that were recently released?" the woman asked, motioning to the chair. "Would you like to try some?"

"No, that won't be necessary," Katheryn said and walked toward a perfume display.

"Welcome to Bergdorf Goodman," said yet another woman. "Looking for anything in particular?"

"No, darling, just browsing." She picked up one of the bottles of perfume and sprayed it into the air. "This is a rather interesting fragrance," she remarked, taking in a deep whiff.

"That is Molecule 01. The aroma changes depending on one's PH balance!"

Katheryn looked at the woman and then back to the counter. "Interesting."

She became momentarily distracted by a man's voice raised far past library volume. She regained her attention and continued to walk around the counter, examining the design of each bottle, but eventually could not avoid the distraction of the commotion. She walked toward the noise. Something she heard sounded familiar.

" . . . birthday," the voice was saying. "Bumbling idiot . . ."

Katheryn walked closer, listening intently but pretending to still be browsing.

"We will need you to gain your composure," she heard another voice say. This one sounded familiar.

She moved closer to see if she was right. "Julian!" she said. "Julian, darling!"

Julian turned quickly in an attempt to dismantle any further unwanted attention that had been brought to the situation. When he saw Katheryn, he was immediately sobered.

"Well, if it isn't Mrs. Weinberg! Please give me just one moment," he said and whispered something to the woman behind him. "If you could excuse me, Mr. Tiller. I will be back momentarily."

Julian grimaced, then turned to approach Katheryn.

*　　*　　*

He always looks stunning and put together, but then again why wouldn't he? It seems as if he's done something different with his hair, or maybe it's that he's grown a little stubble since I saw him last. But that is none of my business. What is my business . . .

*   *   *

Julian moved in close and looked into Katheryn's eyes. "So, what brings you in today? If I'd been expecting you, I would have—"

"I do apologize, darling," Katheryn interrupted worriedly. She thought he had been informed. "I thought Marshal would have called to let you know we were on our way."

"Don't worry about that, no apologies needed," he said and looked over his shoulder to monitor Julia's reaction and assessment of the situation. "Is there anything in particular I can assist you with?"

Katheryn was confused and hurt that he didn't automatically insist on taking her to the private viewing room where they'd bring out the clothing racks and serve her dirty martinis and gossip over celebrity sightings since her last visit.

"Well," she said, "I was wondering if you could show me some of the upcoming fashions of the fall collection."

"Absolutely! I just wasn't expecting you today and will need to arrange a few things, but it shall happen."

This felt odd, as she believed she shouldn't have to ask. She grew even more nervous when her eyes fell on Joe standing in the back lounge. There was a woman there standing beside him who appeared to be keeping him under close watch.

"But the more important question," Katheryn said, "is why that woman is guarding my grandson. Has he done something wrong?"

"Grandson?" Julian sputtered. "I beg your . . ."

Katheryn didn't understand why she should have to repeat herself. Doing so made her feel like an average guest. "Yes, my grandson. I heard the commotion, and that is why I came over. Upon a closer and more detailed inspection, it's clear Theodore is receiving less than exemplary treatment. So, what seems to be the problem here?"

"Well," Julian began and stumbled over his words. "I . . . umm . . . It appears there has been a mix-up, which we are attempting to address."

She didn't understand. "Issue to address? Well, whatever it is, I'm sure we can find an immediate solution that my grandson may move about his day."

"Again, Mrs. Weinberg, we are attempting to resolve this issue for Mr. Tiller . . ."

Joe interrupted Julian before he could finish. "Grandmother," he said and walked over to greet Katheryn with a kiss on the cheek. "I've been sitting here for the past twenty minutes, secluded in this tiny room."

Katheryn was incensed after Joe told her about the entire debacle. "I'm appalled by the way you've treated my Theodore and seriously reconsidering doing any further business here. Now please just resolve whatever may be the issue so that he may join his grandmother for brunch."

Julian doubted the nature of their relationship but thought maybe it was a coincidence they were both here at the same time. "I'm truly sorry for the confusion," he told Katheryn, "please go with Julia. She will provide you a complimentary manicure while I resolve this with Mr. Till—"

"Theodore," Joe interrupted. "You go along, Grandmother. I will find you momentarily."

"Are you certain, darling?" she asked, wondering if she might be able to help further. "Please, Julian, please help Theodore with whatever he needs and bring him to me when you've finished. I need his assistance finding something special for Veronica and Lilian." She turned to follow Julia.

Julian began scanning the area and called Nadia from his

earpiece. Then he turned to Joe. "Mr. Tiller . . ."

Joe took it as an opportunity to play dumb and determine how he might benefit from this situation.

"Mr. Tiller . . ."

"Don't you mean Mr. Weinberg?" Joe said and looked Julian directly in the eye.

"Yes, Mr. Weinberg." Julian saw Nadia approaching. "Please excuse us."

After he pulled Nadia aside, Julian berated her. "While you have been distracted by the likes of Rihanna and Beyoncé, I'm assuming you've never heard of or knew the work of Katheryn Weinberg . . . I mean York . . . Apparently, the man in the back room is her grandson, Theodore Weinberg—the last living heir of her estate! I don't care what you have to do, but this needs to be resolved immediately. And Nadia, if I should find that he leaves today feeling he received less than satisfactory treatment, you, my dear, might want to consider going to whatever hole in New Jersey you crawled out of this morning, because you will never find yourself employed on 5th Avenue again. You'll be working some low-level clearance store down in the East Village!"

Nadia was stricken, struggling to hold back the tears. "Certainly, sir. I will do whatever it takes!"

Julian turned back to Joe. "Mr. Weinberg, I do apologize for this confusion. Had we known . . ."

Joe brought up his hand in an attempt to shut him down. "Let's just get this resolved so I can join my grandmother and provide her the needed assistance to select something desirable for Veronica and Lilith . . . I mean Lilian."

"If you would follow Nadia," Julian said, "she will assist you in preparing the gift for your wife. Please don't let this rupture impact your day. We here at Bergdorf's do not take situations of this nature lightly."

*   *   *

Katheryn looked at the woman giving her a hand massage and closed her eyes. It felt nice, gentle, and relaxed. "What a lovely necklace, darling," she said, to which the attendant smiled.

"Have you enjoyed your day?" the woman inquired, which was the standard question she asked everyone she encountered, believing it was more likely she would be tipped if she schmoozed the person in front of her.

"It's been fine, darling. We took a walk through Central Park, and I decided I would do some afternoon shopping." She thought about Roman and grew worried. "I came in with my companion. I wonder if you might know what is keeping him?" Before the woman could answer, Katheryn told her all about how she'd had to intervene for her grandson. "This is an unforgivable mistake."

The woman pretended what Katheryn was saying was of interest and pumped the bottle for more lotion.

Katheryn could read the expression on her face. "Please be a bit gentler, darling." She began to grow bored, feeling captive. "Could you be so kind and ask Julian to locate Marshal?"

The woman picked up a towel and wiped off the moisturizer from her hand. "Give me just a moment," she said and left to speak with the receptionist. She giggled and regained her composure when she walked back to the station where Katheryn was sitting. "I spoke with Julian and he will be in momentarily."

*   *   *

"Mr. Till—I mean Weinberg. I want to apologize for this mix-up. Please let me know if there is anything I can do," Nadia said, leaning over the counter and exposing her cleavage.

Joe straightened his tie, then gulped and took a deep breath. "I . . . I . . . I . . ."

"Yes, Mr. Weinberg, you just let Naughty take care of everything," she said, speaking seductively. "Are you absolutely sure you would like to continue with the Burberry? We have many other fragrances that might be of interest." She held up a bottle of another expensive perfume.

"What did you have in mind?" he asked, readjusting himself as he'd become aroused by her flirtation. "What do you have in mind?" he repeated.

She felt repulsed by what Julian had implied, but if it meant never having to return to Nordstrom Rack, she was willing to do anything. "Well, I'm sure we can work something out," she said, placing her hand over his.

Joe took in another deep breath. He couldn't stop blinking. "I . . . umm . . . I . . ."

* * *

She totally wants me, but who wouldn't?

I knew from the moment she laid on those baby blues that on her next fifteen-minute break, she might find herself in one of the private restrooms rubbing one out to good old JT.

I'm sure she's been saving it for some time and will add this to her mental spank bank. She's probably thinking about what it would be like if I were fucking her titties.

I'm sure when I inform her why we'd never work, she'll show up at one of those women's marches wearing a pink pussy hat and flashing a big sign that demonstrates why she's a feminist: I AM WOMAN . . . HEAR ME ROAR. I may be a lot of things, but I'm not stupid.

*   *   *

"Please just package the perfume so I can move on with my day," Joe said and withdrew his hand from under hers.

Nadia was afraid she'd been too forceful, and she wondered if she should go to her locker to gather her things—walk away with what little dignity she still had. "And which bottle should I package for you today?"

He found himself at a standstill, unable to locate the same or at least a similar bottle to the one his mother used to wear. "It's light, dark brown with a red ribbon imprint."

She knew the fragrance department well but didn't know what he meant. "Are you sure, sir?" she asked, trying not to sound like she was questioning him.

"Yes, I'm certain. Please just wrap it up so I can be on my way."

Nadia grew suspicious. The packaging he described had never been sold there. "Let me just check one thing," she said, conducting a search at her computer terminal. She was able to locate other fragrances created by Burberry, but not the one he described. "Well, it appears we've never sold what you're describing. Maybe I could interest you in another fragrance?"

She gathered a few bottles and testing strips. With each squirt, she said, "How about this one?" or "Maybe your wife will experience a long-lasting fondness for this?" but each time, Joe looked at her and the bottle design and shook his head.

"No, she's very specific!"

Nadia realized anything she suggested would fail to please him. "Well, it seems we've found ourselves in a bit of a predicament," she said and continued making suggestions for other fragrances popular with women in their mid- to late-thirties. "We do have a fragrance by a new designer, a bestseller of sorts." She grabbed the nearest bottle, sprayed a testing strip, and handed it to him.

"I didn't come here to be pushed around. My daught—I mean my wife is not going to be happy knowing her birthday was ruined because some woman working the register tried to pawn off some imposter fragrance. I don't care what you have to do, but this needs to be resolved immediately." His clenched fist hit the counter.

Nadia had dealt with difficult people in her time, but never like this. "I'm sure we'll find a resolution." She continued to bargain her way out of something that really had nothing to do with her yet felt it had everything to do with her future at Bergdorf's.

Joe scanned the counter, looking for what appeared the most expensive bottle he could find. "Let's try that one." He pointed to a bottle with alluring packaging that he thought might appeal to JC.

"But sir, that bottle . . ." she said and looked at him.

"That bottle what?"

"That is one of our finest fragrances by Alpharetta Formash. Divine it is, but only a few hundred units are made each year."

Then she told him how much it cost: $13,500.

Joe stared at her blankly, realizing he now had control over the situation. "And . . ."

She didn't know what to say or how to respond and wondered if she should radio Julian. "But Mr. Weinberg . . ."

Joe stood silent and tapped his finger on the counter. "You wouldn't want this getting back to granny, would you? I dare you to involve that stupid little faggot," he said and pulled up the sleeve of his jacket.

She didn't know what she would say or how she would explain this. The remaining two unopened bottles were secured in a safe that only Julian and Gilroy had access to.

"Well, then . . . okay, sir."

She told him that due to its level of sensitivity, it would need to be retrieved by one of the members of upper security.

"Not to worry, this is normal procedure," she said. "Please join Mrs. Weinberg in the parlor for afternoon tea. I will personally deliver this to you, wrapped in a bow. Please follow Julia, who will return you to your grandmother."

She picked up her radio and called for Julia.

All Things Considered

"Welcome to Bergdorf's, what may I assist you with today?" said the woman at the concierge desk.

"I'm . . . my name is . . . I'm looking for a man by the name of Julian," the man said and looked at his watch.

The woman, fiftyish and bearing a blank but inviting smile, asked, "And whom should I say is requesting his presence?"

"My name is Roman White. I'm—"

"Having a lovely day," she interrupted, then stopped and started over, speaking into an almost invisible headset. "I mean, having a wonderful day at Bergdorf Goodman, please hold." She looked over to Roman and added, "Leave your resume with me and I'll be sure to let Julian know you stopped by."

Just as swiftly, she returned to the headset. "Thank you for holding. Yes. Well, if it isn't . . . yes, we most certainly did . . . would you like me to . . . one moment, please."

She transferred the call to an employee working cosmetics, then looked back up, readjusted her expression of discomfort, and smiled.

"Look," Roman said, glancing down at her name tag, "Vera, I don't have a resume and I'm not looking for employment. I'm looking for a man by the name of Julian. I'm the caretaker of a very sick woman who is roaming around your store. Now if you would please contact him so I can locate her."

Vera looked confused. Roman was wearing nothing that resembled that of a caretaker. "Julian is generally very busy, but let me try his assistant," she said, dialing an extension. "Could you please put Gilroy on the phone? It appears we have a situation emerging at Concierge." A few seconds later, she hung up the phone. "Mr. . . ."

"White."

"Yes, Mr. White. If you could please have a seat over there, Mr. Gilroy Sanglores will be down momentarily to assist you."

Roman took a seat on a nearby plush chair, trying to hide the frustration he felt over the way she had spoken to him. *A fucking job my ass. You couldn't pay me enough to work with these tight-ass social climbers,* he thought, focusing on the decorative rug beneath him, identifying a pattern that reminded him of something familiar from his childhood.

A few moments later, he saw a man in a suit walking alongside a very well put-together woman on the way to the concierge desk to consult with Vera. Roman couldn't hear what was being said but watched as the man he assumed was Gilroy stood before, Vera shaking his head and clutching his imaginary pearls. "I will take care of this," Roman heard from a distance and saw the man walking toward him.

"Welcome to Bergdorf's," Gilroy said. "What may I do for you today?"

Roman let Gilroy know why he was there. "So you can let Vera know I'm not here for a job interview," he added.

Gilroy felt taken aback by Roman's dismissive attitude toward retail. Years ago, Gilroy had begun his career as a stocker in the women's shoe department and was later promoted to assistant for one of the most powerful humans in all retail. "Well, I see," he said, then asked sarcastically, "and who is the individual for whom you provide care?"

"Katheryn Weinberg. I mean . . . Katheryn York."

A sudden look of fear swept over Gilroy, yet he remained in disbelief. "*The* Katheryn York?"

165

"Yes, Gilroy, *the* Katheryn James York."

Gilroy fought panic as he placed his hand over the top of his collar. His entire demeanor changed. Immediately, he became defensive.

"So if you are the so-called caregiver of Mrs. York . . . I mean Weinberg . . . I'm sure you won't mind providing us some identification, as she is a regular and would never show up without first scheduling an appointment!"

"I certainly will not. Please just get Julian down here now!"

"Mr. White, please lower your voice and wait patiently while I attempt to resolve this," Gilroy said and smiled back to Vera, who was filing her nails and flipping through the latest issue of *Vanity Fair.*

*   *   *

"It appears we have a crisis at Concierge," Gilroy told Julian. "Some man named Roman White says Katheryn York is running around unattended. Have you ever heard of such a thing? Katheryn York, here, spending an afternoon at Bergdorf's . . . unattended?"

Julian sighed. "Yes, I have, you twit, because she found me on the first floor between Cosmetics and Fragrance. I'm a bit unclear why she arrived today, but I have her currently entertained. Please assist Mr. White to one of our lounge areas and treat him to whatever he likes. Let him know I will be down momentarily."

A spark of fear and extreme anxiety overcame Gilroy as he realized he'd clearly overstepped. He began to think of all the ways he could rectify this rupture—the actions he should take and how best to preserve himself.

*   *   *

Gilroy returned, looking shaken. "Mr. White, if you would please follow me this way."

Roman was hesitant to do anything and acted as though he hadn't heard, staring off into the distance.

"Mr. White," Gilroy said, "I've spoken with Julian and he has requested that we escort you to a lounge."

He wanted to refuse despite the fact the situation reminded him of the time he was stopped by the police and placed under arrest. "I'll be just fine right here," he said and readjusted himself.

"If that is what you would like. It's totally acceptable."

Roman didn't respond but pulled out his phone to feign distraction.

Gilroy walked away and returned to Vera. She called Julian, who directed her to bring Roman a glass of champagne.

"From all of us here at Bergdorf's," she said and set the glass down on the end table next to Roman. She put the remainder of the Dom Pérignon in an ice bucket.

Roman didn't understand what was happening. Just minutes ago he was berated. Now he was presented with joy. "You all have a really strange way of demonstrating hospitality."

As much as he wanted to taste the champagne, he was still working and needed to remain vigilant until the end of his shift. He wanted to leave. Instead he sat watching the air bubbles as they rose to the top of the glass.

*　　*　　*

"Mr. White?"

Roman looked to see a man approaching him.

"Could you come with me?"

Roman stood and shook the man's hand, glad he wasn't being approached by the police.

"Please follow me," the man insisted.

Roman looked at the empty glass of champagne and back at the man.

"Don't worry about that," the man said. "Julia, please have Consuela come clear this area."

They walked to a private seating area, where a fresh libation had recently been poured and new bottle of champagne stuck in a bucket of ice. Roman sat down and said nothing.

"Julia, please wait outside," the man said. "Under no circumstances are we to be disturbed." He smiled at Roman and then to Julia, who walked through the threshold and closed the curtains behind her.

Roman worried that if something happened to Katheryn, he could lose his job and his ability to practice.

"Mr. White. Is it okay if I call you by your first name?"

Roman nodded.

"Roman, my name is Julian, I manage the day-to-day operations here at Bergdorf's. I've known Kathy for many years. Probably much longer than you've been alive. She has frequented this store since before I was born. Over the years, I've developed a rather strange but close relationship with her. I realize you normally don't work on Thursdays, which was a bit of a surprise to myself, as she was supposed to arrive yesterday and is generally accompanied by Charles."

Julian went on to inform Roman that Katheryn paid a visit every third Thursday of the month.

"I don't know if you realize it," Julian continued, "but Katheryn is a special friend to myself, the staff, and the Bergdorf family. At one time, it was through her contribution to the Bergdorf collection that we had one of our most influential and profitable years."

"So where is she now?" Roman asked. He didn't know how else

to respond.

Julian sensed his worry and put him at ease. "She's fine. When she arrives, we always pamper her with a facial and hand massage. I'm sorry no one at Hampton Grove informed you of what was happening. I was just surprised when she arrived today, as when she does I always want whatever memory that remains to be pleasant. Now, I understand she is sick and does not remember much, but at times she can be sharp."

Next, he explained the sequence of events that would take place. "After her manicure, we will take her to the seventh floor, where she will pick out a gift for Lilian and Veronica. Yes, I know they both passed away some time ago. We just want to make her last days on this earth pleasant. After, we will move to the eighth floor, which if you notice is not open to the public. I will sit with her, and you can retire to the seventh floor and enjoy a late lunch at BG's. And don't worry, we will take care of the bill, so please make yourself at home."

Roman was surprised to learn Julian was not a figment of Katheryn's imagination, but rather an actual person she knew. "Should I contact Hampton Grove?" he asked.

"No, they are fully aware. She will spend the next few hours looking over the same dresses she has seen. Sometimes we integrate new designs, but generally it's the same. Chanel, Fendi, Versace . . . She will select five to six items that will be packed up and brought down to car service. After she retires for the evening, your replacement should know what to do. They will send the items down to the front desk, where one of my assistants will gather them and return everything to the store. No matter what she does or how insistent she becomes, under no circumstance should you let her place them in her wardrobe, but insist they be placed into the foyer closet. When she asks, remind her that everything must be sent off to be altered."

Roman pulled out his steno pad and began taking notes. When Julian was done, he read back everything he'd been instructed.

"Perfect," Julian said. "Now there is another situation at hand you should be made aware of." He told Roman about the situation with Joe—or Theodore, as she called him. "I'm not saying he isn't her grandson. But it is odd Theodore Weinberg appears to have no recollection that his mother passed away years ago. Decades ago, in fact. There is also the fact that he presented credit cards with different names when attempting to make a purchase. It's not my place to question this, but I thought I would bring it to your attention so you can further investigate and keep an eye on the situation. Katheryn informed me that I am to honor anything he desires, and never do I want to question her, as this could cause her to feel a certain way. I've decided it best to play along."

Roman knew he had to tread lightly. It was his responsibility to care for her but also to make sure she wasn't upset unnecessarily. "Thank you for bringing this to my attention," he said. "I'll be sure to remain observant."

"Now please enjoy yourself at lunch and let me know if there is anything further I can provide," Julian said and motioned for Roman to follow him to the parlor where Katheryn was receiving a manicure.

*   *   *

Joe sat next to Katheryn, guzzling champagne.

"Grammy, is it okay if I get a new suit? This old raggedy one . . . the buttons are falling off," he said, pointing to a button that had become loose on his sleeve.

"Why certainly, darling." Katheryn said. "Anything for you, Theodore. You are my favorite grandson."

"Don't you mean your only grandson?" he said and engaged her

170

in a nervous laugh.

She placed her hand on his cheek and looked deeply into his eyes. "Yes, my only grandson," she said and returned her hand to the woman who was applying a finishing coat of nail polish.

A certain level of excitement had risen within the room, as Katheryn felt secure and joined within herself. She started to hum an old familiar song, but she was unable to recall the exact words.

Joe figured he'd milk this situation for all he could, then find a way to excuse himself—but first needed to obtain the crazy old woman's address. Maybe he could influence her to entrust him with whatever she had.

"I've just been so busy, Grandmother," he said. "I've had little to no time to myself, but I'm thinking of going away on holiday to the southern part of France. Yes, a vacation this winter."

Katheryn listened and smiled politely to the woman painting her nails.

*   *   *

If I asked for a car, she'd probably have it delivered within the afternoon—what a goldmine! To think you've lost all your marbles and are giving out gifts like Oprah on her annual giveaway: "You get a car! You get a car! And you get a car!"

I should feel bad, but this seems a bit too easy.

"Grandmother," I say, "can I have . . ." and before I'm even done asking she opens up her purse and hands over a wad of cash. Maybe Williams will be just as gullible and write a check to old JT on the spot. I swear, I've seen a lot of things in my day, but never anything like this. The old bat clearly just walked in off the street and said, "I think I'll conjure up my grandson."

It's like this was meant to be—JT in the right place at the right time. I'm doing a service that should be compensated: unrequited joy, which I'm sure she hasn't felt for years. This feels like one of those situations where an older man hires a young broad who eventually puts out, but nothing is going up my ass. I bet Naughty likes to take it up the ass and has probably practiced with a cucumber a few times. I bet when she gets home, she's gonna go straight to the fridge and grab one for her ass, one for her flappy cunt, and the other for her mouth—thinking about JT in each orifice.

I could take the old bat for everything she has, but I'm not that cruel. No, I'll leave her a little something for her retard of a grandson who'll probably show up at some point, but by then it'll be too late, I'll be gone—no farewell or forwarding address. I'm assuming this kind of shit happens all the time to women her age. If she were one of my relatives, I would have probably done the same thing, but I'd be smart and get access to monitor the old bitch's bank account. Frankly, I'm surprised this hasn't happened sooner. Some old woman shows up with nothing but herself and a spending account at Bergdorf Goodman.

I need to play it cool to avoid bringing any unnecessary attention to myself. I'm certain somewhere there's someone watching over things. "Grandmother, do you think after this we could take a stroll down the Avenue?"

That's it, engage her, make her think I'm interested and get her alone.

"That is a possibility, dear. We need to locate Marshal and send our farewells to Julian."

Shit, who's Marshal? Maybe one of her imaginary friends, or someone who works here. "Yes, I suppose we should say our goodbyes to our friends here at Bergdorf's."

This is too easy. We'll stroll down the street, into a department store, tell her I need something. I'll distract her, have her hand over a credit card, take a picture of the front and back, and then make an exit for the door.

"I was thinking Gucci or Luis Vuitton. There was a pair of shoes I wanted to show you."

*   *   *

It's nice spending time with him, but something is different. I can't place my finger on it, but there is something about him that feels changed and new. Sometimes I wish I'd not spoiled Brando the way I did, as Theodore might have grown up to be more self-sufficient and less dependent on me. It seems he only comes around when he wants or needs something. I'm assuming this is what most people experience as they get older, yet I still feel young.

"Of course we can, darling," I tell him, but what I don't understand is why he is so persistent about visiting those other retailers. I'm sure if I asked Julian he would bring whatever we requested from the men's department.

He's grown up, and I must say he looks so much like his father. I remember when Brando was his age, starting out in life. Look at him now—he will grow up one day and have children of his own, but for now Grandmother will take care of all things considered. I'm sure he will be gratefully appreciative of my provisions. "Yes, darling, we can do whatever it is you desire."

I wonder what it will be like when I am near death. Who will take care of me? I know Lilian will be taken care of, as her children visit often. I fear I will be left alone, drinking champagne and singing all those old standards to an audience of one. When I die, I hope Theodore will do something in my honor; recite a haiku at my funeral that will be used to define me, who I am as a woman. But something in me says the only time anyone will remember me is when they see my name written along the children's wing at that library in Greenwich Village near Christopher Street. When I die,

I hope they scatter my ashes here at Bergdorf Goodman.

"Theodore, darling, can you see where Marshal is? I'm becoming a bit worried."

*   *   *

Joe didn't know how to respond. He selected his words wisely.

"Why certainly, Grandmother," he said but made no move to do as she asked. "I was thinking maybe after we head down the Avenue we could go to the ice cream shop."

He realized this was deceptive, yet he couldn't resist. Exposed prey she was, but if she had been better attended to, he might never have met her and she would not be prey. A part of him wanted to shake her, wake her up, but he realized it was no coincidence that he'd been traipsing through the subways and along sidewalks only to stumble upon one of the wealthiest women he'd ever met.

"Your father and Felix were inseparable," she said. "I remember the time Hilda had to interrupt my bridge game, frantic. She believed she'd lost them, only to realize they were hiding in the attic."

Katheryn told him that after they were found, she made them sit at the kitchen table and write out an official apology to each of her guest for causing a stir.

"That was the last time your father ever decided to disrupt my time."

Joe didn't know how to respond, so he just nodded. "Grandmother," he finally said, "let's wrap this up already and proceed with our afternoon."

He was growing restless and felt a surge of anxiety. He pulled out his handkerchief, wiped his forehead, and placed it back in his jacket pocket. He knew time was limited and she might be persuaded not to leave.

"Yes, they were inseparable. They used to drive Hilda mad. Have you ever met a kindred spirit?"

"Kindred spirit," he repeated in an annoyed tone, checking his watch for the time. "Grandmother, I hate to cut our visit short, but I really need to be . . ."

"Be going, darling, if you must."

"No, Grandmother, with you. You are the only person I want to spend the afternoon with, but I have a meeting in just a few hours and want to make sure we are able to—"

"Able to . . . ?"

"Yes, able to visit some of the shops on the Avenue."

She didn't like the idea of interrupting anyone, especially her grandson. "Well, I suppose we can, but we need to locate Marshal." She grabbed a few dollars from her purse to tip the manicurist. "Thank you, darling," she said and gathered her things.

Joe felt the same excitement he did when he was little—shoplifting candy from the Penny Saver on West Main Street. "Do you need any help," he said, acting as though he was interested in her wellbeing.

"No, darling, I think I can manage."

He extended his right arm to her, as if he were accompanying her to a red carpet event. "I just need to gather my package that should be waiting for me with Naughty—I mean Nadia," he said and smiled.

She grabbed his arm and began walking. "I've seen many things in my day, but never have I been so proud of my grandson."

"Don't you mean your *only* grandson?" he said and provided her a provoked laughter.

They walked through the lounge and to the fragrance department, where Nadia was standing at attention with another associate.

"We're here to gather the package," Joe said in a snotty tone.

Nadia felt scattered. She didn't think they would have finished up this soon. She'd not yet even prepared the perfume nor thought to contact Julian or Gilroy.

"Give me just one moment," she said, picking up the phone, "we just need to wrap up a few loose ends and you should be on your way."

"It appears there's been a bit of a snag, Grandmother," Joe said. "Honestly, I don't know why you put up with these people. I think we should hire you a personal assistant who can take care of things."

"Mr. Tiller," Nadia said and corrected herself. "I mean Weinberg. I spoke with a member of our management, and unfortunately they are not able to grant your request."

Joe became visibly enraged and increased his volume. "You're telling me, after all that, that you weren't able to grant my request?" he snapped, throwing "grant my request" in air quotes. "My grandmother and our family are respected members of the community. I have more pull in my pinky than you do in your entire body."

"What seems to be the problem?" Katheryn asked Nadia, who recapped the events leading up to this moment.

"We do apologize for this mix-up," Nadia said, "but the fragrance your grandson is requesting is $13,500."

Katheryn wondered why he couldn't select a bottle of perfume more reasonable. "Well," she said, "it seems we do have ourselves in a bit of a situation. Theodore, do you think you could find something a bit more . . ."

"But it's Muffy's birthday, and I fear she will be deeply disappointed."

Katheryn couldn't recall to whom he was referring, as Theo's wife's name was Laura. "Who is Muffy, darling?" she asked.

"Grandmother, my wife," he said and laughed loudly.

Katheryn decided it best to withhold any further engagement, recalling the time Theodore was sixteen and didn't get the car he wanted.

"Grandmother, this will not do," Joe went on, pounding his fist on the counter. "We mustn't ruin her birthday over something this minimal."

"Mrs. Weinberg," Nadia said, "we have agreed to provide him an in-store credit of three hundred dollars to compensate for our shortcoming, but it's out of our power to grant his request at this time."

"Well, darling, I think it is time that we consider another option," Katheryn said, looking up at Joe.

"No, you old . . . I mean Grandmother . . I won't possibly accept this as something so egregious." He put his head on the counter.

It wasn't like Katheryn to allow any member of her family to make a scene in public, as it felt undignified and unbecoming of a Weinberg. "Nadia," she said, "please remedy this situation, have the bottle brought to the front counter that we may be on our way."

"Certainly, madam."

"And please, darling, call for Julian, as I would like to thank him for such a wonderful afternoon and to let him know we won't be needing a viewing."

"Certainly, Mrs. Weinberg." Nadia picked up the phone and called Gilroy. "Please gather a bottle of the Alpharetta Formash for Mrs. Weinberg and let Julian know she has requested his presence." When she hung up, she said to Katheryn, "He will be with you momentarily."

Nadia directed them to a waiting area, where she informed them that Julian would bring down the perfume and presented them with registration papers. "Due to its sensitivity, we recommend it be insured in case of an emergency or theft," she said and told Katheryn a form of identification was needed.

Katheryn opened her purse and began to rummage. "I can't seem to find mine, darling." She turned to Joe, who seemed hesitant.

"It doesn't matter who provides identification," Nadia said, "we just need this on file, as we will need the number to associate with the perfume."

"Go on, Theodore," Katheryn motioned to Joe.

"Is this really necessary?" he asked.

"Oh, yes, sir. Again, your information is not shared, but we require this before it can leave the store."

Joe was reluctant to cause a scene. "Can I just write down the numbers?"

"Unfortunately, I must see the ID, as there is other information I need to enter," Nadia said and smiled.

"Well, I guess if this is what you need, who am I to question the likes of someone like Naughty?" he remarked and handed her his driver's license.

"It will only be just one moment. Let us provide you with a glass of champagne while you wait."

Joe rolled his eyes, took in a deep breath, and exhaled—but realized if he wanted to get out of here with Katheryn and the perfume, he would need to comply.

"Sure, that would be fantastic," he said, annunciating each syllable.

"If You Break It, You Bought It"

"Thank you for bringing this to my attention." Gilroy said. He hung up the phone and placed another call. "Vera, please let Julian know it's imperative I speak with him immediately and to meet me at Concierge within the next few minutes." His words came out rushed.

"He's standing in the lobby with Mr. White, would you like me to gather his attention?" Vera responded pointedly, as she thought eventually she would be moved from the front desk to a more valued position with increased responsibility at Bergdorf's.

"What do you think?"

"Certainly," Vera said. She set the receiver on the counter and walked out to Julian.

"Vera, what are you doing?" Julian said. "You know it is never okay to leave the front desk, under any circumstance."

Vera felt panicked and didn't know what to do. "It's . . . umm . . . it's Gil on the phone, and it sounds rather urgent. He told me to have you stay here and he would meet you momentarily." She looked at him attentively, like a dog waiting for its master to provide affirmation or reward.

Julian turned to Roman. "Mr. White, I do apologize, please have a seat while I assess the urgency of this situation." He followed Vera back to the desk, admonishing her the whole way. "And what is it you think you're doing? What if someone would have called for car service or, better yet, an emergency happened? Vera, I don't think you understand the severity of this. I will be speaking with Delfina," he said, referring to the director of Human Resources.

Roman could hear the commotion but thought nothing of it. He didn't want to bring any further attention to himself. He pulled out his phone and scrolled through the news—nothing had happened that was significant, yet if something had it would've been just another day living in the city. He leaned back and took in a deep breath. Even though he'd never met any of these people until today, he knew Katheryn was in good hands.

Meanwhile, Julian continued to berate Vera. He had threatened before to speak with Delfina, but never had it gone this far. Vera tried to contain her panic but couldn't hold it in any longer and burst into tears.

Julian felt concerned, as not only did he have the immediate situation to deal with, but he also had to deal with Vera falling apart at the entrance of Bergdorf's. "Calm down, now," he said and handed her a tissue he kept for situations like these. "It will be okay. Now, please just regain your composure."

"I was . . . I was just trying to . . ." Vera stuttered, unable to form a complete sentence.

"I know you were, we'll deal with this later, but for now just please compose yourself. We cannot have any of our guests witnessing this breakdown." Julian picked up the phone, dialed, and spoke into it. "Please tell Julia to drop whatever it is she is doing and send her to Concierge immediately. I understand she is . . . please just tell her she needs to make her way here."

Julian hung up and scooted Vera to the side, serving as a visible barrier between her and anyone who might witness her crying.

Moments later, Julia arrived with Gilroy. "Julia," Julian said, "please relieve Vera and stand post here until I send for you."

Roman sat in observation of everything transpiring before him. Julian and Gilroy walked away as another associate came to collect Vera. Gilroy spoke into Julian's ear in low tones.

"Oh, my," Julian said with his hand on his chest. "This is certainly a quandary. Umm . . . I will handle it. Now please take Mr. White to her."

Julian and Gilroy approached Roman.

"Sir," Julian said, "I do apologize, but there is a pressing matter I need to tend to, please follow Gil and he will bring you to Mrs. Weinberg." He turned to Gil before walking away and said, "Great work. This is why we no longer have you stocking shoes in Women's."

Gilroy felt compelled to spout off something snarky regarding his rise up the retail ladder but resisted. "Mr. White, please come this way."

Roman stood and followed him through the lobby to the fragrance department, where he saw Katheryn sitting next to someone he didn't recognize. The man was laughing uproariously.

"Grandmother, you are a gas!" he said and took hold of her hand, then sobered at the sight of the two men approaching. His dementor changed from joyous to reserved, and he immediately disengaged her.

Katheryn saw Roman coming and said, "Marshal, darling, while you were away, I stumbled upon Theodore."

Roman was hesitant to say anything. He wanted to assess everything that had happened since he'd last seen her. "Well, isn't that a coincidence," he smiled.

The entire exchange felt awkward to the point that everyone fell silent.

Gilroy interjected. "Madam, I spoke with Julian and he is preparing the room."

Joe felt a sudden panic, as he'd not figured this into the equation. "Grandmother, I thought we were going to walk down the Avenue?"

Katheryn felt conflicted, as she had promised him, but recalling why she'd come to Bergdorf's in the first place, she thought twice. "Darling, I did promise, didn't I? But . . ."

Joe made sure his frustration was visible to everyone. "But . . . but . . ." he said, attempting to establish guilt in the hope he could persuade her otherwise.

"Maybe another day, darling. Julian has graciously gone out of his way to clear his schedule so I may get a sneak peek at what will be displayed in the fall."

Joe realized he had to change his approach, as there were now other variables present, and that he would need to demonstrate some reserve if he had any chance to whisk her away. He grabbed her hand. "I suppose that will be fine. Maybe tomorrow or another day."

Katheryn smiled and put her hand over his, glad she wouldn't have to entertain another outburst. "I think before this private viewing ensues I would like to visit Seven and find a gift for your mother and Lilian."

Joe looked at her and slowly removed his hand. "Anything to make you happy, Grandmother," he said and shifted his attention to Roman and Gilroy.

*   *   *

Theodore is acting rather queer today—I don't understand why he's become this invested in detaching me from this moment. It all seems strange, and I'm wondering if there isn't something more he isn't telling me. He knows that when I'm here I become preoccupied and mustn't be distracted.

I don't believe he has ever stepped foot into this building. Maybe something is going on with Laura, as he would normally send his assistant to do all of his shopping. This is something to be mindful of, but regardless, I will not become distracted, as a dinner party is to be scheduled. I cannot allow myself to be diverted from selecting something special for the ones I love. Maybe he's upset I didn't include Laura in this venture.

"Theodore, please remind me when we've reached Seven that I must also purchase something for Laura."

That should be enough, I'm sure. It's a very delicate situation, and I can see how his feelings could be hurt if he believed I'd forgotten her.

The question now becomes what I should get them? Maybe something themed or an alike chromatic scheme. I'm generally very good at this, but sometimes I've been known to be off in my judgment. It's good to know I'm surrounded with such strapping young men who can assist me in selecting something from a masculine perspective.

It's not just a gift but something that says I care. Something that indicates style, but more importantly that says Katheryn York. Maybe they will be happy with a new set of china, but I think they may have enough. Maybe something functional to display on special occasions—when their guests arrive and are eating dinner, they will make known it was from me and I will be honored, regardless if it is a month or ten years from now.

Should they ever decide to put me in a nursing home, they will feel and experience increased guilt, as when they look at what I've given them they will be reminded what they've done is unbecoming of a Weinberg, and they will retrieve me immediately.

I just wish the show wouldn't have been canceled and that I could have performed for my fans—it does feel strange to think that while I'm sitting here being lavished in luxury, someone is sitting disappointed. I do hope they will forgive me and remain fans instead of foes.

I often think of the girls and all the stages we played: London,

Paris, Spain—and now it's difficult to think or believe a financial barrier stood between me and my art, my pleasure, and is now causing me severe pain and discomfort. I hope I am able to move past this.

*   *   *

Roman extended an invitation for Katheryn to take hold of his arm.

"That is okay, Marshal, darling. Theodore is here to serve as my guide."

He didn't attempt to interfere but smiled to her and then to the man she called Theodore. They'd spent the entire day together and she had never once mentioned a grandson. Still, he decided it best to keep these thoughts to himself.

"Yes," Roman said, "I guess he is." He secured her purse underneath his arm and handed her the walking cane.

Joe looked concerned that all he had was access to her body. "I will take that," he said and ripped it from Roman's arm. "Grandmother, you need to be more aware of who you are handing things to." He scanned Roman up and down.

Roman let him take control and continued to chaperone.

*   *   *

Makes sense the old lady would have a servant—the only thing missing is the "yes and no, Massa."

I'm sure he's been in one or more of these situations, taking orders from white people. It doesn't surprise me. I'm sure that's why he grabbed her purse. Probably for the same reasons as me. It doesn't make sense why she would trust a fat-lipped bastard who probably grew up with a mama that worked the welfare system like a night crawler. I wouldn't doubt if he's scamming the old bitch now—but she's clearly delusional and doesn't have a clear understanding of what day it is.

I'm assuming on his days off he sits around with his associates laughing uncontrollably, fist bumping his bros and saying something to the effect of "yeah, dawg" while taking shots of Mad Dog 20/20 and chasing it with Mountain Dew—they like citrus drinks while listening to Snoop Dog and talking about how they're going to make it big, imagining they'll one day make out like Jay Z.

I see them on the train, swinging around the rafters of the subway cars like monkeys and doing tricks with loose baseball caps or whatever other articles of clothing are available, which always seems to piss me off. It's like they think because they showed up, everyone has to stop and listen—and the worst part is they walk around with plastic bags targeting tourist for whatever loose change they can get their hands on.

The little bastards are the worst, walking from car to car selling Welch's candies or whatever snackable, all while claiming they're trying to raise money for their high school basketball team to "keep them honest," they say.

I'm sure they aren't paying taxes, and neither is the welfare recipient that hands them a dollar. I believe you need a peddler's or food handler's license for it to be legal. I wouldn't doubt those little bastards take a big shit and were never taught to wash their hands. Last year there was a hepatitis scare, which I'm assuming was from one of those little fuckers. The New York City Mayor's Council needs to do a better job of regulating our subway systems.

*　　*　　*

They approached an elevator that appeared out of service, but patiently waited as it might seem strange for a group of people to beeline in single file up the escalator.

Gilroy touched the button again. "Well, this is unfortunate," he said but was saved by the electronic numbers that descended down to the lobby.

As the door opened and they filed inside, two women in their mid to late twenties appeared confused as to why the elevator didn't stop on the third floor at Advanced Designer Collections.

"That's awkward," one of them said and pressed the button to activate and close the doors.

The silence felt uncomfortable, so Gilroy broke it. "Mrs. Weinberg, I hope your afternoon has been pleasant. I'm almost certain we will find something fitting." Katheryn appeared to be concentrating on something, and he wasn't sure he should disturb her. "I was up there earlier this morning, and there was this absolutely lovely vase collection. I was thinking it might be something someone like a sister would absolutely adore . . ."

He stopped when he realized she wouldn't entertain him in conversation. Bothered by her lack of interest, he waited for the elevator doors to open.

"Well, here we are," he said and exhaled.

The door opened, and one of the women huffed, "Elevators are not studio apartments! People should learn how to move. Excuse us, we need to get through!" They reminded Joe of the woman with the IKEA bag on the subway earlier.

Gilroy extended his arm to prevent the door from automatically closing. "Here you are, ladies, enjoy the rest of your afternoon," he said, and they exited.

Joe was standing beside Katheryn but behind Roman and Gilroy. Discreetly, he stuck his hand inside Katheryn's purse, unfastening the clasp, but soon realized he was faced with another obstacle—he would have to unzip it without causing a stir. To create a diversion, he began to cough loudly while moving the zipper backward but stopped when he realized he couldn't fit his hand in far enough.

"Theodore, darling, are you okay?" Katheryn sounded alarmed.

"Yes, Grandmother, it's just something in my throat." He wasn't ready to concede to a zipper and began to cough even more loudly.

"Theodore, darling, do you need a cough drop?"

"No Grandmother, I think I got it that time."

Joe slowly moved his hand inside the purse to scavenge for anything of value: a pen, a brush, some cosmetics, and an organizer, which was where he assumed she kept all of her credit cards. Struggling to undo the button clasp of the organizer, he continued to fidget, not sure if he'd found credit cards or just a few random pieces of paper. He didn't want to draw any more attention to himself so he decided to stop until he could be alone to rifle through her things.

The elevator doors opened and Gilroy used his arm to stop them from closing. Roman exited first, followed by Katheryn and Joe.

"Welcome to Seven," a voice said, then whispered the announcement that "a very important person" had arrived to the woman working a small yet inviting area of the showroom. They stood with their hands behind their backs, patiently waiting to provide assistance. One of the women stood statuesque in a black dress with a hemline to her knees. She did not look particularly ecstatic to be there but was reminded of the potential commission she might make.

Katheryn looked amazed by the layout of the showroom, appearing to be seeing it all for the first time. No one attempted to remind her otherwise.

"My, oh, my. What a wonderful display," she exclaimed tearfully, the same way she did when Roderick brought her here decades earlier. "It just feels all so majestic!" She continued to lose herself in the belief she'd somehow missed this in the past. "Your grandfather used to bring me to a place like this to calm my nerves before a concert and provide me with a distraction."

She grabbed Joe's arm. "He would always remind me that one day I would be able to walk in and point to whatever my heart desired, and it would become a reality. Darling, can you call your grandfather and let him know I will be home a bit later than expected?"

Joe didn't know what to say or how to respond. "Of course, Grandmother, of course I can," he said and continued walking alongside her.

He felt as though he were being held prisoner, with the only exception being he was his own captor. He wanted to contact Gloria, to hear a familiar voice, but realized it was not an opportune time.

Roman was consumed, as he'd never stepped foot in a place like this. He was brought to a memory of his grandmother, who would often take him by this building but never stopped off for a manicure or lunch. His only thoughts now were to consider what his life would have been like if he'd grown up with money—having a grandmother who was able to lavish him with gifts or whatever else he wanted.

The thought was sobering, and he was glad he grew up poor. He'd had a close relationship with his grandmother, a relationship that didn't rely on material objects to substitute for love.

Gilroy walked alongside Katheryn. "I think you will find something of interest here," he said as they approached the woman in the black hemline dress.

Katheryn disregarded him. She had become captivated by a vase that was ocean blue and transparent. "Absolutely divine," she said and held it up. She looked to Joe. "I absolutely love the works of

Rene Lalique." She glanced at its price and echoed its description. "A Persepolis blue. How divine."

She described how while performing in France she and Roderick had gone shopping and purchased a vase very much like the one she was now holding. "The show was absolutely amazing. We were required to check our luggage. I remember the entire flight home, I found myself obsessing and mentioning to Roderick how one day Rene would be recognized in the States. Look at him now," she said, pointing to another of his works. "The Carpes Koi." She motioned for Joe's attention. "When I returned to Paris later that year, I bought one similar to this. The impeccable eye for clarity is something only a few aspire to obtain, so clear yet not translucent. I wish I would have met him before he died. I did, however, pay my respects and visited the Père Lachaise Cemetery in Paris. I always wondered what it would have been like to converse with him. We are fortunate to hold his memory and legacy in our hearts through Bergdorf." She looked at Joe to gauge his reaction. "Maybe Muffy would enjoy something like this."

Roman picked up the blue vase and examined its price, which brought forth an increased level of discomfort. It was difficult for him to comprehend why someone would choose to spend thousands of dollars on something that would most likely be placed on a coffee table for display, only to be experienced with commentary during the high holidays or by the staff at Hampton Grove. He carefully set the object down but wondered what would happen if it fell and shattered. He assumed the "if you break it, you bought it" rule would stand.

"I'll take one of those," she said, pointing at the large pewter flower vase, "and have it wrapped for Laura."

"Most certainly, Mrs. Weinberg," the sales associate said. "We will have this sent down to Concierge."

Katheryn was delighted and relieved that she was being taken care of and found it even more exciting to inform Julian of the purchase she'd made for Laura. "Darling, I really think she will enjoy this new addition to your home."

Joe stared blankly. He couldn't remember if he'd used the name Muffy or Mitsy but figured it didn't matter. "I'm sure she will be taken by your exemplary taste," he said, trying to sound refined, believing the word *exemplary* to be commonplace amongst the wealthy.

He'd forgotten that her purse was on his shoulder but was reminded when Katheryn asked for it so she could reapply her lipstick. "Oh, Grandmother, let me get that for you." He unzipped it so he could continue scanning for anything of value, fishing for anything that felt like a tube of lipstick.

She found it strange he would make himself welcome in her purse and thought it unbecoming for any man, especially a Weinberg. "Well, aren't you the helpful one. Really, darling, that isn't necessary."

Before she could stop him, he pulled his hand out and handed her a tube of mascara. "Here you are, Grandmother."

"Darling, thank you for your assistance, but it appears you have . . ."

Joe dug in again, worried she would publicly rebuke him, and exclaimed in a raised voice, "Aha! Here it is!"

"It most certainly is," she said and took the lipstick from him.

Joe looked like an ostrich with his head crouched into the crevices of her bag, unable to identify anything of value. "Damn it," he said.

The papers in the organizer were now spread out and mixed in with the other objects. He decided to call off the search. Not waiting for her, he purposefully dropped the bag on the counter. "Here you are, grandmother."

It was an uncomfortable scene for everyone including the sales associate.

Katheryn finished reapplying her lipstick as Joe grew increasingly irate. "Darling, you do not need to wait on me. In fact, Marshal has agreed to help me finish up here. You can go."

Joe felt the latter part of his afternoon had been wasted on her. Knowing it would be impossible for him to conduct any further inspections of her purse with everyone standing around, he knew he had to do something quick. With one hand, he grabbed the bottom of the purse, acting as if it had slipped, and poured all of its contents onto the floor.

"Theodore! I don't know what has gotten into you today."

"I'm so sorry, Grandmother! I guess my hand slipped." He scanned the spilled contents but saw only a few receipts, a hairbrush, some newly used cosmetics, and loose papers.

Katheryn was unsure what to say or how to resolve the commotion he'd created. She looked at him and then to the contents scattered across the floor.

"Your house boy can clean this up," Joe said, motioning to Roman.

Katheryn was taken aback by the offhanded comment. Roman stood speechless.

"Theodore," she said, "that is inappropriate. Please show Marshal and your grandmother some respect." She motioned to the sales associate who was watching uncomfortably. "Darling, could you please . . ."

"Yes, Mrs. Weinberg." The sales associate went about the task of cleaning up the mess, in anticipation her kindness would erase any memory of what had just happened. Once she'd retrieved everything, she used the glass counter as support to help her stand, and handed Katheryn the purse. "Here you are, madam."

Katheryn was upset by Joe's behavior but felt limited in her capacity to mediate the situation, thinking about the assistance

Hilda had long ago offered to manage her children and sometimes grandchildren.

"Thank you, darling," she said and set the handbag on her arm, avoiding any further engagement with Joe.

Roman turned his attention elsewhere. "Maybe your sister would like something like this," he said and pointed to a Ralph Lauren frame. "You could find an old photo from when you were children." He wondered why anyone would spend almost two hundred dollars on a five-by-seven frame that was most likely manufactured in China but only recognized for its value because of lettering that read Ralph Lauren. The description indicated it was a Huston Frame, but he didn't know the difference between that and the Michael Aram, which was silver with animal designs and retailed for a similar price.

"Or this one." He pointed to the Michael Aram.

"That is a rather interesting idea, darling, and something Lilian would find endearing," she said, still thinking about the awful comment Theodore had made. "I'm so sorry, darling. I just don't know what has gotten into Theodore today. I'm assuming it has something to do with his wife, but don't you worry, when he and I are alone I will address this."

Then, attempting to defuse the tension in the room, she continued to scan the objects on the shelves. "I think this would be more suited for Veronica." She held up a silver vase by Match that retailed for nearly five hundred dollars. It was filled with orange daisies that were noticeably synthetic yet provided an example of what it would look like to a potential buyer.

"I'm not really familiar with this designer," she said, trying to make sense of its value.

"Match was founded by David Reiss in the mid-nineties," the sales associate said. "He is an up-and-coming designer who is a recent addition within the Bergdorf collection. He was successful in his ability to combine an Italian framework aesthetic with pewter metals."

The associate went on to explain how since its inception the company had grown in popularity.

"The artisan craftwork is impeccable," Katheryn said, reaching for a picture frame that retailed for much less but was still not something you would find at a discount retailer. She was intrigued. She loved new things and always included a receipt to ensure the gift recipient knew its value, but more importantly that it could be returned in exchange for store credit.

"Yes, I think this will be sufficient, and it does speak to me. I just hope you're correct that it would fancy Veronica the way it has myself. Please make sure to include a receipt."

The sales associate began to push harder, imagining parleying the commission into a pair of Jimmy Choos—the ones she'd been eyeing that had recently gone on sale. "And if you like this, I'm thinking you would also be interested in the Beaded Footed Oval Basin that was recently released to the showroom."

Katheryn found it inviting but remained reserved as she was unfamiliar with the designer.

"It can also be paired with the Garda Platter," the sales associate went on, "but are giving all our special guest a thirty percent discount."

This was not what she'd offered when Katheryn purchased the large pewter flower vase. Katheryn understood what she was doing.

"Don't be so eager, darling. It's never good to see a woman grovel." She looked at the woman with contempt. "I think this will be all for now, but maybe next time."

Katheryn looked to Roman for help. He intervened. "Shall we be going?" he said and offered Katheryn his arm. The sales associate took that as her cue to return to the register, acting as though she'd not been too presumptive in her approach.

"That is the thing about those saleswomen," Katheryn said, "they will try to pique your interest in anything if it means they will receive a commission."

She moved on, perusing for a gift for her sister, and was greeted by another sales associate. "Welcome to Bergdorf's, is there anything I can assist you with today?" the woman said in an inviting tone, looking Katheryn up and down to determine her taste but unable to. She was familiar with the bag Katheryn was carrying, but less so with the dress she was wearing. "That is a lovely dress, madam. Isabel Marant?"

Katheryn froze, unable to remember the name of the designer. She looked up to Roman for assistance.

"Sascha Jason," he whispered.

"Sascha Fashion," Katheryn said loudly, to which Roman corrected her. "I meant Sascha Jason. I'm friends with the designer," she made sure to let the woman know, "she's up-and-coming but has yet to be included within the Bergdorf collection."

"Well, whomever she is, she does have an eye. Is there anything in particular I can assist you with today?" The sales associate smiled with her recently implanted veneers. She wore a contoured cocktail dress and straight brown hair. Generally, she was good at assessing the aesthetic of a guest, pairing them up with something she felt they might find of interest. She saw Katheryn as an old soul who teetered within the Victorian but was also a bit modern for her time.

"I'm actually looking for something for my sister. We will soon have a dinner party, and I wanted to find something divine that will show I was thoughtful. That I cared. Something that says Bergdorf Goodman. Something refined." She looked at the display of small, familiar-looking figurines, yet nothing she saw fit into her previous experiences.

"Well, I think I have something that may be of interest. I'll be back momentarily," the woman said, opened the display case behind her, and pulled out a figurine five inches long and nine inches tall. "This is a Jason Strongwater. He has worked with Oscar de la Renta and designed jewelry for many of his runway shows. Later, he moved into creations such as this."

Katheryn held the figurine and examined it closely—the pastel colors felt inviting, and she found herself lost within them. The glass bird was mixed with hues of blues, reds, and gold. It looked Oriental, like something observed on display in an upscale Chinese restaurant. She turned it over to read the price tag, which showed it retailed for nearly three thousand dollars.

"Tell me more about this, darling."

"It was made in the United States," the woman said. She went on to explain that it was fourteen-karat gold and hand painted by the designer himself. "Which explains why it has found a temporary home at Bergdorf's," she added. She was working for her commission but understood the boundaries of their relationship.

Katheryn was taken; it looked like something Lilian would find appealing. She was hesitant of its value, as she was unfamiliar with the designer, but the connection with Oscar de la Renta piqued her interest.

"Oscar de la Renta, you said?"

"Yes. He spent many years with him. Some say they were once lovers."

Katheryn found herself infatuated by the figurine. It reminded her of Lilian and the times they visited Central Park, sitting for hours with a pair of binoculars trying to identify different types of bird species while Lilian paged through a field guide. Her favorite bird were finches because they looked small and vulnerable. Katheryn never understood her sister's obsession with them—to her they were just birds that lived in Central Park.

She wondered how a figurine could bring about so much emotion. She was sobered by the reality that one of them would die before the other, which caused her to become tearful. She couldn't picture life without her sister. She felt that something was off. Something she was unable to identify.

"Something feels rather queer, darling," she directed to Roman and began to concentrate more deeply on the figurine. The color illuminated her and sparked the earlier memories. "There was this time when I was just a little girl." She paused, then continued. "Lilian asked me to go with her. She said she'd sighted this aromatic creature, which is the way she thought of all birds, the aromatic creatures. She convinced me to go into the depth of the park . . . kept pushing and telling me to continue looking for this bird, which she was unable to identify in her book. Well, darling, needless to say we spent the entire afternoon walking through mud puddles because she told me that certain species of bird congregated in the water. The only thing we encountered that afternoon was the cold. When we returned home, our shoes and stockings were covered in mud. Mother was not pleased."

Roman looked at her and smiled. "Is that so?"

"Yes, darling. I didn't speak to her for the remainder of the evening, as I could've spent the afternoon practicing my violin and drinking tea with Mother. Instead, I was running around Central Park looking for a bird that didn't exist." She began to laugh but covered her mouth, as for her it was never okay for anyone to witness a woman engulfed in hysteria.

Roman looked around for Joe. "I think your grandson has disappeared," he said, but she didn't respond. It was evident she was visibly upset, and he decided it best not to mention him any further.

Katheryn continued examining the figurine and its structure. "I think this is the one, darling," she told the associate and smiled. It was strange to find something of value on her first attempt—something that was suitable and might be received with joy.

The sales associate nodded and scanned the barcode. "That will be $3,210.54. Would you like to pay by cash or credit?" she asked, not having been clued in by Gilroy.

"Mrs. Weinberg has a standing account," Roman replied.

"As, I see," she said, confused but not wanting to cause a stir. "And what is the first name that I should search?"

"Katheryn," Roman said, hoping it would spark something, but it didn't. "Do me a favor and speak with Gilroy. He can provide you with the details regarding this situation," he added, then motioned Katheryn away from the counter.

The sales associate called Gilroy through her earpiece. "I need your assistance, sir," she said and put the figurine back in the case with its beak facing north.

Moments passed and Gilroy approached, speaking in a lowered voice. "Just do whatever she asks," he instructed her. Then he approached Katheryn. "So, how are things going? Did we find anything for your sister?" He tried to push the dinnerware, as that was what he assumed all women in their early to late nineties would want, and something he would get his own grandmother.

"No, darling, I found something more fitting," Katheryn said and began to laugh.

Gilroy paused, feeling he may have offended her with his suggestions and deciding it best not to provide any others. "Well, that sounds delightful. Mrs. Weinberg, I spoke with the associate, and she has arranged for this purchase to be sent down to Concierge, which you can retrieve from Vera upon your departure."

Little Gidding

J oe was visibly irritated and continued to strategize on how he might get the old lady alone. He worried his actions would go in vain, as she had no credit cards or anything of value in her purse. Then the solution came to him: "Gloria . . . GLORIA."

"Yes, Mr. Tiller?"

"I need for you to conduct a search and email me the names of every high-end designer, with price points, for all items sold at Bergdorf Goodman, and email it to me at once."

"Okay, sir," she replied, wondering why he needed this and what the urgency behind it was. "Certainly, sir."

He hung up. If he couldn't obtain the woman's credit card, he could at least have his own private viewing and walk away with tens of thousands of dollars in merchandise to be returned later for cash. He felt an extreme sense of calm and continued to scheme how he would make this plan a reality.

He recalled the old lady telling him Julian would bring over whatever he wanted from the men's department. Soon he began to obsess about the time it would take Gloria to send over the spreadsheet. He couldn't wait any longer; he'd already been absent from Katheryn for some time.

Politely reinserting himself, he returned to the scene with a loose apology about how things had been difficult between he and his wife. Joe knew he had to tread lightly in order to get back into the old lady's good graces.

*   *   *

"Grandmother," he said but Katheryn didn't respond. He realized she was still upset with him. "Grandmother, can I speak with you for a moment . . . alone?"

Katheryn examined him with a look of extreme disappointment but followed him to another section of the showroom.

"I do apologize for my erratic behavior, Grandmother. Miny . . ." He paused, unable to recall the pet name he'd given his fictional wife. " . . . and I are going through a very situational time. We just found out the baby we're supposed to have is stillborn, which is why I've come here today . . . to find her the perfect gift . . . in hopes that I might ease her pain."

Katheryn was taken emotionally and placed one hand over her mouth. "Oh, my darling, I'm so sorry to hear this . . . How is Laura weathering through this storm? How are you, my darling?"

While the story was extreme, Joe saw it was being bought, much like the gifts she'd purchased for his imaginary wife, mother, and deceased aunt.

"I know there isn't anything that I could do or say to change this situation," Katheryn continued. "Where is she now?"

"She . . . umm . . . she's at home."

Katheryn was perplexed, assuming any woman going through something as significant as a miscarriage would need to be under the supervision of a doctor—in a hospital, "Shouldn't she be under a doctor's care?"

Never having had children or even been exposed to a birth, live or otherwise, Joe thought fast. "They're with her now, at the house."

This sounded oddly strange to Katheryn. She wondered if she were home, why wasn't he with her?

"It's okay, Grandmother," Joe said, "they said there is nothing I can do. So I decided to come here because I knew you would be.

I didn't know where else to turn."

Katheryn understood why he would think this, as this was the place she often found herself in difficult times, like when her mother would send the estate manager to drag her father out of the bar.

"Well, I am deeply sorry, Theodore. Come with me, darling, and let's pick her out something that might relieve her pain," Katheryn said, having forgotten everything else she'd purchased up to this point.

"I will need to get a suit for myself," Joe said, "a dress for her, and something for the baby to be presented in at the funeral."

Katheryn felt an immense amount of pain for him yet witnessed no trace of emotion on his face. "Of course, darling, whatever you need."

Joe tried to present something that would insinuate the loss of something significant, and realized it was possible to milk her for more. "Yes, it is sad. Things have been hard this year with the business, and now this. We just weren't prepared, and we didn't think we'd be burying little Brody." He felt that was a name suited for a situation such as this; a name he would've picked for a firstborn son.

He observed Katheryn's reaction, tearful and saddened, visibly upset. He removed the handkerchief from the lining of his interior coat pocket and handed it to her. "It's okay, Grandmother, little Brody just wasn't meant to be."

She felt a surge of emotion, as it reminded her of that which she'd lost throughout her own life. She wondered if that grief, once a distant memory yet now staring her in the face, would ever recede. "Whatever you need, darling. Do not hesitate to let Grandmother know."

Roman observed what was unfolding—he didn't understand how in one moment she could be chastising him and in another, latching onto his arm. He assumed this was the way white people handled situations. He noticed the strange grin on Theodore's face, as if he'd just gained something valuable: her trust. He saw the white in Katheryn's eyes appeared bloodshot, which further raised his concern.

"Darling, please have Gilroy phone Julian. I must speak to him immediately!"

Roman was alarmed. "Katheryn, is everything okay?"

"Please," she said, "just get Julian."

He thought maybe something significant had occurred—maybe she wanted to return to Hampton Grove, or maybe she just felt she needed some air. Roman went to Gilroy and gave him the message, then waited in silence. His job was to not interfere in situations where he was not invited, unless they were life threatening. Concerned, he observed carefully to see if she were showing signs of a heart attack or low blood sugar. He asked if he could further assess the situation, to which Katheryn declined.

"No, no, darling," she said and motioned for Joe to guide her to the nearest chair where she could rest.

Everyone stood around her, waiting. Everyone except Joe. He was gone again, trying to figure out a way he could turn this to his financial advantage.

*   *   *

"Sir," Gilroy said into the telephone, "she said she wanted to see you immediately. It sounds urgent. She didn't say . . . umm-hmm . . . well, that's unfortunate . . . I will let her know."

Fearful of offending Katheryn, Gilroy decided to try to resolve this himself.

"Madam," he said, "it appears Julian has become tied up, but he said he will be down later this afternoon for the viewing." He smiled, not knowing what else to do. "He asked that I provide any further assistance and be of service to whatever it is you need."

Katheryn sat unamused with Joe's handkerchief in her lap, clasped with both hands. Gilroy could see something was out of place and decided it best if he sat down next to her. When he did, she began to sob. Gilroy looked up to Roman for help as if he had never witnessed a woman crying.

Roman motioned for Gilroy to move over. "It's okay, Katheryn," he said and sat beside her, taking one of her hands. "I'm here for you."

She did not respond. Roman observed her deep sadness. It had been sparked by more than just a memory. It was as if she had experienced something she hadn't in a very long time. He waited for her to speak, but it didn't seem anything would come. At that moment he felt a strange closeness to her, remembering when his grandmother was on her deathbed and passing into the next life.

He'd always thought what happened after death, wondered if what the Bible said was true—that all of his grandmother's work in life would be praised and she would have something posh to look forward in the afterlife, rewarded for all she did and the impact she had on others. It was the reason he had decided to become a nurse. He knew his job was more than pushing medication, but providing a holding space in moments such as these. In the end, he thought, the size of the wooden box would remain the same.

"We are in the midst of an emergency," Katheryn said. "A very sad emergency, at that."

He didn't know how to respond. "Whatever it is, we'll get through this together."

"Theodore informed me the reason he came to Bergdorf's," Katheryn said and fell silent, taking a deep breath before continuing, " . . . his wife . . . the baby was stillborn."

Like Katheryn, Roman found this strange and wondered why he was here. "If it would make you feel better, we can go to the hospital."

"They're not at the hospital. He said the baby is stillborn, and the doctors are at the house."

This felt suspect to Roman. He was familiar with in-home births and women who had non-surgical abortions. A doctor would need access to certain medical equipment in the situation she described.

"It's not that she is losing this baby . . . as when a child dies in utero I'm always drawn back to the assumption that the unborn soul was called back to Heaven. It just brings back so many memories of that time when . . ."

She stopped, grabbing Roman's hand, at which point Gilroy realized this was the perfect time to exit (he had no desire to hear memories of the fluids that once flowed out of Katheryn York's vagina) and stepped away.

"I'm going to tell you something, darling, and you must never repeat it to anyone. Not Theodore, Julian, or Roderick. Especially not Roderick. I was tiny compared to other women for the majority of my pregnancy. During the second trimester, Berta and the girls began to question if something was happening, as I was gaining weight rapidly and could no longer use the excuse that I was overeating. Marques decided it best that I not perform until after the baby was born. I remember sitting around my apartment and asking myself what I was going to do.

"One day, curiosity got the best of Berta, who stopped by uninvited. 'Paris is real nice this time of year'—which is what Marques told them, that I'd taken a four-month sabbatical to study voice—'my mama may have raised a lot of things, but never did she raise no coon.' She burst into my apartment."

Katheryn paused before continuing. "Darling, at that moment I broke down and began to sob. The jig was up, and I was worried. In those days, it was illegal for colored and white folks to mix, let alone have a child. I remember Berta saying, 'I will take care of this.' I told her I wouldn't kill my baby, that I'd heard of women who went to doctors to perform abortions and never walked out alive.

"That was when she told me she had a 'friend of a friend' who was a doctor in Jersey City. 'When the time is close,' she told me, 'you let Berta know and I will arrange everything.' I was so scared, darling. Yes, New York was liberal compared to most parts of the United States at that time, but segregation was still running rampant.

"A few months later, I went into labor. I called Berta, who was warming up with the girls at Polly Parker. I remember calling in a panic, and Berta screaming, 'Marques, its time!' They rushed to my apartment. There was the strangest expression on Luna's face when Marques opened the door to my apartment and there I was, sitting at the kitchen table, when she'd been told I was in Paris.

"We got in the car and drove to Jersey. It started to storm. Berta told him to call Christ Hospital and ask for Dr. Matthews, who was the doctor who would deliver the baby. We pulled over on the arm of the highway, where Marques got out to make the call to the hospital. A man jumped in the car and tried to drive off. Luna kicked and screamed, and he and Marques got into an altercation. I believe Marques shot him, but I never asked.

"We arrived to the hospital that evening and I gave birth to Eliot. He was six pounds, two ounces. Everyone was staring at me because I was the only white woman in the colored wing of the hospital. The next morning, Marques called Berta, who told us she was going to take care of it and that we should meet her at the Polly Parker. We showed up that evening. I never again saw little Eliot. I named him after T. S. Eliot and left him with a blanket and *Little Gidding*, a book of poems I was reading at the time. I never asked

Berta where she took him, but she told me he went to a good home. Sometimes I find myself taken back to that moment and wonder what became of his life."

*   *   *

Roman didn't know how to react after hearing her story, but quickly sobered when he realized that regardless of her wealth, she was just like all other women who'd ever lost a child—in Katheryn's case, the one she'd given up for adoption. A part of him judged her, but he knew her life was complicated in those long ago times.

"Thank you for sharing this, Katheryn. I promise your secret will be guarded."

"While I do not understand what it's like to experience the death of a child," Katheryn said, "I do understand what it means to lose one. A part of me wishes I would've never given him up, that I had cared less about what the world thought. If I knew then what I know today, I believe I would have made different choices. But enough about me. I need to speak with Gilroy."

Roman got up and went to the counter, where Gilroy was showing the sales associate his phone. It was a picture of a man he would be meeting for a date later that evening. ". . . and don't worry, honey, he'd better think twice before I put out."

"Excuse me," Roman said, tapping Gilroy on the shoulder, "I'm sorry to interrupt."

Gilroy readjusted himself and returned to the role of Julian's assistant. "Yes, sir, what may I help you with?"

Roman looked to Gilroy and felt a strange warmth overcome him. "I umm . . . I . . ." Latching his eye to Gilroy's, Roman found it difficult to speak and began to adjust his tone. "Mrs. Weinberg is ready for you now."

"Well, yes, let us be on our way." He brushed his hand against Roman's shoulder and smiled, attempting not to appear irritated that he'd been interrupted.

As they walked toward the sofa where Katheryn sat, Roman suddenly found himself consumed with thoughts about Gilroy's body and what it would be like to be alone with him.

"Mrs. Weinberg," Gilroy said, "how may I be of further assistance?"

Katheryn didn't want to divulge too much but was compelled to communicate her needs at that moment. "It seems there has been a change in the events that have unfolded. Please see to Theodore and help him with whatever he needs, and please do not ask questions. We will need to have him fitted for a suit in addition to being presented with formal clothing that would be worn by an infant. Again, do not ask any questions but assist him with anything he should need."

Gilroy pulled out his steno pad and began taking notes. "Certainly, madam. Should I present him the catalogue? We can certainly arrange for someone to bring different options from our men's department." The thought was unsettling to Gilroy, as men's garments weren't normally brought to the women's section. "I suppose the twain shall now meet," he said under his breath and went to contact Julian and let him know about the change of events.

*   *   *

Joe was meandering through the store and closely examining the value of every object.

"I need you to do me a favor," he said to the woman behind the counter, "I need for you to identify anything on this floor that is of significant value. I am ready to spend an obscene amount of money."

He envisioned himself as Richard Gere in *Pretty Woman*, emphasizing the word *obscene*, and smiled. "My wife and I are preparing to remodel some rooms in our brownstone, and Grandmother told me I can have anything I want."

The woman felt she could now recover from Katheryn's previous accusation that she was groveling. "And how obscene are we talking?"

"Let's just say this. After this spree, you're going to have enough to pay for those new set of ta-tas you've always wanted."

He laughed, but she was offended by his comments and looked down at her chest. She had never questioned the size of her breasts in the past.

"You can envision them being triple-Ds. And if you're nice, maybe Uncle Joe will come back and take them for a test drive."

While she had been harassed by many men—and sometimes women—throughout her time a Bergdorf's, this was by far the most direct anyone had ever been.

"So let's just hurry and get down to business while old moneybags is preoccupied with the faggot and house Neg—"

He stopped himself, realizing he'd become too comfortable with her.

"Look, Candy," he said, using the name he'd given her as it was what he imagined she'd go by if she worked in the adult film industry. "Yeah, you look like a Candy. Anyone ever call you that?"

She was deeply insulted but realized she would need to put her feelings aside if she didn't want to walk away empty-handed. She decided to focus on the potential commission. "No, I haven't, but I can be a Candy, if that helps."

Joe scanned her body for any inviting expression. The entire exchange felt forced, but this didn't bother him. He was in control. "So, Candy . . . let's get down to business," he said, staring at her chest. "Is there a way to identify the highest priced items sold here? Like a registry of some sort?" He'd given up getting the list from Gloria.

Candy felt pressured to offer a solution. "Have you visited the website?"

Joe looked at her with a blank stare.

Candy pulled out two iPads—one for Joe and the other where she could place his order—and said, "Why don't you come with me?" She went to another associate and whispered something inaudible. Then she returned to him and motioned to a location where it would be difficult to be disturbed. "Here you will find everything," she said, handing him the iPad, "that can be found on the seventh floor. And some additional items."

Joe took the iPad and sorted by price, from highest to lowest. Six Dolce Gabbana refrigerators priced at $50,000 each populated the top of the listing. He kept scrolling, thinking about how he wanted to leave unnoticed. "Does this come with free delivery?" She shook her head. Joe kept scrolling. "Ah, this is nice," he remarked, examining the Parler Seul by Joan Miró—a limited-edition tableware set by Bernardaud, which retailed for over $25,000.

"I think I will take two of these," he said and pointed to the iPad.

"Good choice, sir," Candy said, keying in the order.

Joe was enthralled with the idea he could walk away with all these home furnishings. "And I'll take two of these," he said, referring to the Ardent Medium Waterfall chandelier by Kelly Wearstler that retailed for nearly $13,000. "You can never have too many chandeliers."

Candy felt overwhelmed. It felt like a birthday or a wedding proposal. "Yes, sir," she said as he continued to add items, or "Good choice!" She thought about how she could finance a vacation or maybe make enough to cover tuition in the fall.

Joe mentally calculated the total cost but felt it wasn't enough. "Do you work in handbags?" he inquired, as he assumed women spent lots of money on purses and shoes.

She realized where he was headed but knew handbags couldn't be processed or ordered from the seventh floor. Instead, she refocused the situation. "Yes, we do carry an assortment of handbags," she said, grabbing the necklace around her neck, drawing attention to her breasts and trying to steer him toward something that would earn her more commission. "Your wife is one lucky woman." She loosened one of the top buttons of her blouse.

Joe grew distracted, fantasizing about what it would be like to caress her breasts in the middle of the department store. Seeing that he was focused on her chest, she put her hand on his leg. "As they say, the way to a woman's heart is through another's home decor."

Looking up, Joe saw Gilroy hovering. "Umm-hmm," Gilroy said, clearing his throat and looking at the sales associate. "Excuse me, Francesca, can I see you for a moment?"

Francesca (AKA Candy) felt like Winona Ryder after being detained for shoplifting at Saks Fifth Avenue. "Of course, sir. Excuse me, Mr. Weinberg, I will be back momentarily."

When she got up, Joe focused his attention on the back of her legs.

*   *   *

Gilroy looked at Francesca and examined her condition. "Ms. Peate, what do you think you're doing?"

This was not the first time she'd unbuttoned her blouse—she was known for making advances on married men in the past and ringing up high-priced items that were not in her discretion.

"We cannot go through this again. You know we cannot risk another complaint!" he said, referring to a previous incident where a woman reported having a large shipment of chandeliers and vases delivered to her residence.

Gilroy took the iPad from her hands and examined the items in the queue. "I hope we don't have a repeating incident, Francesca, as another occurrence could lead to disciplinary action . . . including termination."

She feigned confusion although she understood what she'd done. "Sir, he has requested that these expenses be placed on Mrs. Weinberg's store account, and as you've taught me, it's never okay to question a customer."

"I see," Gilroy said. It was true. Associates were never to question, but he assumed she would have used discretion. "Well, please return to your assigned location and I will finish up with Mr. Weinberg."

*   *   *

Joe anticipated her return, only to realize she'd walked past him as though they'd never met. "Excuse me, Candy," he said with a smile.

She turned her head slightly but avoided making eye contact, winking quickly and moving ahead to approach a woman eyeing one of the vases in in the middle display. "Welcome to Bergdorf's, is there anything I can assist you with today?"

Joe felt dismissed, but was interrupted mid-thought by Gilroy. "Oh, great," Joe said with dissatisfaction.

"Sir," Gilroy said, looking at Joe with disdain, "would you please come with me? I believe your grandmother is requesting your presence." He extended a hand in the direction of Kathryn and her party.

"Excuse me, Gilbert," Joe said, purposefully emphasizing the *bert* even though he knew this wasn't his name. "Candy and I were in the middle of something. So if you could please send her back, that we may finish what we began."

Gilroy didn't want to engage in confrontation or bring any further attention to the situation. He said, "Please come with me and I will explain later."

Joe felt this was unacceptable and that he wasn't being treated appropriately. "Don't make me call that other fa—I mean your boss. Because I will."

It wasn't the first time someone had thrown a derogatory term at him, but Gilroy wasn't as offended by Joe's insult as he was by Katheryn's association with someone like him. He decided to minimize any further engagement. "I understand you were finishing up with Francesca. Maybe there is something I might interest you in?"

"Could you please just get Candy," Joe said, looking at Gilroy with contempt. "I'd much rather deal with her."

Gilroy realized he was not going to win in this situation, but this was not his first time dealing with someone this uncooperative. "I do apologize, but it does not appear that she will be available anytime soon."

Joe was unable to bite his tongue. "Just place the fucking order," he snarled and muttered something underneath his breath only he could hear.

"Certainly, sir," Gilroy said, "that will be $77,500, which does not include tax." He waited for Joe to pass him his credit card. "How will you be paying today?"

"It's going on Granny's account," Joe said and stared at Gilroy, who just blinked the way a mother does when she's expecting a different answer. "Charge her fucking card so we can get on with this already," Joe spat in a deep Bronx accent.

"Certainly, sir. However, we will need to receive formal approval from the account holder before we can move forward."

"So why don't you go talk to Granny and let her know her darling grandson has done some retail therapy?" He pulled out his phone to see if Gloria had emailed him back. "And please have everything delivered to my office no later than this evening."

Gilroy clenched his fist. He didn't want it getting back to Julian that he'd in some way insulted Katheryn Weinberg. "Certainly, sir. Just come with me that you may rejoin your grandmother and Mr. White."

Sascha Jason

"Darling, I do apologize for becoming overly emotional," Katheryn said to Roman. "It's never appropriate for a woman to display anything but pleasantries in front of a man, or for that matter to the public. It's a wonder how all these years Roderick has been able to manage me."

"No need to worry," he said, thinking to himself that it had been an extremely long day. He looked at his watch. "Maybe we should consider letting Gilroy know we are ready to proceed to the viewing."

She smiled at him with delight, as this allowed her to refocus her attention to her favorite pastime. "Yes, darling, I do think you are correct. But where is Theodore?" she said, realizing she'd not seen him for a while and blowing her nose into the handkerchief in her hand.

Revisiting these intimate parts of her life was stressful, but she did not want to die knowing she'd never disclosed them to Marshal.

"In those days, things weren't cut and dry. In fact, they were complex and difficult."

Roman wondered what had happened to the baby and if he'd gone to a nice home. He wondered what he would do if he was put in her shoes.

"Maybe I should go and find Gilroy?" he said.

"Marshal, darling, please let him know we're ready to proceed to the viewing."

He wondered what it was like for her to live in this cycle, coming to a department store where she purchased things that would never be hers. Her life had been bought and sold within the industry—and if she'd made different choices and not ostracized the ones she loved, maybe someone would have remained. Her life was nothing more than an empty apartment on Park Avenue now occupied by strangers.

A look of excitement appeared on her face when she saw Joe returning with Gilroy. She was worried he'd disappeared. "Oh, Theodore!" she said, waving him over, to which he forced a smile.

"Oh, Grandmother," he said and kissed her on both cheeks.

She turned to Gilroy. "Darling, I believe we're ready to go to the viewing room."

"Certainly, madam." He was unsure of how to proceed; this was normally Julian's responsibility. "Please give me one moment as I check on something."

Gilroy was afraid that if he inquired with Julian, he would appear incompetent and would find himself returned to the women's department stocking shoes.

"Just one moment," he added, "as I want to make sure everything is prepared for you. Can I offer you a glass of champagne while you wait?"

Joe was distressed at the thought of finding himself sitting through another chapter of Katheryn's life sober. "Yes," he said, "that would be nice" and once again checked his phone. He thought of all the possible scenarios under which he could leave without anyone questioning. "Grandmother, I was thinking," he began but stopped himself when he realized he was surrounded by an audience. "Do you think we could be excused for a moment? I need to speak with you."

"Just a moment, darling," Katheryn said, frazzled. She was preoccupied with the impending viewing. "I need to wait on Gilroy to return so that he may escort us." She dismissed his request and returned her attention to Roman. "I do hope they have secured the Gucci. Or maybe we shall witness and be honored with the luxury of Val and Oscar," which were the shortened names she used to refer to Valentino and Oscar de la Renta, "I must find something that will further exude my talent. Something that will hit me in the right light."

Roman smiled and refocused his attention on Joe. "Were you saying something?" he asked, as if he had missed some important piece of information, insinuating Joe had better ways of spending his time.

Joe was shocked and felt this was some ill attempt to discredit him. "Grandmother, I really need to speak to you," he said and waited for her to respond.

She was not taken by him and appeared worn by everything that had happened over the course of the afternoon. She purposefully did not respond but looked to Roman. "Marshal, do you remember that show, the one where I practically tripped over the microphone? Luckily, big Jim was standing right there and I fell into his arms."

She laughed and smirked. "Those were the days. When my fans would show up in anticipation. I would walk out and they would cheer. Now I'm finding myself hiding out, fearing the paparazzi. Sometimes I wish fame would have marched past my door and on to the next." She smiled at Roman and held her composure. "Here you go, darling," she said, handing Joe back his handkerchief.

Joe began to scheme how he might create a crisis but was interrupted by a new voice. "Well, if it isn't Katheryn James York," a woman said. Katheryn was confused, not recognizing the woman who was calling for her attention. "I was hoping you received the care package I sent, and it looks like you have!"

Although she didn't remember receiving anything, she decided to be polite and play along. "Yes, darling, I did. Thank you for thinking of me."

"Well," the woman said, indicating the dress Katheryn was wearing which she'd had delivered to her by her first assistant, "it looks like it fits you well."

Katheryn looked at the woman again. She stood about six feet and had long, flowing brown hair. She was wearing something similar to Katheryn and appeared to be waiting for further recognition.

The woman turned to Roman and smiled, appearing annoyed that no one had said anything. While her line had not yet been presented at Bergdorf's, the showroom represented her aesthetic. Promises had been made suggesting she'd be featured by the fall, and she wanted to make sure she wouldn't be placed next to Isabel Marant—or anyone else who might take away from her spotlight.

She thought maybe Katheryn was overwhelmed by all the commotion surrounding her and decided to excuse herself. "Alright . . . well . . . if you would like me to send over more samples, don't hesitate to contact my assistant." She leaned down to provide a European style kiss and walked away.

Waiting until she was no longer in view, Katheryn held a smile, which was what she often did. "Marshal, darling, please remind me who that was. I cannot recall how I know her or where we met."

Roman stood beside her. "I do believe that was the designer."

"Who?"

"The designer. Sascha Jason." He waited a moment to see if it sparked her memory. "The woman who created the dress you are wearing."

Katheryn felt embarrassed, realizing she was in fact wearing the woman's dress and had met her in the past. "Well, that is unfortunate, darling. Absolutely unfortunate. I hope she wasn't offended." She looked at him as though he should track her down to restart the conversation. "Oh, my . . . well, I just hope that she will forgive me for this mental lapse. I can only imagine what I'll be like when I'm old and losing my marbles."

Roman thought of Katheryn meandering through Bergdorf's and believing those who passed were living and that those surrounding her were merely placeholders for the dead, and began to laugh. But rather than judging her, he pinched his leg and redirected the focus.

"I'm sure she will forget the entire thing," he said, wanting to suggest that if and when she encountered her again she would retain a note in her mental registry, but thought that highly unlikely.

*   *   *

I can't believe I was unable to recall her. This all seems queer—the entire day, actually. It feels like I don't even know myself. Everything feels off. I don't understand why I couldn't recall who that woman was and why Theodore is being so persistent. It's as if he's become distracted and unsettled by the situation—and now me.

It does not feel right. If Roderick ever left me at home during the midst of a miscarriage, he wouldn't have a wife. When I get home tonight, I'm going to have a serious talk with him about the young man Brando raised. I think I've reached my tipping point with him, and for that matter, Brando.

To think that this has happened and no one informed me before I left the house this morning! And poor Laura. If someone had told me, I wouldn't be here. I would have stopped by their home and brought her some soup, a sympathy card, and flowers.

It's difficult to think that this is happening to my family, but especially to someone like Laura. I should advise Gilroy to have the viewing canceled, as I'm uncertain if I can even concentrate.

"Darling, please let Gilroy know that it's imperative I speak with Julian."

It's as if no one hears me, that I don't exist. Surely Marshal can provide an explanation, a conclusion. It feels he's judged me for the decisions I've made. But then again, he is not a woman and wouldn't understand.

I wonder how my life would have turned out if I had kept the child. Deep down I know I should have, but I also know the world is unforgiving, and the tabloids would have had a field day with that story. No, I made the decision and as hard as it seems and difficult as it was, I refused to marry regret.

Yet, as hard as I try, I feel nothing but regret.

I chose a life that made sense to me. That is something I will have to live with until the day I pass into the next. I realize that he judges me, that I'm to blame, and if I never gave that child up maybe my story would have been different.

Maybe, just maybe, I would never have made it onto this stage—my life.

*   *   *

She was ashamed of what she'd done but kept it to herself for fear of any further judgment that might ensue. She decided to keep silent within her feelings and allowed herself to re-experience the guilt that again presented itself. She didn't understand how this could be a life worth living, knowing her child would have been perceived a bastard.

She found herself tearful again but tried to contain her emotions. She felt as if she'd cried too many times on a day that was supposed to be filled with joy and hope. So she distracted herself with thoughts of what it would be like when she arrived to the viewing room.

Gilroy stood indecisive, then interrupted the uncomfortable silence. "Well, it looks like . . . or should I say, the viewing can . . ."

He was interrupted by an unfamiliar hand on his shoulder.

"I do apologize, Katheryn," Julian said, "it has been an absolutely crazy day. Thank you for your help, Gil. I will take it from here. I was detained by a crisis in handbags."

Katheryn looked up at Julian in relief, excited to proceed. It was as if she'd forgotten about everything that had transpired and was again eager to be escorted to an undisclosed location where she and Julian would sit and gossip about the women she'd seen.

"The room is almost ready," he said, "I just need to check on one last thing. If you will excuse me." He left to go speak with Francesca.

Katheryn, eager for a change in scenery, looked up to Roman and smiled. "I never thought this day would come," she said, but in truth this happened every third Thursday of the month.

He smiled at her and then looked at Joe, who was visibly irritated and thinking of a clever but believable story he could deliver that would enable him to leave Bergdorf's with thousands of dollars in merchandise, stiffing her with the bill.

Baby, I've Got Your Blues

Julian returned and motioned for them to gather their belongings. "If you will come with me, please," he said.

Katheryn immediately began to re-center herself and reached for Roman. "If you would be so kind, my dear, and provide a woman a hand." She waited in expectation for him to assist her, to which he extended his arm.

Julian stood with a stoic yet nervous look only visible to Francesca, who'd witnessed this expression on a few occasions. "Everything has been arranged and will be ready when we arrive," he said and looked to Roman, recalling he had suggested he go to the diner while the viewing took place. "And you, sir, are more than welcome to find respite in the lounge, where lunch will be served."

Roman was apprehensive. He didn't want to leave, even though he was overcome with hunger. "Maybe I will join you."

"Certainly, sir." Julian felt maybe it was worth having him accompany them, but he hadn't arranged for extra seating. He looked to Francesca and in a low, faint voice said, "Please make sure there are four flutes."

"Very good," Francesca said. "Everyone please follow me."

They all gathered their belongings and walked toward the elevator. All except for Joe, who stayed behind calculating all of the items that would be delivered to his office.

"Mr. Weinberg," Francesca said, "I believe your party has departed."

Joe gave her a look of disgust. He felt betrayed and seemed to be waiting for an explanation as to why he was left behind. Francesca didn't engage him but wondered if she would get at least partial commission for her efforts.

"Please follow me," she said to Joe and held her arm out toward the elevator, avoiding any further eye contact.

Joe scanned her body again. "Nice work, Candy," he said and walked past her with the residual of a lifeless expression that lingered.

*   *   *

"Oh, darling, I do hope that we're able to enjoy the remainder of our time," Katheryn said and looked back to mentally place where everyone was. She focused specifically on Joe to see if he'd left, but noticed him straggling behind some twenty feet away.

Her annoyance was beginning to show, but she refrained from any visible display as she readjusted herself to Roman's arm. "It's as if I've been here before, darling. Several times. Yet something seems profoundly different."

Roman was cautious in his response. She had been here the week prior, but with another nurse. "Well, I believe life is what you make of it. Something my grandmother used to say."

"I never met your grandmother, darling, but if I did, I would inform her what a lovely young man you've become." She brought him in closer and focused on her steps.

Nearing the elevator, Julian told them, "Please do not enter unless it is empty."

Joe just rolled his eyes.

No one questioned Julian, not even Joe. Instead, they stood silently and waited for the elevator doors to open. When the doors opened, Julian recognized the two women from before.

"Give me just one moment," he told his waiting party. Then he smiled and gave the women the standard welcome: "Welcome to Bergdorf Goodman." They simply laughed and exited the elevator.

Julian held his breath against the reek of alcohol and expensive perfume as they passed, then let out a long, grateful exhale when they were gone. He rolled his eyes but was immediately sobered by his surroundings and wondered if anyone saw him holding a look of disgust. Proceeding to distract them, he looked at Francesca, who ushered everyone to enter.

"Come this way," she said. It felt to her as if she were herding sheep. She looked down to see a mouse scurrying past and almost let out a scream but was quickly reminded what Delfina had taught her during last year's annual emergency management meeting: "Whatever you do, under no circumstances are you to bring attention to a crisis."

She looked at Julian, who returned a look indicating he was fully aware and waited until everyone had entered the elevator before saying anything.

"Could you please hold this button?" he asked Roman. "I just need to speak with Francesca for a moment."

Roman nodded and followed Julian's direction.

*   *   *

"Did you see that?" Julian said in a low voice, mouthing the word "mouse" and clutching his pearls, exaggerating the size of the creature with his hands.

Francesca nodded, wondering what she should do as this was the first time she'd ever seen a rodent meandering through the department store.

"Please, Francesca, just get with Gil. He will know exactly what to do."

Julian returned to the elevator. Francesca appeared annoyed, but she was reminded that if she ever wanted to be considered for a promotion she had to refrain from commentary and remain solution focused. To her, mice and rats were normal—her cat would often be waiting at the door to greet her with what he'd caught earlier in the day.

*   *   *

Julian entered the elevator and smiled. "Thank you, sir," he said to Roman and removed a set of keys from his pocket, inserting one into the lock and pressing the button to activate the eighth floor.

Everyone stood in silence as the doors closed, waiting in anticipation for what they would witness—with the exception of Joe. Realizing they were now a captive audience, Julian told everyone what should be expected. "Please stay close together, and under no circumstances is anyone to veer away."

The eighth floor, he told them, was closed off to the general public. Anything that was observed, he added, should not be shared outside of Bergdorf Goodman.

*   *   *

The elevator doors opened, providing a view of the lobby that was as decorative and beautifully furnished as the other floors. Everyone stood in awe, taking in the majestic experience that created a feeling of home.

"Julian, darling, why has such a gem been kept from the general public?" Katheryn remarked, to which Julian took a pause and smiled.

"This area is restricted to all but people such as yourself. It is where only a select few are permitted."

Katheryn became tearful as a part of her remembered what life was like when she first became famous—having her assistant contact various department stores in the city to arrange for privacy while she shopped. "I remember when . . ." she began but quickly stopped as the memory of those times escaped her.

She latched onto Roman's arm in anticipation that he would continue to serve as her guide. "Darling, this is just so exhilarating," she said, internally reflecting upon her experience. "I've not been mesmerized for some time."

"It's breathtaking," Roman responded, remaining focused on Julian.

"I've arranged for a light lunch that has been prepared by our head chef," Julian said as he walked them down the long hallway. "He's never been one to disappoint. I think you will find his selection fitting."

He stopped speaking when a member of his team interrupted him.

"Sir, Miss Jerma—" the young man said, then halted himself abruptly. "She has been waiting for the past thirty minutes on Lagerfeld's assistant to arrive. I'm a bit concerned, as she appears to be growing restless and mentioned her early dinner plans with her fiancée. Would it be possible to stop in and send your regards while I identify the ETA of his assistant?"

Julian grew concerned. The rooms were scheduled by the hour, and the next appointment would arrive shortly. "Certainly, I'll be there momentarily. If you could please let her know I will see her shortly. In the meantime, please offer one of our finest glasses of whiskey . . . the Balvenie," he said and smiled, continuing to escort Katheryn's group down the hall.

Something was different about this floor compared to the others. It felt empty and disconnected, yet private and exclusive— much like a gallery, where everything is visible and there is an understood expectation to never touch.

Three men stood statuesque along the wall, equally separated in distance. They reminded Katheryn of the soldiers who guard Buckingham Palace.

"Here we are," Julian said with a reserved level of excitement as he opened the door numbered 864, which was strange as they didn't follow any particular order. He never asked or cared to know what exactly happened in these rooms, however it was sometimes reported by the cleaning staff that loose condom wrappers and other forms of illegal paraphernalia were left behind. This made sense, as a non-refundable charge from Bergdorf's was more discreet than a charge from one of the local boutique hotels. Julian never asked questions but just assumed it was never his business. He thought maybe in his next life he would focus his efforts on being a private investigator.

As the door opened, Katheryn looked around excitedly. In the room was a long sofa and two chairs that held a satin pattern that broke up the color scheme. In front of the sofa sat a circular coffee table and a large vase filled fresh lavender and roses.

Katheryn walked over to the flowers and took in a deep breath. "How delightful, darling!" She looked around, wondering when the dresses would arrive. "The anticipation is killing me . . ."

*   *   *

Brody, you bitch—we thought we'd lost you. No need to go to Rainbow Bridge just yet because Daddy is coming to save the day. She'll never know what hit her, as this is perfect. I'm going to tell her a miracle has occurred and that Picaboo, or whatever pet name I gave my imaginary wife, has "overcome one of life's most difficult challenges." That's the way I'll phrase it, but I'll put a little more *oomph* into its delivered meaning.

I need to make sure the expression is captured perfectly. If not, this entire scam might be exposed. If that happens I'm walking away with zilch, nada, nothing—I need to find a way to really bring on the crocodile tears like women always do.

I've heard that during filming, directors tell actors, "Think of your saddest memory." Think, Joe, think! There has to be something that bothers you, something unresolved. Hmmm, it's not registering. Maybe I'm just callous, or maybe I just had an outstanding childhood. But if I can't think of anything, maybe I'll imagine one of those ASPCA commercials where they show an emaciated dog chained to a fence that hasn't eaten for days. If my mother hadn't been such a bitch, maybe I would've had a dog—let alone a memory to glean from.

Think, Joe, think . . .

*   *   *

"Theodore, darling, are you as excited as I?"

Katheryn looked at Joe, attempting to repair her frustrations.

Joe looked up at her and tried to think of something sad. He thought to himself *if all else fails, I'm going to spit in my hand and begin rubbing it in my eyes* and smiled because that was all he knew to do at that moment.

"It really is something, isn't it, Grandmother?" he said, placing emphasis on the word "mother," which came off strange as the inflection sounded like one of those commercials the Federal Communications Commission had banned for violating the established volume ordinance—to supposedly prevent heart attacks of the elderly and incidents of domestic violence.

A man in slacks and a black button-up shirt presented them with four champagne flutes and began to pour. "Here you are, Mrs. Weinberg," he said and handed Katheryn a flute.

Roman was concerned, as she was prohibited from consuming

alcohol—it could be fatal if it interacted negatively with her blood pressure medication. "Maybe we should hold off on that for a moment," he said, but she pushed his hand away.

"Darling, I've already had a glass, and if it didn't kill me, neither shall this."

After everyone's flute was filled, Katheryn took one of the knives and began to tap it against her glass, raising it. "I would like to propose a toast."

Everyone raised theirs in union.

"While today has found us in moments of uncertainty and sadness, I would like to thank Julian and my family here at Bergdorf's for everything they've done to prepare for this moment."

Julian smiled with his glass raised. "Hear, hear."

Roman didn't want to disrupt the informal celebration but found himself glancing over to Julian with concern. After everyone took a sip of their champagne, which tasted more like sparkling water, Julian interrupted. "It is an absolute honor to be here today and share in this moment."

Kathryn looked at him and ushered in a "cheers, cheers, let us celebrate."

Roman felt relieved that he could sit easy knowing she was consuming sparkling juice that tasted similar to a Rose Kennedy—minus the alcohol.

Each time Joe tried to say something, he found himself feeling disregarded, constantly interrupted. "Grandmother, would it be possible for me to speak to you privately for just one moment," he said.

Katheryn became irritated at his insistence on interrupting her during a moment she had been waiting for. "Darling," she said and paused, seeing that he had become tearful. "Theodore, my love, I understand that this is a very difficult time for you and Laura, but maybe you should excuse yourself until you can regain your composure."

She felt horrible saying this, yet her emotional cup was full and needed this mental vacation to distract her from the reality of what was happening.

"I do apologize for snapping," she added. "Maybe you should go be with Laura, as I can't imagine how difficult this must be for the both of you."

*   *   *

Essentially, it comes down to how I'll walk away. I just need to get the attention of her darling Julian—tell him I'm leaving, then head for the door.

There's no easy way to do this without being noticed. Shit! I should have thought about that.

Maybe I'll give them the address to my office, and if they ask any questions I'll just tell them Joe Tiller & Associates is the undisclosed location where I have all deliveries sent "to preserve my privacy."

But what if they ask more questions?

I'm just going to provide that address and say it's an "undisclosed location" and that under no circumstance should it be shared, and that they're to remove it from their system after everything has been delivered.

Once everything arrives, I'll have Gloria contact each distributor and have cashier's checks written directly to the firm, then signed over to me. That way if I'm ever audited by the IRS there is no paper trail and I will have a plethora of receipts that can be used to show business expenses.

I couldn't have come up with a better idea.

*　*　*

"Grandmother, I agree. I should probably head back home and see how Laura is doing." Joe wiped an imaginary tear from his eye. Katheryn returned a look of pity. His experience hit too close to home for her. She grabbed both of his hands to offer her condolences.

"Well, please send her my regards, and once things have calmed down please let me know so I can help make arrangements with your mother and Lilian."

Joe appeared contemplative, wondering if this was the best time to leave. "Excuse me," he said to Julian, who was sipping the sparkling apple juice, "I need to speak with you in private."

Julian didn't engage him but only smiled. Finally, he said, "Certainly, Mr. Weinberg," and set his flute on the side table.

He'd overheard the entire conversation between grandmother and grandson but acted as if it were the first time he'd heard it. "Give me just a moment, sir," he said, then finished up what he was saying to Roman. ". . . and that is how I met Mrs. Katheryn Weinberg." He reached out and grabbed her hand. "If everyone would excuse me, Mr. Weinberg needs to speak with me. Katheryn, I think you will be pleased with today's food selections: an arugula salad with dried cranberries and a hint of fromage."

She hadn't expected lunch to be served and reacted excitedly, imagining what the combination would taste like as it mixed around on her pallet. "That sounds absolutely delightful! You always know how to go out of your way for a gal like me."

"I will be sure to take care of your grandson," Julian said, "and make sure he is seen out appropriately."

Joe felt a distant yet familiar nervous excitement in his stomach, the same way he did when shoplifting that bottle of Burberry from the J.C. Penney. He stood silently, waiting in expectation that all he had to do was provide an address where everything could be delivered.

Julian stood up. "Mr. Weinberg, if you could just give me one moment. I must make sure everything is properly arranged for your departure."

He headed for the door just as a server walked in with four silver liners covering the salads plated underneath.

"Well, Grandmother, it sure has been a pleasant time." Joe smirked and quickly recomposed himself. "I mean, an eventful day."

"Here you are, madam," the waiter said, uncovering the platter and placing each salad in the center of the table. "I hope these will be to your liking."

Katheryn's mouth began to water as though it was the first time she'd experienced this, yet it was the same thing she was served each third Thursday, in addition to a large cut of salmon that would follow. The only difference was this time there were two additional plates.

"Darling, I'm sure it will be perfect. As you were saying?" she said, directing her attention to Joe.

He sat speechless, awestruck by how unbelievably easy this was, and reached for her hand. "Yes, Grandmother, I'm sure Picaboo and I will make it through this trying moment. No parent should ever be placed in this position, but with your kind contributions I'm sure we will be able to manage."

Something about the tone in his response made her feel extremely uneasy, yet she didn't want to draw more attention to the uncomfortableness of the situation. "Well, darling, I'm here for you," she said and looked to Roman for something to say that might further ease the situation. He had nothing to give other than the awkwardness of silence.

"Just call Grandmother if you should need help with the

arrangements."

"Certainly, Grams. Most certainly." Joe glanced down at his watch to determine how much time had passed and when he'd need to leave to avoid being late for his appointment with Barney Williams. "I have an appointment this even—" he began, and immediately stopped himself mid-sentence. "I mean I have to be home shortly to check on Picacho. So yes, I will be leaving shortly to make it home in time for dinner."

Roman flinched, as this response sounded odd, but was reminded of his place when Katheryn looked at him.

"Whatever you need, darling, your grandfather and I are here for you and Laura." She opened her purse for the compact mirror to reapply her lipstick—a ritual she always engaged in before proceeding with a meal—but remembered this was something she usually did in private. She closed the mirror and sighed. "Oh, my," she said, looking around to gauge everyone's expressions, "I think I should excuse myself to the powder room."

She began to collect herself but felt suddenly unfamiliar in her surroundings. "Excuse me, gentlemen," she said and grabbed her cane and scooted to the front of the chair, placing one hand on her knee, to which everyone stood.

"Do you need assistance?" Roman asked but found himself shooed away.

"I'll be just fine, darling," Katheryn said and stood. The more Roman persisted the more she disengaged. "Like I said, I will be fine. Please just direct me to the ladies' room."

The man refilling the champagne glasses interjected, "Once you exit the door, you will make a left, and it will be on your immediate right."

She felt a change in scenery would help her readjust and prepare for the viewing. "I will be back momentarily."

Once in the hallway, Katheryn found herself disoriented and

unable to remember which way he said to go. She figured if she got lost she could inquire of one of the men standing guard.

"It sure is a lovely afternoon," she said, passing by. "For the life of me, I'm unable to recall if he said take a left or right." She looked at the man in anticipation of assistance.

"Left or right," he responded with a look of uncertainty.

"Darling," she said, "I'm just trying to find my way to the powder room."

"Ah, yes, it's right over there," he said and pointed to a door that was labeled with a capital W.

She pushed the door open and wondered why it was designed with no handle—forcing her to pull while exiting at the risk of contaminating her hands.

*   *   *

There was a woman in the bathroom talking feverishly into her phone when Katheryn walked in.

"Can you please tell him that it's Ms. Jermanotta? No, I can't hold. Mr. Lagerfeld's assistant and I were scheduled to meet thirty minutes ago. I'm at Bergdorf's . . . Barneys . . . this is completely unacceptable. No, we cannot reschedule. Let him know I will be there within the hour."

Katheryn listened and wondered why anyone would schedule an appointment outside of Bergdorf's but instead focused her attention on the perfect way to reapply her lipstick. She heard the toilet flush and the stall door open. A woman emerged, walked to the sink, washed her hands, grabbed a paper towel, and threw it in the dispenser. She opened her clutch and pulled out a tube of lipstick and began to apply a coat similar to Katheryn's, but a richer shade of red.

"At the end of the day it feels like a man's world, and we're just living in it," the woman said.

Katheryn took in a deep breath. "Oh, darling, you don't have to explain this to me. I'm fully aware. They wouldn't know their left from their right if it weren't for us."

The woman appeared taken by Katheryn immediately.

"I've been around much longer than you," Katheryn continued, "and I can tell you this: It only gets worse."

The woman looked at her reflection in the mirror and took in a big sigh. "I can only imagine." They both laughed.

Katheryn admired at the woman's inventive approach to fashion. Her clothing looked antique yet modern. She reminded her a bit of herself.

"I adore how you've put this together," Katheryn said, referring to the shoes, dress, and hat the woman was wearing. "It has been some time since I've witnessed something put together in such a way."

The woman finished applying her lipstick and turned around, leaning on the sink. "Sometimes I wish fame would have passed my door and moved on to the next person. Maybe I would have been a housewife living on the Upper East Side with two kids, a dog, and a husband. I just don't think Timothy and I will survive my next tour."

"You're a performer?" Katheryn inquired, to which the woman just nodded. "I am as well. I have performed on many stages in my life."

"Do go on," the woman said, interested.

"I once recorded a song with Frank Sinatra," Katheryn said, to which the woman's eyes became enlarged.

"You recorded with Frank?"

"Yes. 'Baby I've Got Your Blues.' It was recorded with a string quartet."

Having just finished recording a bunch of old standards with

Tony Bennett, the woman's jaw dropped. "You performed 'Baby'?" For a moment she was speechless, and then she said, "Katheryn James York? I can't believe I've just met *the* Katheryn James York!"

"Yes dear, that is me." Katheryn wondered who the woman was and if she should have said anything at all. "I was just twenty-seven then. So young and naïve. But Frank, well, he was a true gentleman. It was unfortunate that I'd married Roderick, as Frank told me if things didn't work out to give him a call."

"My name is Leah . . . Leah Angelina Jermanotta," she said, feeling she should provide her full name since she'd used Katheryn's full name. "I'm a huge fan of your work! Tony and I recorded that number. It's set to release sometime in the fall. It would be something if we performed it together! I'm performing at Carnegie next month . . ."

Katheryn was flattered by the offer but took pause before responding. "As much as I'd love to, I can't really show my face right now." Leah appeared confused. "I . . . well, I had a performance scheduled for this evening that was canceled. Apparently there was something . . ." She stopped herself mid-sentence. ". . . it doesn't matter."

"Well, if something should change or you change your mind, please let me know," Leah said and asked if they could exchange numbers. She held up her phone, waiting for Katheryn, then appeared confused when Katheryn pulled out a small notepad, to which she wrote down her number.

"I forgot to say what a lovely dress you're wearing," Leah added. "I absolutely love Sascha Jason."

"Yes, she is a good friend of mine, up-and-coming they say." Katheryn felt proud of herself that while this collection was not included within the family of designers at Bergdorf Goodman, it was receiving rave reviews.

"I should give her a call, please send her my regards," Leah said, adjusting a piece of hair that appeared out of place. "Well, Katheryn, it's been an absolute pleasure meeting you. I hope one day we will collaborate together." She picked up her clutch and walked toward the door singing, "Baby I've got your bluzzzz . . . Stranger . . . I was no stranger to you . . ."

At the door, she stopped, turned around, smiled, and winked. "Take care of yourself, babe."

"You as well, my darling, you as well."

Katheryn smiled, realizing that while she was not performing tonight she still had at least one fan who would see her through thick and thin. Realizing she was alone in the bathroom, she looked in the mirror and began to sing, thinking about the night in Paris where she'd performed that number with Berta, Luna, Candace, and Sandy.

"Baby, I've got your blues . . . Stranger . . . I was no stranger to you . . . Baby, we've all got the blues." She picked up her purse, pointed at the mirror, and said to the woman she was: "You still got it, babe. And don't let anyone tell you any different."

Ashes

Katheryn emerged from the bathroom looking helpless and disoriented. "Sir," she said to the man in the hallway, "could you please direct me to where I might find the viewing?"

He remembered her but hadn't been paying attention and forgot from which direction she had come. "What room are you headed to?" he asked.

"Let me think," she said and grabbed a mint from a candy dish on a tray in the hall. She unwrapped it, took the candy, and returned the wrapper to the table. "Just do me this favor. Could you point me in the right direction?"

He pointed, and Katheryn followed his direction, humming as she walked down the hall. She examined the door numbers as she went, seeing if something sparked her memory—moving slowly to see if she could hear the sound of glasses or silverware clanking together, but the farther she went the more silent it became. She didn't know each room was soundproof.

Well, isn't this a rather interesting predicament I've gotten myself into, she thought and turned around.

As she continued on, she was comforted by the thought she'd been here before on a day much like this, unable to recall where she was going, drawn deeper into the floral pattern on the carpet.

She found herself emotional. The moment felt like opening a Pandora's box where the past intersected the present. *I remember being here once, but I can't recall.*

She considered randomly opening doors. She thought this

might provide an experience of something familiar, but quickly realized none of it made sense—just phantom memories she was trying to experience but couldn't. She felt a strong sense of déjà vu that lasted longer than any she'd experienced in the past, and decided it best to continue walking.

Staring at the floral pattern in the carpet, she became distracted by the size of her hands. They reminded her of a waitress who worked at a truck stop diner where the wrinkles represented stories—but she'd never done manual labor.

She thought about the times she relieved Hilda, returning to her own life and children. She tried to remember what her mother's hands looked like but could only see Effie's, as that was the woman who'd raised her. She thought about what life might have been like if she'd never been discovered.

The hallway represented parts of her life. It felt empty. Filled with remorse for the child she'd given up, wondering what became of him. She wondered what it might have been like if the times were different, if she were black. She knew she'd been naïve and absorbed.

She wondered what they'd say about her after she died. Would anyone truly understand her life? Would the family crest be tarnished, or should she take this truth to the grave?

She found a sofa and sat to reorient herself, but her stare found the carpet again. It gave her a familiar and comfortable feeling.

There was a round mirror on the wall across from her with a table underneath it. On the table was a vase filled with pink and white roses. *Absolutely breathtaking,* she thought.

*   *   *

Julian peeked in the room to observe Joe and Roman in an awkward silence. "Where is Mrs. Weinberg?" he asked.

Joe looked down at his phone and then up to Julian. "Are you ready?" he said, completely dismissive of what he had asked.

Julian appeared perturbed by Joe's response. He composed himself and glanced over to Roman.

"She went to the restroom," Roman said. "I should go to check on her."

"Are you ready?" Joe interrupted, looking at Julian impatiently. "I really need to be going."

Julian, not wanting to engage him, took a moment to pause. "Yes, but I must first check on your grandmother."

Joe took in a deep breath and returned to his phone. "Well, let's hurry it up already."

Roman understood Katheryn was his responsibility and broke the standstill between the two men. "Don't worry about it, I'll go find her."

Out in the hallway, Roman approached the hallway attendant and asked where the ladies' room was. When he reached it, Roman opened the door and called for Katheryn but there was no response.

He approached another hallway attendant nearby. "Sir, did you see an older lady with a cane come this way?"

The attendant looked at him. "Yes, I've seen many women today."

"Recently," Roman said, annoyed. "Within the past twenty minutes?"

"Oh, yes," the attendant said but hesitated. He had been instructed that unless a member of the staff inquired about the whereabouts of a customer, he was under no circumstances allowed to respond. "But I can't tell you," he finished with a lifeless expression.

"It is very important that we find her. She is not well."

The attendant didn't flinch or react. "But I suppose if there were a woman who was lost . . . I'm sure you will find her."

Roman realized he wouldn't get any assistance and turned to go back to the room. Rounding the corner, he saw Katheryn sitting alone, staring off into space. "Katheryn," he said and let out a deep sigh of relief.

She looked up, and he saw something was bothering her. He said nothing, letting her have her emotional space.

"That night we left the Polly Parker," Katheryn said, "Berta's irritation was beginning to show. She told me that if something happened to her, I would be held responsible. I said nothing as she drove down Amsterdam Avenue. She could see the look of concern on my face and decided to remain silent and focus on the road. She told me everything would be okay but that she wouldn't go into the park. I felt scared. I didn't want to go alone. Maybe Marques was waiting for me, but then again maybe he ran off to meet that woman who'd been frequenting the club. I didn't want to be the jealous type but needed to speak with him. She asked me what I saw in him and that I should just count my losses and move on with my life. Part of me wanted to, but there was something about him that made me see life differently. He and I shared a deep connection. Something that very few find in this life."

Roman listened as she continued her story, unsure where it would lead.

"We made a left on 59th. I could feel the adrenaline coursing through my body. Berta was on edge. I can only imagine what it was like being a Negro woman in those days and wondering if and when you'd be harassed by the police at a routine traffic stop. 'Let's just get this over with,' she said and asked me why I'd never gotten my license. 'That's the problem with you white people, you think everyone should cart you around New York City.' That made us both laugh uncontrollably. 'I'm just giving you guff,' she told me. Then she said, 'I'm sure he's fine, he probably just got caught up with something.' She put her hand on mine to comfort me."

She took in another deep breath and continued. "We veered off one of the side streets and I remember her saying 'I got ya this far, now you're on your own.' I didn't want to go into the park alone. There had been an increase in muggings, and people were told to avoid the park late at night, especially women. I told her I was terrified and that she would feel horrible if something happened. She sat there with her hand on the ignition trying to decide if she should come with me."

Roman leaned forward eagerly. "So what happened?"

"Here is where things got interesting," Katheryn said and grabbed his hand. "Berta began to argue with me. She didn't want me to go in alone, but she was just as scared. I promised I wouldn't let anything happen to either of us. We walked across the street to the west end of the park, beginning at Columbus Circle and into the darkness. We held one another with both hands. We were scared, but that didn't stop us from moving forward. She was much braver than I. What she didn't know was that if someone did try to act funny, they would meet Lue's friend Bobby."

"Bobby?" Roman said. "I thought you two were alone?"

"We were, darling!"

"So who was Bobby?"

"That was the name Lue gave his gun. I told him I needed backup in case us gals got into any trouble."

Roman's jaw dropped. Something about Katheryn carrying a gun seemed out of character.

"At one point, she told me we should turn around. I told her to take it easy and showed her the gun. It seemed like we'd been walking for an eternity when I saw lights flashing." Katheryn began to weep. "A section of the park had been closed off with yellow tape that read DO NOT ENTER. Two police officers were standing guard. I asked what happened and they told us to stay behind the line. Then I heard one of them say, 'They strung up another one.' The look on Berta's face was one I'd only seen a few times in my life."

She looked up at Roman with her mouth open and her lips quivering. He assumed this was the expression Berta had given her. He sat in the heaviness of that moment. He knew an overwhelming sense of emotion was about to unleash. Like a dam about to burst.

"Marshal," she said, sounding almost like a toddler calling out to a parent. She took in a deep breath and exhaled. "I remember it as if it were yesterday. She said, 'Kathy, don't look!' and tried to shield me. But there it was. It was Marques . . . hanging from a rope . . . swinging . . . his body lifeless. It can't be him, I screamed! Then I saw those wing-tipped loafers I'd given him as a birthday present . . ."

A sudden emotional shift overcame Roman, wondering if something like that could or would happen today in a place like New York City. He was speechless, and his eyes grew tearful. He turned away, not wanting Katheryn to see his reaction.

"Berta picked me up from the ground," she continued. "I remember running for the police. Then two men, one at the top of a ladder and the other holding the ladder in place . . . trying to cut him down . . . saying there might be a chance to save him."

Roman understood what was about to happen and stared at Katheryn, spellbound.

"His face was unrecognizable, and his suit was ripped and dirty . . . They cut him down and he hit the ground, and I started digging through his pockets for something, anything. Then I found this."

She opened her purse and handed Roman a worn, tattered piece of paper folded four ways, a certificate of authenticity from the Central Park Conservatory. Roman didn't understand what he was looking at.

"That was the reason he was late," Katheryn said. "It was not because he was seeing another woman. He was waiting on this. He was going to give it to me that evening." She began to wail as if it were happening all over again. "My darling Marques . . . he was murdered. If I'd been there, maybe he would . . . This was my fault. I am responsible for his death."

Katheryn paused to blow her nose and compose herself. "Later that summer, two more Negro men were lynched. Right in the city. The *Times* never covered it, and the police never investigated. It was as if nobody cared."

Roman was overwhelmed by the idea that such a horrible crime could be viewed as just another undocumented occurrence.

"Berta and I left the park and followed the ambulance to the hospital. The lights on the top were no longer flashing. When we arrived, we waited in the lobby and finally were taken into a room with a body in a long plastic bag. When they unzipped it . . . I knew he would never find me at Central Park or the Polly Parker. He was gone. I realized at that moment what a mystery Marques had been to me, despite everything we'd shared. The Polly Parker closed its doors for the rest of the week. A wake was held, New Orleans style. That was where he was from. I'll never forget when we walked to the Hudson River and Berta led the procession with an old spiritual and we spread his ashes. After the service, Berta handed me a tiny canister. It was Marques, or at least what remained of him. She gave this to me so I could carry a little part of him with me into the afterlife."

Katheryn took a small container from her purse and held it up.

"Darling, when I die, please make sure that his are mixed with mine."

A dark sadness overcame Roman and he thought about his lost love, Jacob. "Sometimes love just isn't enough," he said, repeating the final words Jacob had said to him before leaving for Paris. The plane had gone down somewhere in the Atlantic. It was a pain Roman had not yet fully processed, a healing made more difficult by the fact Jacob had never come out to his family.

"Does it ever get easier?" he asked.

"Darling, it does. But grief is like a raft on the ocean. We go through the motions, which find us at any moment. Yes, it does get easier, but the body has a strange way of never letting us forget. To this day, I wish I had just five more minutes. I don't know what I'd say. I'd probably just hold him, to remember his scent. But life doesn't work that way."

They sat together in silent remembrance of the ones they'd lost.

"Well, Katheryn," Roman finally said, handing her back the folded piece of paper, "I think we should be getting back to everyone."

She put it back in her purse but remained still, hesitant to move, trying to remember Marques's scent and the last interaction they'd had together. "If you wouldn't mind, darling. I would like a moment to gather myself."

"Certainly. Would you like me to come back?"

"No, darling, I will find my way. Please just remind me what the room number is."

"864."

She kept her focus on the floor as she spoke. "Alright. Please let Julian and Theodore know I went to the powder room and will be in momentarily."

He handed her a tissue, as her mascara had run. "I will let everyone know."

Betsy von Muffling

Julian opened the door for Joe and directed him into the hallway. "Mr. Weinberg, if you could please follow me. Everything has been prepared and is ready for you at Concierge."

A twinge of delight ran through Joe as he followed.

"I understand you would like some things delivered," Julian added. "Please let Vera know to what address you would like everything sent, and I will ensure it arrives."

Joe felt a sudden burst of energy and began to scan the hallway. "I will let her know," he said, walking alongside Julian.

"Before we leave, would you like to say goodbye to your grandmother?" Julian asked.

"No! That won't be necessary," Joe said, mentally calculating the total of all the merchandise, wondering if this is what it felt like to be a contestant on *The Price is Right*. "Just let her know I will be in touch later this evening."

Julian felt a hint of suspicion as they rode the elevator down to the first floor. "Are you sure that you have everything?" Julian asked. "There is still time to do some additional browsing."

Joe could sense a hint of sarcasm in Julian's voice but dismissed it. He assumed this was a normal reaction when sending a guest off after a long day of shopping. "I think I have everything I need."

As they descended closer to the first floor, Joe thought about how he could avoid any further questioning by placing a call to Gloria—telling her she would need to stay overnight, as an important delivery would be made that she'd had to be present for.

The elevator doors opened to the first-floor lobby. Joe prepared himself to leave but was interrupted.

"I do apologize," Julian said. "Did I say the first floor? I meant the lower level. We have a special exit that is used for our premier guests." He put his key in the elevator and pushed the button to access the basement.

Anxiety began to creep up Joe's spine as he stared straight ahead.

"Mr. Weinberg," Julian said abruptly. "Or should I say Mr. Tiller?"

Joe said nothing and waited for the elevator doors to open.

"Or should I say Mr. Bloomfield . . . or maybe Mandy Holloway?"

Standing paralyzed, Joe fumbled for his keys nervously like someone heading to a parking lot to retrieve his car.

"I wouldn't know which one," Julian said, "as the credit cards you attempted to use earlier today in the fragrance department would provide anyone increased confusion. Yet upon reviewing your identification, it indicated you are Joe Tiller. So, for this purpose, I will refer to you as Mr. Tiller."

Joe tried to think of something to say and how he planned to proceed once the elevator doors opened, but Julian pressed the emergency stop button and everything came to a halt.

"You see, Mr. Tiller. Mrs. Weinberg's grandson is vacationing with his family in Europe. You're probably thinking how someone like myself would know this. Well, I called the residential facility where she lives and they informed me that he called earlier this morning to inform them he'd be returning from Paris next week."

"If you would give me just one moment," Joe said, "I can explain everything."

"Yes, you will have plenty of time to explain yourself. The police are waiting patiently. And, Mr. Tiller, please know this. It is a felony to extort the elderly, which I'm sure will come with additional charges once you've settled in with them.'"

Joe pulled a BB gun out of his pocket and pointed it at Julian's face. "You son of a bitch! You better take this elevator back to level one!"

Julian threw his hands in the air. "Anything you say, sir!"

"And don't try any funny business, you dumb faggot," Joe snarled in a southern Brooklyn accent.

In all the years he'd worked at Bergdorf Goodman, Julian never thought he'd be held at gunpoint. He was terrified. "Whatever you want! Take whatever you want!" he said, echoing the words Delfina had said in the annual Security and Safety training a few weeks earlier.

Joe moved the gun down to Julian's side. "Here's what we're going to do. You're going to get on the radio and direct good ol' Vera to have everything brought down to the lobby, and we are gonna leave together."

"Whatever you want, Joe," he said, remembering that in the case of a robbery it was important to go on a first name basis, as this could cause some sort of compassion—"become humanized," as Delfina would say.

"I have a wife, Carol," Julian lied. "Daughters. Marsha . . . Jan . . . and Cindy. Waiting for me at home . . . they cannot live life without a father." He didn't feel guilty about using the names of the female characters in *The Brady Bunch*.

"Shut up, faggot, and call Vera!"

Julian pressed the button on his earpiece. "Gil, I'm with Mr. Weinberg," he said, sounding panicked and stuttering. "H-he has decided he'd like to transport everything himself . . . please move immediately on this. We're on Seven and will be taking E3 down in about twenty minutes . . . Just have everything ready. And one more thing, Gil, can you please reschedule the afternoon appointment for Betsy von Muffling?"

Joe didn't know, but this was the code phrase used to indicate an emergency.

"I will personally be accompanying Mr. Weinberg to help with the delivery to his residence," Julian continued. When he finished, he turned to Joe. "It looks like everything is set."

Am I going to have to sit with this faggot for the next twenty minutes? Joe wondered.

He hadn't thought about what he would do with Julian once they'd left Bergdorf's. "Looks like we're going to hang right here until they bring down the merch," he said, keeping the gun in Julian's side.

The faggot probably thinks this shit is loaded, Joe thought and almost laughed.

"And make sure to include a couple bottles of that nice champagne as a parting gift," Joe said, motioning to Julian's earpiece.

"Gil . . . yes . . . yes, and please make sure we include three bottles of our finest champagne for Mr. Weinberg as a parting gift. Thank you, yes. And please let Ms. von Muffling know I'm terribly sorry but will contact her later this evening to send my personal apologies and reschedule for sometime within the week."

Joe felt secure in this decision to hold Julian hostage but knew if he looked close enough, he'd be able to see the pistol was a toy.

"How do you faggots do it?" Joe said. "You know . . . taking it up the ass?"

Julian tried to avoid engaging him. "I wouldn't know. I'm married, sir."

"You're telling me that a romp-roaster like yourself has never taken a roll in the gay hay?"

"My wife Carol would be appalled by your assumptions," Julian said, making sure to place emphasis on the word *wife*. "I wouldn't know."

247

"I'm sure you don't," Joe said and shoved the gun deeper into Julian's side.

*　　*　　*

Ten minutes later, Gilroy's voice came through the earpiece. "Sir, everything is set."

"Perfect, we are on our way down." Julian pressed the button to go back to the seventh floor.

"What the fuck are you doing?" Joe barked.

"Sir . . . I mean Joe . . . we must make this appear normal. Gilroy has informed me everything is in car service and ready for our departure."

Joe wondered how he'd gotten himself in this predicament. It wasn't his intention to have this happen. "Just make sure that no attention is drawn and we are free to go," he said, switching the BB gun to his other hand.

"Certainly, Joe."

Julian watched the numbers at the top of the elevator as they descended to the lobby. The elevator stopped at the second floor, and the two women Joe had seen earlier that afternoon stood irritated.

"OMG, we never thought this day would come," one of them said as they started to enter.

"Excuse me, ladies," Julian said, "but this elevat—"

They paid no attention and barged in with shopping bags on each arm.

One of them looked back to Julian and winked at Joe, making a sexual innuendo with her lollipop. She turned back to her friend and laughed. "I'm pooped, Trisha!"

Julian was struck with a terrified thought, imagining the outcome if anything happened to these women or himself, but fortunately the elevator doors opened and the women exited.

"Thank God he hasn't cut me off!" Trisha said as the two moved in the direction of Cosmetics. "Let's go treat ourselves to some mannies and peddies!"

A sigh of relief overcame Julian at the thought there would be two fewer fatalities on this June afternoon. Then he looked up and saw Gilroy.

"Everything has been loaded and car service is ready," Gilroy said, trying not to act nervously. "Mr. Weinberg, I hope your afternoon has been filled with joy. Thank you for choosing Bergdorf Goodman."

"Thank you, Gilroy," Julian said, fighting panic.

Joe and Julian exited through the lobby. As they passed Vera, she began to cry.

"What's her problem?" Joe said.

"She was informed this afternoon she would be terminated at the end of her shift," Julian said with little confidence, focusing his attention on the door and wondering if he'd make it out alive.

"Well, it sounds like someone else I know," Joe said, thinking about Gloria. As they approached the glass exit doors, Joe felt a rush of excitement. "It sure has been a lovely afternoon—"

He was interrupted by the voice of a man shouting, "PUT YOUR HANDS IN THE AIR MOTHERFUCKER!"

His eyes not yet adjusted to the light outside, Joe looked around confusedly.

"DROP THE GUN!" came a woman's voice. "DROP THE FUCKING GUN!"

Julian looked to see the sidewalk shut down by six NYPD cars sitting in front of the building.

"And if I don't?" Joe screamed back.

"RELEASE YOUR WEAPON!" another officer yelled.

Joe didn't know what to do. "It's just a TOY!" he screamed. "It's just a TOY! See?"

He waved the plastic gun in the air. This was followed by a deafening barrage of bullets. Joe fell forward on Julian's shoulder and then to the pavement. Blood ran from his body onto the concrete.

Unharmed, Julian looked down to see Joe choking on his own blood.

"It was just a toy," Joe said. "Just a toy gun . . ."

"For Just One"

Roman walked back to the viewing room and found everyone gone except for an attendant and a waiter.

"Where did everyone go?" he asked the waiter.

"Julian accompanied Mr. Weinberg down to the lobby," the waiter replied.

Roman thought he should request a change of venue now that Joe was gone but didn't. Maybe this was the room that was originally planned for.

"How long have you been working here?"

"For a while now," the man said, hesitant to engage in conversation.

Roman wondered what anyone would find appealing about this place. To him it seemed dark and without substance. "I'm sure you've seen plenty in your time," he said, to which the man grimaced but said nothing.

The entire afternoon felt strange to him, but he realized this was the price of working with uppity white folk with money and few worries.

"It's my first time here," Roman said. "I've never been in . . . a place like *this*."

The waiter was offended by Roman's tone but removed the champagne bottle from the basin filled with ice chips. "Can I offer you another glass of champagne?"

Realizing his shift was almost over, Roman raised his glass and watched the waiter pour. "That's enough, thank you."

The waiter wasn't accustomed to customers saying thank you.

"You're welcome, sir."

"I'm sure you've dealt with a lot of bullshit in your time," Roman said as he took a drink. "Maybe you should join me. For just one toast."

He took one of the empty glasses from the table and motioned for the waiter and the attendant to sit.

"Come on, I won't tell a soul. I'm just waiting for her highness, the great Katheryn James York, to grace us with her presence. That we all may be gathered together to see the family of designers included in the . . . how did she put it? The family of designers at Bergdorf Goodman." He raised his glass, feeling a bit buzzed as he'd not yet had lunch.

"Well, sir," the waiter said and laughed.

He was interrupted by the sound of an alert that began to sound on their phones at the same time. Roman didn't think much of it until he saw the look of dread on their faces.

The attendant and the waiter exchanged whispers. "Sir," the attendant said, "not to alarm you, but Bergdorf Goodman is under lockdown. There's an active shooter in the building."

Roman jumped up, sobered by the fact he'd left Katheryn sitting on a bench in the hallway. He dropped his glass and ran for the door. Racing through the hallways, he came upon Katheryn, who had not moved from the place he'd left her.

"Katheryn!" Roman said as he approached, but she did not respond. He slowed down and approached her gently, thinking maybe she was taking a nap. He touched her shoulder. There was no movement.

He put his index and forefinger on her throat. Katheryn had stopped breathing. Roman began to panic, not knowing what to do. Then he pulled her to the floor and began CPR. He stopped when he realized his efforts were in vain. All the life that had once resided within her had left her body.

He took a pillow from where she had been sitting and gently placed it under her head. She looked peaceful and relaxed—no longer to carrying that which had burdened her for most of her life.

Grabbing Katheryn's purse, Roman peered inside and noticed a small compartment where he found thousands of dollars in loose cash, a handful of credit cards, and a few sealed, unmarked envelopes. There was a crumpled piece of paper in Katheryn's hand and he took it, looking at it closely. It was the certificate of authenticity from the Central Park Conservatory she'd shown him earlier.

Roman leaned back, wondering if everything he'd learned in nursing school was useless. Then understanding dawned on him. There was nothing more he could do. Perhaps today Katheryn had lived through him . . . through Marshal . . . and through the lives of those who worked at Bergdorf Goodman.

Epilogue

Roman's telephone rang.

"Can I please speak with Mr. Roman White?" a woman said.

"This is him," he responded with a hint of annoyance in his voice. He didn't like telemarketers. "Can I help you?"

"Mr. White, this is Loretta from Banks & Freeman. I'm calling today to—"

"I'm going to stop you right there, ma'am," Roman interrupted and hung up. The phone rang again. Roman snatched up the phone and answered. "I told you, lady, I don't want to save ten to fifteen percent on my car insurance."

"Sir, that isn't why I'm calling."

"So why are you calling?"

"We've been trying to reach you. Your presence has been requested with Mr. Banks at 9 a.m. on Thursday."

"For . . . ?" he asked cautiously.

"Sir, I've just been told I needed to call and speak with you. It's a legal matter regarding Mrs. Katheryn Weinberg. Mr. Banks represents Mrs. Weinberg."

Roman felt uneasy. "I told the detective and Hampton Grove everything that I know. The cause of death was heart attack."

"Mr. White, I understand. I can't go into detail at this time, but your presence is required. We're located at—"

"Hold on. hold on," Roman said, trying to find a pen. "Okay, go on."

"We're located at 20 W. 37th Street. Suite 4702. Please bring identification, as you will need to present this to the front desk."

*   *   *

Exiting the platform on the N Train at 34th street, Roman walked toward 5th Avenue.

I'm starving, he thought, debating whether he should stop by Starbucks or Dunkin Donuts for a latte and a breakfast sandwich. He didn't; he felt too nervous to eat. He wondered if he should call Loretta and tell her he was sick but decided to keep going.

As he walked, he thought about Katheryn and that afternoon at Bergdorf's.

Maybe I should've done CPR longer, he thought, but understood there was nothing he could have done for her.

Looking down at his phone and up at the address before him, Roman realized his meeting was at the Empire State Building. He wondered what it must be like working here, then thought again: If he wanted a nice view of the city, he could take a job at New York Presbyterian on 168th.

He walked through the revolving door and looked around, finding the concierge desk where a man in his mid-thirties was finishing up with a woman. "You will take the middle elevator up to the fourteenth floor," the man said, then turned to Roman. "And you, sir! What can I do for you today?"

"I have an appointment at Banks & Freeman on the forty-seventh."

"Ah, yes, Suite 4702," the concierge said and paused, waiting for Roman to speak.

"I have an appointment at 9 a.m."

"I see. Identification, please?"

Roman handed him his driver's license.

"Here you are," the concierge said, handing Roman back his

ID. He also gave him a sticker with his last name and his first initial, and a sheet of paper Roman would have to scan to get past security before getting into the elevator. "You're going to take the third elevator from the left to the forty-seventh floor."

Roman put his driver's license back into his wallet, slapped the sticker over his right lapel, and walked to the elevator. Once he was inside, he was overwhelmed with a surge of anxiety and hit the button for the forty-seventh floor. Standing in the empty car as it rose, he grew nauseous and thought again about leaving, but before he knew it the door opened again and he was greeted with a hallway. Looking to the left, he saw a glass door with the logo for Banks & Freeman.

He approached the receptionist desk and had to speak fast— the phones were busy and the lady behind the desk was working quickly.

Moments later, the woman who had called Roman came out to greet him. "I'm Loretta," she said and asked Roman to follow her.

"This is a really nice space," he said as he followed, making polite but nervous small talk.

Loretta didn't respond but led him into a large conference room. "Sir, this is Mr. White."

Conrad Banks stood, directed Roman to enter, and pointed to a chair in. "Please have a seat, Mr. White," he said, then turned to Loretta. "Please close the door behind you."

As Loretta left, Roman remained standing, surveying the room, planning his escape.

"Please," Conrad said again, "have a seat. Might I offer you a latte or espresso?"

"If you want to ask me anything," Roman said, "you can read the report I provided to Hampton Grove and the police."

"Hampton Grove . . . Police?" Conrad said confused. "I'm sorry, Mr. White, I don't quite understand."

Roman was also confused but refrained from further comment. Conrad redirected him to sit. "Please, there are a few things we need to go over before the other party has arrived. Mr. White, I need for you to remain absolutely silent throughout this entire process."

Feeling blindsided, Roman watched Conrad press a button and speak into an intercom.

"Loretta, please send in Mr. Weinberg."

Roman looked alarmed. Conrad placed two fingers up to his lips. "Shush!" he said, then stood to greet the man entering his office. "Hello, Theodore."

The man named Theodore, who was not the Theodore that Roman had met at Bergdorf's, looked annoyed to be there. "Now that the old bat is gone, let's get this over with." He looked at Roman. "And who is this?"

"We will get to that momentarily," Conrad said and smiled.

What the fuck is happening? Roman thought but sat silently.

Theodore turned nasty. "I want to know who this is and why he is here."

"Sir," Roman said, "I was the nurse who took care of your grandmother at Hampton Grove."

"So, if she's dead, why are you here?"

"We will get to that momentarily," Conrad interrupted, explaining that Katheryn had wanted an impartial third party present for the meeting.

Loretta handed Conrad an envelope, which he took and opened. He pulled out the packet of papers, spread them on the desk.

"Today, we are gathered to read the last will and testament of Katheryn James Weinberg."

A look of confusion overcame Roman and he moved to stand. "I can go . . ."

"No, Mr. White," Conrad said, "I believe you will want to be here for this." Then he began reading. "'I, Katheryn Weinberg, residing in New York, New York, declare this to be my last will and testament, and I revoke any and all wills and codicils I previously made. I direct my executor, Eliot Shutter, to enforce and administer my estate. I give all my tangible personal property, assets, royalties, and life insurance policies to Eliot Shutter.'"

"What the fuck, Conrad? This must be a joke!" Theodore interrupted.

"On the contrary," Conrad said. He reiterated the fact that everything included within the estate was to be given to Eliot Shutter—and that Katheryn had drawn up the will after Marques's death.

"And what does that have to do with me?" Theodore interjected.

"Before she met and married your father," Conrad said, "she conceived a child with a man by the name of Marques Shutter. The child was named Eliot and was given up for adoption."

"I don't believe it," Theodore said. "What does this mean for my inheritance . . . the family crest . . ."

Conrad took in a deep breath and exhaled. "It's very complicated." He opened a manila envelope and pulled another sealed envelope. "Here you are," he said and handed it to Theodore.

Roman didn't know what was happening or why he was here. Trying to avoid eye contact, he looked down at the table and then to Conrad.

Theodore opened the envelope and began skimming the document. His eyes widened to the size of watermelons. "It says here I get nothing but a set of silverware, a rug, and some used china."

Conrad could see Theodore was upset and tried to defuse the

emotion in the room. "Theodore, I'm sure your grandmother had your best intentions and a good reason for her decisions."

"So who is this?" Theodore said, pointing to Roman. "I don't even know why I'm entertaining this with some home health aide and you."

"I'm a nurse, sir," Roman corrected him.

"Well, whatever you are," Theodore said, directing his attention to Conrad, "I will be contesting this. You will be hearing from my attorney."

Conrad adjusted himself and provided a stern yet sympathetic expression. Theodore responded with a look of deep disgust. He couldn't believe what was happening, but more importantly why this was happening to him.

Conrad told him that while he could attempt to contest the will, it would get him nowhere, as Katheryn had been specific in her instructions. He turned the copy of the will toward Theodore and pointed out the clause.

"If you would let me finish," he said, "your grandmother clearly stated here, and I quote: 'UNDER NO CONDITION is this will to be contested, especially by my son, Brando, or any of his children.' Your grandmother was very specific in the way she wanted her estate to be handled. Prior to your grandmother marrying Roderick, she had this will established with Banks & Freeman."

Theodore was appalled and nearing panic. He was relying on his inheritance to send the children to college, but more importantly, to get out of debt. "So I guess I'm worth nothing more than some used china and a rug."

"Well, there's always the family crest," Conrad responded condescendingly, to which Roman chuckled.

"I'm sorry," Roman said. "I do apologize."

"Well, you haven't heard the last of me," Theodore said,

standing. "Theodore Weinberg will not be mistreated."

"Please feel free to have Loretta set up an appointment, and we can go over this," Conrad said, but Theodore cut him off: "FUCK HER, FUCK YOU AND FUCK THE FAMILY CREST!"

He shoved his chair aside and stormed out of the room. Conrad followed him out, leaving Roman alone. After a few seconds, Loretta popped her head into the room.

"Can I offer you a latte or espresso while you wait?" she asked, to which Roman replied: "Coffee would be great, thanks."

She returned a minute later with a cup of black coffee and a sugar caddy filled on a small tray. "Here you are, Mr. White."

"Thank you," Roman said and poured a splash of creamer into his coffee. "Do you by chance know when Mr. Banks will be back? I have to report to work in a few hours and would like to stop by the library to return a book."

"Any moment, I'm sure," she responded with a smile. "I love going to the New York Public Library. I always imagine myself like Carrie Bradshaw in *Sex and the City* where she gets married to Big."

Roman felt connected to her, as this was one of his favorite series that was later turned into a movie. "It's a great show. Hopefully they'll do a reboot."

Realizing she'd overstayed her welcome, Loretta began to exit. "Mr. Banks will be back any moment."

"Yes, I will," Conrad said from behind her. "Thank you, Loretta, you can see yourself out."

This felt completely uneasy for Roman; he wanted to escape. Conrad looked at Roman and said, "Mr. White, can I please see your ID?"

"First tell me why I'm here," Roman said.

He was confused and afraid and found himself growing tearful. This whole thing reminded him of the time he was pulled over in an Uber, taken into custody by the police, and questioned and held for twenty-four hours by an SVU detective at the 32nd Precinct—only to be told it was a case of mistaken identity.

"You seriously don't know why you are here?" Conrad inquired.

"No, sir," Roman said and looked down as his eyes filled with tears. "I don't." The emotion began to overtake him.

"Well, today is your lucky day," Conrad said, pushing a box of tissue across the table at him. "There's no reason to cry. Katheryn was a very special woman to us here at Banks & Freeman. We all knew one day this moment would come."

"I don't quite understand," Roman said. "What does this have to do with me?"

"Your grandmother, Roberta White, was a very extraordinary woman," Conrad said.

"How do you know my grandmother?" Roman asked, more confused.

"There is a lot about you that I know. Your father, Eliot Shutter, was a good man. He lost his life in a car accident when you were just a baby."

"I'm sorry, but my father's name is James White," Roman interjected, "not Eliot Shutter. I've never met an Eliot Shutter."

"On the contrary," Conrad said, handing Roman an envelope, "James E. White *was* Eliot Shutter. The information in the envelope will explain everything."

"What's this?" Roman asked, taking the envelope.

"Just open it," Conrad said.

Roman opened the envelope, took out a folded sheet of paper, and began to read.

My Dearest Roman,

Darling, by the time you read this I will have walked through death's door. I truly hope you will forgive me for this abrupt moment;

however, this is the way I often conduct myself: abruptly. Right now, you have many questions, to which Mr. Banks will be able to walk you through everything.

Tonight, we had salmon and potatoes, which I'm not fond of, but Marques was—his favorite dish. I hoped this gesture would've allowed you to connect not only with your father but also your grandfather. This was the last meal your grandfather and I shared before his life was taken by those men at the park.

I've always ensured that Berta, your father, and you were taken care of.

From the time you were born, I put away a small trust to take care of all your needs, educational cost, and extra expenses that might arise. I wished you would've pursued music like your grandfather and attended Juilliard, but I understand that your calling was to become a nurse practitioner.

I wanted to find a way to connect with you, to have a relationship, and when I found out you were finishing up your undergraduate studies at Columbia, I spoke with Berta, who assured me that you would come to work at Hampton Grove.

Too often I wanted to disclose to you who I was, but I understand we must not interrupt God's work. At times I feel like I don't know who I am, finding it difficult to recognize those around me, and more often than not I'm finding it difficult to recognize even myself.

I write this now while my faculties are presently intact, but I find myself more often than not confusing you for Marshal. Had you of known him, your life would have been changed for the better. He made my life a better place to live in, and for that I am thankful.

I understand how this must be confusing for you, and I hope that you will one day forgive me for giving your father, Eliot, up to Roberta. Had Marques not been murdered, I never would have signed that contract with Lennon Talent Agency—but after his death, I did not know what to do or how to live.

I sometimes wonder if Roderick did not have a hand in Marques's death, but I cannot allow myself to mentally visit that place.

I see you here studying in the foyer, working on your Master's degree, making a life for yourself, for your future, for the family crest. You look so much like your father, but also your grandfather.

While I am in this state of clarity, I wanted to write you this letter, which will be presented to you at the reading of my will and last testament. With this, I resign my estate to you, my darling Roman, as the last living heir who will carry on the name of your family, our family, but most importantly the vision of your father.

P.S., I've always been more fond of lavender and roses, however I've enjoyed your kind gesture of white daffodils.

All my love,
Katheryn J. York

Roman sat speechless, wondering what he should say. He felt overwhelmed and thought about what this meant for him.

"When your grandmother Roberta adopted your father, his name was changed to James E. White. The E stood for Eliot, which I assume you now understand. It was Katheryn's intention to come get your father from Roberta after his birth, but because of the times this wasn't possible. Katheryn became consumed with her own life after Marques's death, and she felt guilty she'd signed with Roderick Weinberg at Lennon Talent Agency. On the night of his murder, Marques was waiting for Katheryn in Central Park to present her with the certificate of authenticity from the Central Park Conservatory. He had a white man by the name of Lue Tremont to make the purchase, as it was not permitted for African Americans to do so at the time. If Marques had tried to purchase the plaque himself, it never would've been permitted. So, he had

Mr. Tremont do it instead."

Conrad pulled out the certificate and handed it to Roman.

"This was crumpled up in Katheryn's hand at the time of her death," Roman interjected.

"This was a gesture of Marques' love that would later be placed on the bench. While they could not be open about their love because interracial relationships were illegal at the time, the public display of this plaque would unknowingly allow the world to know who they were. See, Mr. White, Katheryn never intended to sign with the agency, but to meet your grandfather in Central Park, get baby Eliot, and leave New York to build a life in Canada. She would have left it all that evening."

Roman sat in awe and wondered what all this meant and what it would mean. "So, what you're saying is that I . . ."

"Yes, Roman, you are the heir to Katheryn's estate. Now, if you could let me see your ID, we have much work to do."

*   *   *

Visiting the office at the Central Park Conservatory, Roman presented the receptionist with the certificate of authenticity. The woman behind the counter typed in the identification number listed on the document.

"That's odd," she said, "generally the plaque will be engraved with a name, and it will also indicate from whom it was given."

Roman gave her a polite smile and waited. She took out a tiny slip of blank paper and wrote down the bench number. "It's bench 507, near the entrance of Colum—"

"—Columbus and 59th," he interrupted and took the piece of paper. "Thank you."

As he walked there, he felt a sense of resolution. Approaching the bench where he and Katheryn had sat on the afternoon she used the nail file to chip away at the green layers of paint, he saw a man sitting there.

"Sir," Roman said, approaching the man, "do you think I could occupy this bench?"

Looking around confusedly, as the park was empty and there were many unoccupied benches, the man said, "Well, I guess," and stood up.

Roman thanked him and sat down. Looking down at the seat, he understood one thing about Katheryn: She had been an eccentric woman. Anticipating what he would find written on the plaque, he turned his head around and read the inscription:

OUR LOVE WILL SURVIVE
MIS & KJY
1957

Gazing up at the sun after christening a corndog with mustard purchased from a street vendor, he stared out into the distance of the park.

"Oh, Katheryn," he said, "you were a very complicated person."

Acknowledgments

That night at the Palace Theatre in New York City I watched Glenn Close perform Norma Desmond in *Sunset Boulevard*. Something about that performance moved me in a way that I cannot explain. It was at that moment *Afternoon at Bergdorf's* was conceived. Thank you, Glenn, for inspiring the birth of this story.

I would like to thank and acknowledge my parents, William and Kathleen (Molly Shea, who is also a writer), who inspire me. To my partner, Chris, thank you for supporting me in every personal and professional endeavor I pursue and being such an amazing cat-dad. To my extended family in Los Angeles (Karine, Sona, and Peter), thank you for always making me feel welcome. To my friends Lindsay, Melissa, Gabby, Asa, Hakki, Amy, Gabriel, I would like to thank you for making my life a better place to live in.

Laike, I hope you know not a day goes by that I don't celebrate your life. I look forward to that moment when we meet again.

I would like to thank and acknowledge Bergdorf Goodman, as this New York City staple served as a focal point of this story (I still wonder what's on the 8th floor). To the designers and cultural icons mentioned in this book, thank you for providing me inspiration.

I would like to thank Vince Font at Glass Spider Publishing for treating this project with such care—you made her ready for the dance. To Judith San Nicolás at Judith S. Design, thank you for creating such breathtaking cover design and artwork.

Most importantly, which I do not say or use lightly, I would like to thank God, who continues to guide and direct all my steps in this life. While we live in these uncertain times, I hope we all can be inspired and guided by the principles Jesus outlined in Matthew 25: 35-36.

About the Author

Dr. Richard M. Mills is a New York City-based writer who resides with his partner and two cats (Al and Bob) in Astoria, Queens. In addition to writing, he holds a Doctor of Education and Master of Social Work and is a Sex Therapist and host of the podcast "Talk Sex with Dick."

To find out more and connect with Richard, please visit:

www.LaikeRisingTherapy.com

Instagram: @LaikeRisingTherapy
Facebook: @RichardMillsTherapy